Don't Cry Aloud

DENISE ROBERTSON

Don't Cry Aloud

HOPCYN PRESS

To Mark and Nicky Webster, in the hope that one day they will be re-united with their children.

Hopcyn Press
42 Russell Rd
London W14 8HT
Tel: +44 (0) 20 7371 6488
Email: info@hopcynpress.com
www.hopcynpress.com

ISBN 978-0-9928933-2-3

'It must never be forgotten that, with the state's abandonment of the right to impose capital sentences, orders of the kind which family judges are typically invited to make in public law proceedings are amongst the most drastic that any judge in any jurisdiction is ever empowered to make. When a family judge makes a placement order or an adoption order in relation to a 20-year-old mother's baby, the mother will have to live with the consequences of that decision for what may be upwards of 60 or even 70 years, and the baby for what may be upwards of 80 or even 90 years.'

Sir James Munby, President of the Family Division
of the High Court of England and Wales

CHAPTER 1

Celia

It was the same dream, and the same bleak awakening. One moment the warmth of Michael's body, safe and warm. The next, patterns of morning light on the ceiling, the furniture swimming into focus, and then the loneliness of the empty bed. '*Celia*,' he had said, '*Celia*.' She had put out a hand and touched him, felt the firm bulk of his shoulder above her. And then he was gone. The pillow beside her was cold, and there was no indentation where his head would have been, his lovely head with its curling black hair.

She had had the dream before, the same joy, and after it the same bleakness on awakening. In the days after Michael's death, she would have got out of bed and padded through to Gavin's room, climbing in gently so as not to disturb his sleep, but needing to make contact with a living human being. With Michael's son. Now she was less selfish, but the dreams continued. There was nothing in the textbooks about dreams after bereavement, not even in the one she had written herself.

She turned on her side and looked at the clock: 6.25, which was a lot better than 4.25. If she woke that early, she had to decide whether to lie tormented in the dark or get up and sit downstairs, listening to the World Service retailing the miseries of some Third World country ... which ought to have made her count her blessings, but seldom did. However, 6.25 was bearable. There was news, and familiar voices were talking about politics and show-business and sport. You could lose yourself in those things.

She turned over and tried to distract herself by thinking about the meals for the week. She would do spaghetti tonight, and use the leftover mince. Fish tomorrow. Gavin would moan, but he'd still eat it. It gave you Omega 3 oils ... or did that only come from sardines? She had to make sure he ate well. He was all she had.

She raised herself on an elbow and plumped her pillows, lay down again, closed her eyes. But trying to lull herself back to sleep by thinking about mundane things wasn't working. She allowed herself the luxury of a long stretch before she got out of bed and made for the shower. In the warm flow she thought about the day ahead. She needn't get Gavin up until half-past seven. If she skimped her shower, she could have 30 minutes of bliss with coffee and the papers and John Humphrys burbling away, before her son started demanding gym kit and snacks for break.

She might even be spared Sean's music starting up above. He was into rap at the moment, a change from his devotion to blues. All the same, getting a lodger had been a good idea. It had made the house at once smaller and less lonely. And the rent was handy, too, which mustn't be overlooked. Not to mention the occasional baby-sitting. Sean was good for Gavin, too ... half mentor, half big brother. 'He's cool,' had been Gavin's verdict, and she had known it was going to be all right.

She stepped out of the shower and huddled into a towel for a moment, unwilling to emerge and reach for body lotion. If only she had more time for baths, long, luxurious soaks in bubbling water, not two-second plunges with the alarm clock on the end of the tub telling her she should be somewhere else. You never felt cold getting out of a bath, but emerging from the shower was different. Once outside the glass door, you were in the Arctic.

Looking at herself as steam cleared from the mirror, she realised that Sean's being a gay man was somehow less threatening to her, which was crazy. She couldn't cope with men now. Except in the office, and in dreams ... and in them there was only one man. As her mirror image stared back at her, she decided she would hardly need to fend off unwelcome attention, even if it existed. Her eyes seemed faintly red against the dark shadows underneath. She didn't cry much now, but months of secret weeping had taken their toll. She ran a hand through her hair, and it felt dry and scratchy. Perhaps she was drying up, withering. 'Sere' – the word popped up from nowhere, and reminded her of schooldays. You never used the word sere in conversation, only in essays.

She thought about work. She would have to stay in Anxious Alley all day, no time even to nip out for lunch. With the recession, her postbag had almost doubled, and the promise to answer every letter, made so blithely when she had started the Agony Aunt column, was becoming something of a millstone. Still, occasionally, just occasionally, she could make things happen, which was a buzz. And at least today was Friday. Tonight, after Gavin had gone to bed, she would give it the works: candles, soft music, a glass of something nice …

She blow-waved her hair while the kettle boiled, making a mental note to get her colour done soon. Must keep up appearances, even though she no longer gave a damn about how she looked. There was no one left to admire her, no one who mattered. Gavin never looked at her, except when they were rowing, and Sean's current passion was a black, six-foot architectural student who answered to the name of Dom.

As she carried her coffee through to the sitting-room and collected the papers, she reflected that, if it weren't for her job, she would never get out of a towelling robe, would renounce moisturising, and let her natural mouse grow back untrammelled. Which sounded like bliss. But her weekly TV slot was well paid; and, regardless of how good you were at the job, if you didn't look the part on screen you were toast. She must never go back to those weeks when a madwoman with sunken eyes had looked back at her from the mirror. 'For God's sake,' Charley, her boss, had said, coming round to roust her back to work. 'He's dead, but you're not. And you have a child. Pull yourself together, and get a shower.' It had been brutal, but it had worked. She had pulled herself together. Almost.

The newspapers were full of the usual rifts in the political system. It was no way to run a country. There was a whole page on the latest royal romance, and a new girlfriend for a royal prince. Given the way anyone who married into the royal family was hounded by the press, it was a wonder the girl concerned hadn't headed for the hills. Celia was half-way through her horoscope, six lines of platitudes followed by the usual exhortation to ring in to discover something magical, when the music began in the room above. It was going to be a blues day. She folded the paper, downed the rest of her coffee, and went to waken her son.

He was lying on his back, one arm above his head, the dark hair he had inherited from Michael matted on his brow. Michael's son. She felt tears threaten, and blinked them back. None of that nonsense today! She reached out and touched the sleeping boy. 'Wakey, wakey.'

The lashes that fanned his cheeks lifted to reveal blue eyes. 'I wasn't asleep!'

'You were giving a pretty good imitation. Anyway, you said you wanted to check your kit and it's 7.30 already. And you can't ...'

'... go out on an empty stomach,' he finished for her, and rolled over on to his face. She went back to the kitchen and started to make his toast. He was a good boy, really, and would be up before long. Above her, blues had given way to some cool jazz. That wasn't Sean's usual bag. Perhaps he had brought someone new home last night? The ease with which gay men slipped in and out of relationships still surprised her, but she couldn't wish for a better tenant. He had made all the difference since Michael had died.

She felt tears threaten again and, as soon as the toast was finished, buried herself in *The Independent*. It was the same rubbish, slanted against the Government. Which made a change from the *Daily Mail,* which thought that same Government walked on water. At least her own paper, *The Globe*, tried to be impartial, and say that most politicians were flawed. Yes, Charley was not only a good editor, he was a fair man.

When Sean appeared from upstairs, he was alone, and said he was more than ready to baby-sit at 4 p. m. 'No trouble, I'll be back by then. Except the little bugger makes me play Scrabble and he effing knows I can't spell. Still, you get out and enjoy yourself. One of us might as well. Is it the big feller, the boss? Charley Wotsisname?'

She forbore telling him it was pressure of work that would make her late. If he wanted to think she was having it off with her editor, let him. Instead, she gave thanks that his job in IT had wonderfully elastic hours. Or else he only went to work when it suited him. In any event, it wasn't her problem.

She dropped Gavin at the school gate, urging him to contact Sean if there was any trouble. 'I've told you, Mum, I don't need a baby-sitter. I'm nearly 12. I can manage on my own.'

She said all right, but just in case; and then threaded her way through Holborn to the South Bank and *The Globe* building. She had her pass ready in case it was the fierce Lithuanian lady on Security, but it was Errol, beaming at the sight of her and insisting on carrying her briefcase as far as the lift. It was a bit odd, but the sight of a black face on the gate made her relax. West Indians were always kind and helpful, and never, ever moody. Which made a change from some of the rest of her colleagues.

Gracie was already in Anxious Alley, the name that the crew had bestowed on the corner of the newsroom where she and Gracie operated the agony-aunt column. 'Hi, Ceely,' she said. 'Coffee's on, and today's post is entered and logged. I'm on to the emails now. Just the usual in the post, nothing startling. I'll tell you about this lot in a moment.'

As Celia settled herself at her desk, she tried to remember who had dubbed their corner 'Anxious Alley'. It had been Simon ... or Petra, or ... anyway, the name had stuck. Someone had even had a plaque made: it stood on her desk now, holding down a pile of memos. The desk was orderly, and not in the mess she had left it in last night. God bless Gracie, face of an avenging angel and a heart of gold. They had been together since 1996 ... or was it '97? She herself had just taken over the agony page in *The Globe*, and Charley had given her Gracie as a general factotum. *'She'll keep you right ... as long as you do as you're told.'* He'd been spot on there: Gracie brooked no argument.

She was plonking Celia's coffee in front of her now and glancing down at the pad she always carried. 'Paul Fenton of *Search* wants you on his programme on Tuesday. Next week, if you can't make this Tuesday. A new series about the heartbeat of the nation, his PA says. Women with their finger on the national pulse, etc. Men too, except their fingers are usually up their arse, if you'll pardon the expression. Now, these are the regulars, those are the invites, and these are the urgents. And don't take all day, because we still have to finalise tomorrow's copy.'

Celia took a gulp of scalding coffee, and began to read. It was always difficult to concentrate at first, faced with a pile of multi-coloured emails and the odd hand-written letter. Gracie used pink paper for affairs of the heart, yellow for legals, blue for potential jumpers off a bridge, and white for everything else. Celia dithered between the piles: which first, legals or romance? What would she wear for *Search*, if she agreed to do it? Nothing she wore for her own breakfast TV appearances on *The Hour*. Evenings were different: prime-time, big deal. Not that she cared much for what she'd seen of Fenton. 'Too clever by half,' had been her first impression, and she'd seen little since to make her change her mind.

Still, Tuesday was days away. She picked up the legals. Two

bitter marital breakups, someone facing repossession of their home, a row over possession of a land-cruiser, someone facing prison. She ploughed on through the pile, putting aside the possibles for the column, those needing a personal answer, the urgents needing action right now. And then she picked up the letter that began '*You are my last resort.*'

Chapter 2

Celia

The next day, on waking, the letter was the first thing that came into her mind, making her wish it wasn't Saturday, so that she could do something about it. She couldn't quite make out why. God knows, it wasn't the first complaint about the Social Services she'd had. They could paper not only Anxious Alley but the entire newsroom with the letters. All of them were heart-breaking, all insoluble. The first time a letter had talked of 'emotional abuse', she had looked at it in disbelief. '*I try not to cry when I'm with them, because they stop the contact if you cry. They call it emotional abuse. So you keep smiling, but you cry inside.*' What sort of a world was it where you couldn't cry aloud at the sight of your children?

In the beginning, she had seen the Family Courts as relaxed places where justice would be tempered with humanity. Now she was beginning to see them as Star Chambers, and whatever they dispensed, it didn't usually seem to be justice. She did what she could for the letter-writers, sending them to Family Rights, or Parents Against Injustice, or the website of John Hemming, the one MP who seemed to give a damn about what was going on. There was no chance of airing their grievances on the front page of her newspaper, or during her TV slot on *The Hour*, which was what they were all hoping for when they wrote to her. The paper's lawyers had made that very clear and *The Hour* was terrified of anything remotely legal, apart from which most of the letter-writers had had gagging orders slapped on them, which meant they were forbidden to talk about their case to anyone, on pain of imprisonment. So had the writer of this letter, but she was clearly past caring.

'*You are my last resort,*' the letter began. '*I could go to prison for contacting you, but I can't just sit here while they take my children away for ever.*' Poor bitch, she didn't care whether or not they sent her to jail for speaking out: she was clutching at straws, regardless of the consequences. '*Last resort*' – stark words, but understandable in the circumstances. In a few weeks' time, the writer and her husband were going to lose their children to adoption. Celia could see the page in her mind's eye, and the words written there: 'Orders' and 'Contact' and 'Placement'. It would be called a hearing, but the Family Courts, she feared, tended to rubber-stamp whatever Social Services recommended. What had that social worker written to her last year? Something like, '*I won't do child protection now. The mothers are on a hiding to nothing.*'

As light filtered into the bedroom, she tried to think how many letters she had had about forced adoption over the past few years. There must have been 250 at least, since Michael died. She winced at the thought that she was beginning to date everything from that day. Over the years ... concentrate on that, not on Michael. How many had she had in her whole career? At first a trickle, and then, as she used some of them in the column, a rising tide. After the tragedy of Baby P., a flood.

Sometimes Celia could see why Social Services had stepped in to intervene in a family, but too often there seemed no rhyme or reason to it. And the process, once begun, seemed remorseless, even cruel. One woman who had written to her was allowed to see her child only for one hour a year. What else was that but a form of torture? A grandmother, who was still young and was a health visitor, was not being allowed to keep the granddaughters she loved, but had been told to write each of them a farewell letter. Aged nine and two, they were being adopted separately. It hadn't made sense even to Gracie, who was less inclined to sympathise with writers.

'She's fit to care for them, so why won't they let her?' Gracie had opined. 'And what about the poor kid who is losing her baby sister?' But it was in the days when the Blair government was giving cash rewards to councils for hitting adoption targets. 'The little one is blue-eyed and blonde,' Gracie had said, looking at the photo the grandmother had enclosed. 'Adoptable. The older one will be harder to place.' She had turned on her heel then, accepting the inevitable. Celia had tried to help the mother, but the decision had rolled remorselessly through.

Now she turned on her side, and tried to think of something less unsettling. It was 7.15, and it was Saturday. Even if it had been a working day, there would have been nothing she could do at this time. She could turn over now and try to sleep for another hour at least, but the bed felt vast and empty. She was better off out of it.

She took the letter out of her briefcase while she waited for the kettle to boil. Why had she brought it home, where she had no resources to fall back on? She read it again. It was the same as all the other letters, a tale of bewildered parents and hostile authority.

'I didn't notice at first. I was too worried about the baby. But then I realised the nurses weren't friendly any more. And the doctor was abrupt. He shut Stuart up when he asked a simple question. And then two people came in, a man and a woman, and they said I couldn't be alone with Darren, and they were taking the other two children into care. I started screaming then, but they didn't care. Their faces never changed. You could tell they were used to doing it, taking people's children away. I remember I asked a nurse for a tissue and she just pointed to a box. I could see she believed I'd hurt my baby.'

Celia sat for a moment, ruminating. Nothing she could do today. If she still felt uneasy, she'd confer again with Gracie on Monday. Perhaps give the writer a call. She folded the two closely written sheets and put them back in the envelope.

When at last he appeared, sleepy-eyed and tousle-haired, Gavin turned down her offer of a pizza lunch in town.

'Shopping sucks,' he said.

She put out a frozen cannelloni for later, and urged him to eat some fruit. 'And call Sean if you get into any trouble. I'll be back before tea.'

She caught a bus to Oxford Street. She had long ago ceased to go anywhere in London by car unless she knew there was parking waiting for her. She would have to stop relying so much on Sean to keep an eye on Gavin, though. He was good nature on legs, but you could push even the good-natured too far.

Planning ahead, shopping had seemed like a good idea. Retail therapy, every woman's remedy. But as Celia wandered from store to store, she saw nothing to excite her, and there was a limit to how many skinny lattes you could get down in between boutiques. When Michael was alive, they had had glorious Saturdays, right from the beginning, when there were just the two of them. And afterwards, packing everything Gavin needed into the car and taking off, or spending afternoons curled up on the sofa, the baby sleeping peacefully in its crib. '*I miss you!*' The cry hurt her throat, and she looked around, terrified that she had spoken aloud. But no one looked startled, or even interested. They were all wrapped up in their own lives. Mourning a lover of their own, for all she knew.

She darted through the next doorway she came to, and tried to lose herself in the world of posh handbags and silk scarves. It was useless. She wandered through lingerie and plus-sizes, and then she spotted the bar. It was only 11 o'clock but one gin and tonic would do no harm. She settled in a corner booth, and watched the other customers as she drank. All in pairs. What was that poem … she had done it for O-levels? By Shelley. Percy Bysshe Shelley. Oh, how they had agonised over how you pronounced Bysshe – as if it mattered. 'Love's Philosophy', that was its title. She had had a crush on the head boy, then. Her first love. The sight of him in the corridor could make her legs shake, and she had pictured him all the while she was parroting the words: '*The fountains mingle with the river,*

And the rivers with the ocean; The winds of heaven mix forever,
With a sweet emotion; Nothing in the world is single; All things
by a law divine In one another's being mingle; Why not I with
thine?'

'Why not?' She took a sip of her drink, willing herself not
to cry. Not here, in front of all these people, all in pairs.
'*Nothing in the world is single.*' But Percy Bysshe had got it
wrong: some people were single. And it hurt like hell.

She put down a note to cover the bill, and got to her feet.
Kissing. That's how it had finished. '*The sunlight clasps the*
earth, And the moonbeams kiss the sea; What are all these
kissings worth, If thou kiss not me?' Among the racks of lacy
underwear, she wiped her eyes and blew her nose. Poetry must
clearly be avoided, too.

In the end she gave up, and caught a bus home, clutching
her pitifully few purchases. The cannelloni carton was empty on
the draining-board, a plate and a fork in the sink. It was only
12.45.

'What time did you eat?' she asked her son.

'Hours ago. I was hungry. And you didn't leave anything
for afters, so I opened a tin of pears.'

'Did you eat them all?' she asked faintly.

'There was only four! Well, maybe five. And I'm still
starving.'

She felt a glow of pride: he could fend for himself when he
had to. And he never ever whinged. She chuckled, then. He
never ever whinged because he never needed to – he was getting
all his own way, anyway. 'We could go bowling later on,' she
suggested. 'Maybe get something more to eat?'

'OK.' Gavin didn't lift his eyes from his Xbox, but Celia
felt a frisson of excitement. He wanted to be with her. He would
always be with her. For years, anyway. What must it be like to
love a child, and have it taken from you? To see it led away
bewildered, to be placed with strangers. '*You are my last*
resort.' She didn't feel strong enough to be someone's last

resort. There was sweet bugger-all she could do, so it would be wrong to raise the woman's hopes. At least she could tell her that she believed her story. But if she believed it, then she was bound to try to do something.

She tried to put the letter out of her head by making some duty calls. Her aunt in Hove: 'I'm fine, Celia darling, but can you believe the price of food these days?' Her best friend at school, Ginnie: 'Oh Ceely, I think about you all the time, and wish we were nearer. Simon says we'll come up to London soon, but you know you and Gavin are welcome here any time. Day or night. Anything we can do, you only have to ask.' '*You only have to ask*': the wake-attendees' mantra. Except that you couldn't ask because they couldn't give you the one thing you wanted: the man you had loved and lost.

She made coffee, and phoned Michael's parents in far-off Scotland. They had always been good to her, from that first visit, feeling awkward in her heels and knee-high skirts amid the heather. When they realised she had lost both her parents in childhood and now had no family of her own, they had quietly taken that family's place. Today, when they had exchanged reassurances and sighed about the political situation, and the proposed referendum that might separate their respective countries, she carried the phone through to the living-room. 'It's Gran and Grampie. They want to say hello.'

She sank on to the arm of the sofa as Gavin talked with his grandparents, watching his animated face, hearing him chuckle. Even with his father gone, there was still a family. There must be grandparents in the letter-writer's life, too: elderly people wondering if they would see their grandchildren again. She would talk to Gracie on Monday. If they put their heads together ... there wasn't a bloody thing they could do about it, except try. But at least they could try.

CHAPTER 3

Sandra

As usual, the first thing Sandra did when she woke was cock her ear to hear if the children were awake. Stupid after eight months. Eight months and four days. Darren had been five months old then. Now he was one, and she hadn't been there for his birthday, just as they had missed Christmas at home. That had been the worst weekend of her life, sitting in the silent house, trying to pretend it wasn't Christmas outside. It was summer, now, and still, when she woke, she thought they were a family. She would take in the silence for a while before she would remember that the children were no longer there. Silly to lie listening for murmurs, even chuckles, when there were no longer children in the next room. Or anywhere in the house. She felt her throat contract and tried desperately to relax. Mustn't get upset because it showed in her face when she went to the shops.

People were talking already. She could sense it even though they tried to be pleasant. '*No smoke without fire*': she'd said it about other people in the past. '*They don't take your children for nothing. They must have done something.*' She could hear herself saying it. Except that now she knew they did take children without reason. It might have been better if they'd lived here longer, but they'd only just moved in before she had Darren, so the neighbours were still strangers.

She lay for a while, wondering if she would go on thinking about it all the time, even into old age. Even if they never got them back? But if she didn't think about the children, what would she think about? She and Stuart never talked about anything else but getting them back, but they avoided some things, especially what they would do if the children never came home. Once, she had sensed the words hovering on Stuart's lips, but she had hurried to change the subject, knowing that if he said '*What if?*' she couldn't bear it. She felt panic rising again and quelled it. They would come home. They must. She couldn't allow herself to think they wouldn't, even though the solicitor had hinted at it after the last court appearance. 'I think you should prepare yourselves ...' he had begun, and she had cut him short with a question about their next meeting.

Beside her, Stuart was still sleeping, and she lay still so as not to wake him. He worked long hours, longer now because he was convinced extra money would help. It wouldn't, she knew that. The only thing that would help was someone accepting that they were telling the truth. That was why she had written to the newspaper. The woman who answered the letters always seemed fair-minded. She had seen her once on television, and she had seemed as though she cared. Unless it was all an act, and the letters went in the bin. She used to think letters in agony columns were made up, because what people complained of was so far-fetched. Things like that didn't happen in real life. And then it happened to you and you knew they were true.

Suddenly she could hear rain drumming on the window. At least it would be good for the garden. There was always good in things if you looked for it: one of her foster-mothers had told her that, but it wasn't true. Some things were just bad ... all bad ... utterly bad ... no light at the end of the tunnel ... she felt a laugh bubbling inside her. No fucking tunnel! That's what Stuart would say.

Right from the start he had known it was bad. Had raised his voice to the doctors, fought back. Shouted, even. She had stayed silent, like when she was a little girl – she would squeeze her eyes tight shut, put her hands over her ears and wait for it to stop. Wait for Dad to stop braying hell out of Mam and go back to the pub. She had been like that till the council came in a car and took her away. Her mother had screamed when that happened. 'Don't take my bairn, please don't take my bairn.' It

had done no good. Shouting never did. You needed to stay quiet
and pretend nothing was happening if you wanted to get by,
that's what being in care had taught her.

It had been different for Stuart. He had grown up with his
Gran and Granddad, been a proper mummy's boy. Well,
Granddad's boy. She had had 11 foster homes in seven years.
Good ones and bad ones, and then a flat of her own. That was
care, too: Barnardo's Leaving Care. It had worked against her
in the end, being in care. She had seen that in the social worker's
face as she wrote it down, known it before the solicitor
explained it. '*They feel the emotional deprivation you suffered
as a child may have made it difficult for you to parent.*' The
solicitor had widened his eyes to indicate he didn't believe it,
but he did. She had seen it in his face. She was the product of
care, and therefore wanting. But if care was so bad for you, why
were they forcing it on her children?

She felt her nails digging into her palms. Must get a grip.
The letter might help. Newspapers could make things happen.
Perhaps the agony woman would believe them, talk to
someone, pull some strings. Would she have believed it herself
if that letter had come through their letterbox six months ago?
She would probably have decided it was a stunt, and thrown it
in the bin. Back then she had trusted authority; now she knew
better. You couldn't stand up to authority, not if you were just
an ordinary person. It would be different if you had someone to
stick up for you. Perhaps the woman at the newspaper would
do it? But it had to be soon. Already Bobby seemed more
content with his foster-mother. Only Ann Marie was really
pleased to see them at the contact visits. And she was confused.
Last time she had said, when they were walking away, '*Have we
been naughty, Mammy? Is that why we can't come home?*'

Sandra felt moisture on her face. Her nose was running.
She tried not to cry now, because the contact supervisor called
it emotional abuse if you cried in front of the children, and
threatened to end the visit. She could hold back the actual tears

– but her nose would run.

She wiped it on the back of her hand, moving carefully so as not to disturb the man sleeping beside her. Once, at this time in the morning, she would have turned to him, kissed his sleeping face in the hope of waking him so they could make love, quietly so as not to wake the children, loving the sleepy smell and feel of one another. It was months now since they had had sex. The last time had been meaningless. You couldn't enjoy sex when there was no joy in you. It seemed dirty somehow. Besides ... she shifted in the bed, distancing herself. When the doctor had said the baby had an 'unexplained injury', said it outright, in a hard, cold voice, she had seen doubt about her in Stuart's eyes. Just for a second, and then he had covered it up – but it had been there. He could deny it all he liked, but just for a moment he had believed she could harm her own child. They had all believed it.

The nurses, the doctor ... especially the social workers. They'd not only believed it, they'd enjoyed it. They pulled sorry faces and hummed and hah'd, but they enjoyed their power. She hadn't given them the satisfaction of seeing how afraid she was, that was one good thing. Not even when they frightened the shit out of her, she hadn't let them see it. When they'd suggested she could have the kids back if she said Stuart had done it, she'd shaken her head. Afterwards she'd wondered what he was saying, in some other room. Were they offering him the same chance? She'd wondered about that right up until he'd told her about it. '*I told them where to go, Sandra. Told them you wouldn't hurt a hair of their heads.*' She'd wanted to tell him what she'd seen in his eyes that first day, but she hadn't. She'd never tell anyone. That's how bad it was, something that hurt even when you talked about it to yourself.

That first day! Eight months and four days ago. It started like any other day. They hadn't made love, just cuddled for a while and talked about Christmas. She loved Christmas, had always loved it, even in care. They were always nice to you at Christmas, even the ones like Mrs Briggs, who was only in it for the money. Once she'd had her own place, even that first in-care flat, she'd made a lot of Christmas; and when the kids came she'd really gone to town. While they were cuddling, Stuart had promised her a real tree this year, and then she had got up and put on the kettle, leaving him to enjoy a lie-in. She had always liked mid-shift because he was with her at the start of the day and back with her before bedtime.

She had boiled the kettle and mashed the tea, and then she had gone to wake up the kids. Ann Marie had been sitting up in bed, looking at the cot. 'Darren's been grizzling all night, Mam.' She had smiled at her daughter. She was a proper old woman where her brothers were concerned. Bobby had raised himself up in bed then, his face still vacant with sleep, his hair tousled. 'I expect it's his teeth,' she had said, but when she touched the baby he had let out a little cry, more than a whimper.

That's when the nightmare had started. She decided not to remember any more. She was tired of going over and over it in her mind, wondering where they had gone wrong, what they could have said or done to stop the nightmare before it engulfed them. If only they hadn't taken him to the hospital, had just watched over him till he was better. But they had gone because they loved him, and they couldn't bear to run any risks. And now it was too late.

Stuart was stirring. Any moment his arm might come round her. She slid from the bed and reached for her cardigan. 'I'll make some tea,' she said, and headed for the stairs. The door of the empty children's room was half-open, and something drew her in there. Sunlight was streaming in. 'It's Saturday, Mam,' Ann Marie would have said, sitting up in bed, her hair standing up round her head like a halo. 'Saturday, so no school. What are we going to do?'

'What would you like to do?' she would have countered, knowing full well what the answer would be.

'Go down the swingy-park.' It was always that. 'The swingy park' and afterwards an ice-cream at Tony's, if they had the money. They were good bairns. They had never whinged, even when she had to say no to something. And now she might never take them to the park again.

She felt a scream starting way down in her belly, forcing its way up and out into her mouth. But before it could escape, Stuart was there. Putting his arms round her, settling his chin on her head, saying, 'Come on, now. No good taking on.' He was right, of course. It was no good taking on. It was no good doing anything. Not even writing letters to the papers. She put up her face and spoke against his neck. 'When we get them back ...'

But he was shrugging her away to interrupt. 'When we get them back? You're still kidding yourself, Sandra. You saw that letter. They won't let us change to another solicitor, and we both know the one we've got will do sod all.'

He was right about their solicitor. He would do sod all – there was too much smiling and whispering between him and Social Services. The newspaper was lying on the table where Stuart had fetched it from the front door. Would the woman on the paper do anything? And if they did, could she trust them? *The Globe* was a big paper. They must get hundreds of stories like hers, and they couldn't follow them all up.

She pulled her cardigan around her. 'I'll pour the tea.' That was all she ever said now. As if making tea was a magic formula, something to fend off the darkness that was closing in around them.

CHAPTER 4

Celia

'It's not as if there's anything we can really do.' Gracie pulled a face as she spoke. 'I mean, I'm as concerned as you are, but we both know she's had it, poor cow.' Celia pursed her lips but didn't argue. Arguing with Gracie was like battling butter. 'We can give her Family Rights and John Hemming,' Gracie said. 'There's nothing more we can do. And you should be out of here by now. You look pasty, so give make-up enough time.'

'Thanks,' Celia said drily. Today was Monday, the day she did her weekly stint on *The Hour* television programme. She put the letter back in the folder, and locked it in her desk drawer. She wasn't finished with it yet.

'There's your brief ... as discussed,' Gracie said, handing her a folder. 'You're doing the after-effects of rape, family disputes, and the man who pays maintenance but isn't allowed access to his son. Next week, it's domestic violence, and sex with a new partner. The best of luck on that one. And before you go, what am I to tell Paul Fenton? He called again. He's suggesting you two meet up to discuss your coming on his show. Lunch or dinner, it's up to you.'

'If I do it, he'll stitch me up.' Celia's tone was resigned. Paul Fenton's *Search* was renowned for its caustic content, Fenton the cruellest interviewer of all. 'Let's leave it for a while ... see if he goes off the boil.'

Gracie shook her head. 'If you don't do it, he'll come out with a piece on his blog – why are you avoiding scrutiny? That's his style.'

Celia looked down at the desk, knowing Gracie was right but unwilling to concede. Either way, she was toast. But she didn't want to have lunch or dinner with a man at the moment, especially not a journalist, and that was what Paul Fenton was: a journo with a reputation for slicing interviewees in half.

On the way to the studio, she made a determined effort to think about only pleasant things, but they were bloody few and far between at the moment. Besides, the letter kept intruding, which was odd, because she was usually good at keeping her job in perspective.

In the make-up room, she lay back as her hair was sprayed and blow-waved and back-combed into shape, all the while looking through her brief. The after-effects of rape, family rows, and paying maintenance while not allowed access. She could do those three standing on her head, because they were regulars, cropping up in every postbag. At last they were ready to start on her face, and she put the brief aside, holding her breath as foundation was sprayed over her skin. The make-up artist tut-tutted as she applied the Touche Éclat to the dark rings under her eyes.

Celia closed her eyes, the easier to think through her next column – domestic violence: she must try to lighten things a bit; perhaps a teenage letter instead of the sex thing? Not that teenage problems were always trivial, and the lawyers might kick up if the writer was under 16. Her mind leapt ahead to Gavin's teens, and she shivered. How would she cope with a man-child? Michael would have done the birds and bees, taken Gavin to football, taught him to shave. Panic engulfed her, until she remembered Sean. Sean could do those things. If he was still around.

The man in the next chair was rising to his feet, putting aside the protective gown, thanking the make-up artist. He paused beside her. 'Paul Fenton,' he said. 'I won't interrupt you now, but I'm not giving up on that interview.'

Celia mumbled something, aware of the brush poised above her face, and the next minute he was gone.

'He's lovely,' the make-up artist said. '*The Hour* has been after him for ages to do a spot.'

'That's not what I've heard. They call him the male Lynn Barber.' In the mirror the girl regarded her blankly. 'Lynn Barber. She's an interviewer ... eats her interviewees for breakfast. That's why I'm avoiding him.'

The make-up artist's eyes were alive with interest. 'And he wants to do you? Lucky thing, I bet he takes you somewhere nice, and plies you with wine, and gets all your secrets.' The whole room was listening now, brushes poised.

'I haven't got any secrets,' Celia said. 'Besides, I haven't got time.'

As her face began to acquire contours and colour, she marshalled her thoughts. Once she got out of the studio she would ring Jim Horne. She had worked with him on the women's-prison item, and had been impressed by his passion for justice. She would show him the letter, and ask if there was something, anything, she could do. A sound technician was hovering, microphone in hand, and the make-up artist speeded up. 'She'll be with you in five.'

Celia felt the usual rush of nerves as the final touches were applied, and then she was being miked up and ushered along the corridor and into the studio. Paul Fenton was already on camera, talking easily to the presenters about items in the newspapers, until at last they were thanking him, and he was smiling into camera for that last all-important shot.

Then the floor manager was urging her forward, anxious to get her into the chair that Fenton had vacated. She settled herself, made sure her skirt covered her knees, and concentrated on her brief. The next moment, or so it seemed, it was over, and everyone was saying, 'Well done!'

She felt the usual anxiety as she walked off. They murmured 'Well done' to everyone. Had she hit on all the important points? Chosen the right words? Was someone even now tweeting that she'd been rubbish?

The corridor was long and brightly lit, but it wasn't empty. 'I waited,' Paul Fenton said. 'Let me take you for a drink. We both need one. And then I can persuade you to do that interview.'

She was opening her mouth to refuse, to say she never drank before six in the evening, but he went on talking. 'And if I can't persuade you then, I promise I will never bother you or your faithful assistant again. Now that's a fair offer, surely?'

She hesitated. Perhaps she could put him off the idea if they had a drink? Except that interviewers were always fixated on death: that was what he would want, every little detail of her loss. 'Please,' he said, 'I promise not to bite, so stop looking at me like a frightened faun.'

That did it! Frightened faun – bloody cheek! She gave him a Gracie glance, guaranteed to paralyse the opposition. 'No harm in one drink, I suppose.'

The bar he chose was quiet and elegant, and Fenton was obviously well acquainted with it. They sat in an alcove, the hum of chatter around them, making polite conversation at first, both knowing that was not what they were there for. In the flesh, he was slimmer than on television. There was a hint of grey at his temples, and laughter lines around his eyes. If she had met him as a stranger, years ago, before Michael, she might have found him attractive.

'Well,' he said at last, 'let's get down to it. Something has spooked you, because people don't usually try to avoid my show.'

'Perhaps they should,' Celia said, trying to sound in charge, and fearing she sounded scared.

'I'll admit I cut to the chase.' He was trying to fix her gaze, and she met it as bravely as she could. 'I like to think we do things that matter, but I'm after ratings, too. You didn't seem the type to want all the usual flim-flam about saving the world and not giving a damn for ratings.'

'You don't know me. And I don't know why you want to

interview me at all. There are dozens of agony aunts far more prestigious than me – that's what makes me wonder.'

'Not too many doing both newsprint and screen. Besides … you seem interesting.'

Celia decided to stop fencing. 'You say you like cutting to the chase, so let's do that. Your interest in me wouldn't stem from the fact that I was fairly recently bereaved, that my husband was a musician … I mean, I can see it all. You'll paint me either as a nun chained to the ghost of my lover, or someone who has cold-bloodedly put the past behind her and is soldiering on.'

'And you're neither?'

'I'm neither.'

'Which is why you're interesting. Most people fall into one category or the other. So an interview with you would open up a whole new category. Have I proved my point?'

She drained her glass. 'I ought to go.'

'Oh, now you're disappointing me. I didn't think you were the type to chicken out.'

She raised a quizzical eyebrow by way of reply, but her lips were starting to curve in a smile. 'I'm enjoying this,' Celia thought and was shocked by the realisation.

He was smiling, too, as if he knew what she was thinking, and then the barman was appearing with fresh drinks, and it was too late to stand up and take her leave.

'I read about your husband,' he said, when the barman had departed. 'Was he ill for long?'

'A few weeks.' She felt her throat constrict and hardened her voice. He'd love her to break down. He wouldn't need to do a fucking interview then, just describe her disintegration, and probably suggest she was an alky into the bargain. 'Michael could have had longer if he'd had chemo, but it would have been pretty grim, and he wanted good time with our son.'

'You looked after him yourself.'

'You've done your research!' In spite of herself she

sounded complimentary.

'No. My assistant is a fan of your columns ... and you. She told me.' He sounded surprisingly gentle, and Celia felt confused. She had expected to spar with a hardened journalist in search of a story, but this man sounded sympathetic. Perhaps people had got him wrong, after all.

He was changing the subject. 'Tell me about your work ... your postbag. They say it's huge.'

Was he letting her off the hook, or trying to do the bloody interview here and now? In spite of herself, Celia started to tell him of the perennials ... the people seeking justice, forgiveness, a way to re-establish trust. He listened silently, sometimes nodding agreement, occasionally raising an eyebrow, once interrupting to say, 'But don't they have families?' How could she explain why sometimes families were the last people to whom you could turn.

The barman came and went. She couldn't see Fenton giving a signal. Was this some common arrangement: that people were plied with wine while he persuaded them to tell all? And yet it didn't feel like an interrogation.

He was looking at his watch. 'You need food,' he said. 'Tea? Early supper?'

She tried pointing out that she had a child and responsibilities. He didn't argue, but she found herself ringing Sean and throwing herself on his mercy once more. 'I must stop doing that,' she said aloud, and Fenton smiled as though he understood.

They ate in a tiny restaurant, walking to it side by side through a rabbit-warren of side streets. The food was delicious, and in portions small enough to leave you wanting more. They talked of music, stage shows ... they both thought *Les Misérables* a work of art. 'Something new, something you missed, each time,' he said. That first time, when she had been to it with Michael, she had seen his eyes glisten with tears at 'Bring Him Home'.

'I have to be going,' she said at last, and was glad when he did not try to persuade her to stay.

'You will do the interview?' he said. It was a question, not an order, and she nodded.

'Ring Gracie. She'll fix it.'

'Are you sure? She defends you like a Turk,' he said, and she smiled, all the while wondering what she would do if he kissed her.

In the taxi, going home, she tried to dismiss the day as just another day. But it had been something more, and she knew it. Perhaps she was going out of her mind, and would be taken away by men in white coats.

'He's asleep,' Sean said, when she came in. 'Thrashed the life out of me at Scrabble, and went off like a lamb.'

'Sean.' She wanted to hug him, say thanks, say his being her lodger was a godsend, but the words wouldn't come. In the end she said, 'Thank you,' and knew it was enough.

Gavin was asleep when she went into his room. She sat down on the edge of his bed and watched him for a while. He was his father's son, it was there in the resolute chin, his ears close to his head and neat. She had always loved Michael's ears.

She felt strange tonight: sad, as usual, but elated, too, as though something had been achieved. She switched her thoughts to work, anxious to subdue the elation. She had had a drink with a man, that's all. She would do it again no doubt, with another man. Men. The thought of the years stretching ahead was suddenly terrifying. Work was the solution. She would ask Gracie to get out the quandary box tomorrow, the requests for help that had no answer but were kept on file in case one turned up. And she would have another look at that letter. '*You are my last resort.*'

She bent to smooth the hair from Gavin's brow, switched off the lamp, and left him sleeping.

CHAPTER 5

Sandra

Sandra had been awake for most of the night, huddled up on the settee, watching the shopping channel. It was somehow comforting to hear the voices burbling away about jewellery or shoes with sky-high heels and prices to match. She kept the sound low so as not to disturb Stuart. He loved his job, but the work took it out of him, especially when there was a rush job on. He had gone on a course when he left the army: mechanical engineering. He had sweated over textbooks, writing reports in his careful longhand, his tongue poking his cheek in the effort. When she had begged him to take a rest he had his answer ready: '*I want to get on, Sands, for you and the kids.*' She had laughed aloud at that. '*Kids? We've only got one.*' He had laughed too, then. '*One so far!*' They had made love that night, and he always claimed that was when Bobby was conceived.

They had only had Ann Marie then, and a two-room flat with a shower off the kitchen. They used to bath the baby in a blue plastic bath in front of the gas fire, sitting either side, marvelling at the perfect little thing with the starfish hands and the habit of pursing her lips for a kiss. But Ann Marie wasn't a baby any more. '*Have we been naughty, mammy? Is that why we can't come home?*' Sandra felt her eyes sting at the memory of that woebegone little voice. Mustn't cry. Not aloud, anyway.

Stuart was still asleep when she went back into the bedroom, and she put out a gentle hand to touch his arm. He was losing weight. Not surprising because he hardly ever had meals now. He ate whatever came to hand, not much caring whether or not it was tasty or good for you. When they had all been together she had loved mealtimes. Loved seeing them eat something she had made. Something healthy. They had good little bodies. Strong bones. No one could deny that, not even the Social Services. Except that they said she or Stuart had broken that strong little body, or at least done it dreadful harm. How could you harm a baby? They were so fragile, so trusting. You cradled them in your arms, protected their little limbs. The social worker had tried to say that there couldn't be another explanation, but there had to be.

As if she would ever have hurt them, especially Darren. He had been a fretful baby, right from the start. They had picked up on that. They took your words and twisted them.

'So he was a difficult child, Mrs Blenkiron?'

'No, not difficult. Just not as easy as the other two.'

'So he tried your patience – that's understandable.'

'No, it wasn't like that.' But it had gone in the notebook, so it had become fact.

She felt a whimper growing inside her chest, and pushed it back. Not yet. Not till she had locked herself in the toilet. You could cry there, and use the paper to wipe your eyes and blow your nose. Then you flushed it away, and no one knew when you unlocked the door and came out.

She looked at the clock again. Ten past six. She was always awake early on a contact day; thinking ahead, convincing herself that the children would be there, and knowing that at least one of them probably wouldn't be. Perhaps none of them would come this time? The Social Services would say they were running a temperature, or that there was no one to bring them. Sometimes they gave no reason at all, because they didn't have to give reasons. They had all the power, they didn't need to explain.

Some things were constant, though. At some stage, the social worker would try to separate her from Stuart, and would ask the usual question: '*Did he do it, Sandra? Best to tell us if he did. You'd get the children then, and you could be a family again.*' Both she and the social worker knew they would only be a family again over the local authority's dead body – even it one of them blamed the other. It didn't seem to matter which one, as long as they got someone in the frame.

She and Stuart had compared notes that first time, on the long drive home. Contact centres were always distant. 'It's in the hope you won't turn up,' the solicitor had told them. 'Then they can put you down as being indifferent.'

How had it come to this? Over and over again she had asked herself that question. She had even gone back to her old foster home, and tried to find an answer there. They'd been polite, had offered her a cup of tea and all that, but she could see that they weren't really bothered. And at the back of her mind, she wondered if they'd thought she really had done something wrong. Mr. Potts had even suggested she might be better off letting the kids go, and moving on. 'It *happens, Sandra*,' he had said. '*It's sad, but it happens.*'

Well, it wasn't going to happen here, not if she could help it. She'd always managed on her own, right from when she'd left the foster home: money and working, the Co-op at first, and then Marks & Spencer. That had been going up in the world, because Marks were picky about who they took on. She'd visited the Potts to tell them about Marks. 'Well done,' Mrs Potts had said, and had got the biscuits out.

Sandra had been at Marks & Spencer for seven years, shelf-stacking, and then on the tills. She had looked up one day, and seen the soldier she'd met the week before smiling at her – and that had been that. He had been waiting outside when her shift finished, and she had been sorry she wasn't wearing her belted mac.

They didn't speak much at the breakfast table, nor eat much either. Not that there was much choice. Stuart had missed so much work since it all began that the cupboard was bare. 'I'll make it up,' he had promised. 'When we get them back, I'll work round the clock, you'll see.' She had hugged him, and agreed, but, in her heart, she knew nothing was ever going to be the same.

On the drive to the centre, she thought about the price of petrol. She had never thought about it before, but now, every penny counted. If their Legal Aid ran out … the thought made her feel sick, and she started to count road signs instead.

They were allowed to see the children for 90 minutes every second week. Ninety minutes to remind three bewildered children that they were loved. And increasingly, to remind them who it was who loved them. 'They're not sure who we are, any more,' Stuart had said last time, and Sandra had told him not to be silly. But it was true, of the little ones at least.

'We'll give them the juice and the biscuits straight away,' she said as the centre came in sight. 'There'll be more time to play, then. To talk to them.'

But 'they' would be listening to every word. Pretending to talk to one another but, in reality, always watching. Sometimes making notes, if one of the children whimpered or threw a tantrum. And the children did act up a bit.

'They're tense,' Sandra thought. 'Just like us, they realise it's dangerous.'

At least they were all there this time. The baby in his foster-mother's arms was shrinking a little at the sight of Celia's outstretched hands. The foster-mother was kind: 'Here's your Mummy, come to see you,' she said. But Darren was turning away. What else would you do at 13 months old? She had still had milk when they took him, but the doctors had tablets for that.

At least Ann Marie was pleased to see them. Bobby had new shoes, and was showing them off. Sandra felt a sudden spurt of anger. She should be buying his shoes, the ones he liked with the flashing heels.

'Nice,' she said. 'They're lovely, pet. Proper shoes for a big boy.'

'Are we coming home today?' Ann Marie didn't look at her as she spoke.

'Not today, pet.'

'But soon?'

You shouldn't lie to a child but how could she tell the truth. 'Soon, pet. Very soon.'

They had put Ann Marie's hair in bunches, and suddenly Sandra was filled with rage. Her child's hair! She wanted to tear off the striped ribbons, brush the hair out the way it had always been. But if she did they would make a note: '*Behaviour which distressed the child.*' Brenda had warned her about that – poor little Brenda, who had had three children taken, one at a time, and who still kept hoping.

She and Brenda had been standing outside the court when they got talking. She had come out for air, and Brenda was already there, puffing on a cigarette. 'You in court?' Brenda had asked, and nodded sympathetically when she said yes. Brenda had told her what to watch out for, and what not to do. '*Behaviour which distressed the child*' would be the kiss of doom in court. She must warn Stuart about it. He would crack before she did. 'I'm like a tiger,' she thought. 'I'm coiled like a tiger, ready to fight for my children.'

The contact supervisor was approaching. 'Everything all right?' she said. Said, not asked, because even if you told her something was wrong she wouldn't do a blind thing about it. In the beginning, they had told the supervisor things, expected her to care, to be on their side. But she was just one of the rest, no different – whatever her job description.

Stuart tried reading *The Gruffalo* to the children. Ann Marie snuggled up to him and listened. So did Bobby, but only for a while. Eventually he zoomed off, shoes flashing, and climbed up beside the social worker. Don't cry! Mustn't cry! That was emotional abuse, and they could stop your contact. So she clutched the baby, inhaling the smell and the feel of him, trying to convince herself that 20 minutes in which he was still hers was a long, long time.

There were a few tears when it was time to part, but they were no longer tears of separation. They were tears of tiredness and resignation and impotence, because, whatever was to happen, they would have no control over it whatsoever. Little as they were, they knew it. 'Say good-bye,' the contact supervisor said. She didn't say *'Say goodbye to Mummy and Daddy'* – they never used those words. It was part of the process of weaning your kids away from you. Only the baby's foster-mother whispered, 'Kiss your Mummy,' and let Darren stay in her arms until the last minute.

They stopped half-way home and went into a pub. It was deserted at four in the afternoon. Stuart got the drinks, a half of bitter for him and a half-shandy for her, and they settled in an alcove.

'Shall I say it?' Stuart said.

'Say what?' She knew, but she had to ask.

'We're not going to get them back.' It was out, the genie from the bottle. 'We're not going to get them sodding back.'

It was awful to see him cry, but she couldn't comfort him. There was no comfort left in her. 'We need a better solicitor,' he said at last. He was wielding a hanky, across his eyes, then his nose. 'Someone who's on our side.'

She knew what he meant. They had picked their solicitor from a list Social Services had shown them. 'He'll be in their pocket,' Stuart had said at the time. Sandra had pooh-poohed that, but now she knew he had been right. If the solicitor wasn't urging caution, he was suggesting they admit to something ... 'and then they'll see you're co-operating.'

'We didn't do anything,' Stuart had said, desperation in his voice. But it was useless. It was all useless.

She sipped at her shandy, and tried to think about nothing. Stuart was counting the change in his pocket. That meant he wanted another drink. She tried to divert him. 'You haven't rung Granddad.' His grandfather had brought him up after first his parents and then his grandma died, and Stuart loved the old man, had delighted in taking the children north to show them off. No chance of their going to Durham now, not with what they had on their plate.

'I'm shirking it, Sands. Every time he expects me to say the kids are back, that it's all been a mistake. Last time I could hear the doubt creeping in. "They wouldn't have kept them all this time unless there was something."'

She tried to reassure him. 'He wouldn't think that. He knows you too well.' And then a terrible thought struck her. She had met the old man only four times since the wedding: he hardly knew her. Perhaps he thought *she* was to blame, the abuser? She looked up and saw Stuart's eyes on her, and knew that the thought had occurred to him, too. That was what happened when you got involved with Social Services. It dirtied everything, dirtied you so that people's attitude towards you changed, even people who ought to know better.

'Get another drink if you want it, love. I'm OK with this.' She watched him as he walked up to the bar, loving every line of his body. He was mining stock, strong. 'I love him,' she thought. But how long would he go on loving her if they had lost their children?

CHAPTER 6

Celia

'We've given her all the usuals, and she can keep us posted.' Gracie spoke flatly, without conviction, a sure sign that she was fed up with the problem. 'Shall I just file the letter?'

'We're losing enthusiasm over forced adoption,' Celia thought. 'We can do little or nothing for the parents; they never win; so we're admitting defeat.' It had been different in the beginning. She had gone home to Michael, bursting with indignation at a letter she had just received. *'They're taking their baby, Michael. Actually taking it ... imagine if it was Gavin! We'd fight them tooth and nail!'* He had taken her in his arms and patted her hair. *'Well, it's not Gavin, and now they've got you sticking up for them they won't lose their precious baby. I'm going to get you a big G and T, so calm down. It'll sort itself out, you'll see. This is Britain, after all.'*

But it hadn't sorted itself out. That baby had gone, and scores of other since, all swallowed up in the maw of the Family Court. And now there was no Michael to offer comfort.

Gracie was looking at her, expecting her to say, 'OK, file the letter.' Except that this time it wouldn't do. 'I must be getting soft,' she said aloud, 'but this letter has really got to me. Perhaps we could do a feature? Turn the spotlight on it?'

'The lawyers won't let you, you know that. Apart from which, the mother's got a gagging order on her. She's broken that, even writing to us. Put her in the spotlight, and she'll end up in a cell. People have been jailed for less.'

'OK.' Celia was playing for time, trying to come up with a solution. They had a huge mound of letters to consider, and the page still to assemble. 'Send her the usual letter, but keep her letter in the pending tray. I need to think more about it.'

She was sitting in the canteen an hour later, when Charles Lewin, otherwise known as Charley, her editor, sat down beside her. 'Stop frowning,' he said. 'It doesn't become you. No doubt it's one of your waifs and strays you're worried about.'

She wasn't in the mood to confide. 'No. Actually, I'm pissed off with my boss who always makes light of my huge contribution to this newspaper.'

'*Touché.*' He was laughing. 'If you can make jokes you must be OK, so I'll leave you in peace.'

After he'd gone, she found her lips forming a smile. He was one of the good guys. He'd been tough with her after Michael's death, forcing her back to work. But it had been the right thing to do._For a moment she tried to imagine him being gentle, sensitive even, but it was impossible. He was tough-as-boots Charley. People said he'd loved the wife who'd walked out on him, but you would never have guessed it. Except that sometimes he looked quite sad, as if he was remembering. She liked making him laugh when that happened, seeing his eyes crinkle behind the glasses, and his shoulders relax.

She snatched a canteen lunch with Grace, and then they set to work on the page. There was an art to it: you couldn't just take seven letters, and write good answers. You had to think about appealing to all sections of the readership, try to include a letter relevant to whatever was in the news, if possible, and make sure that at least one letter or answer would excite controversy.

It was nearly six o' clock when she pushed back her chair. 'Go home, Gracie ... if you've still got a home to go to. And don't hurry in tomorrow. I won't.' She had made three calls to Gavin since he'd got in from school, telling him what to eat, apologising for her absence, and promising him treats to make up. 'I'm a shit-mother,' she thought and gathered up her things to go home.

'See you tomorrow,' Gracie said as they left the lift. She

turned before she vanished through the car-park door: 'And remember you've got to answer Fenton.' His email had come in at 4.30: 'Are we going to do this interview research the hard way, or over a nice meal in a candlelit restaurant? It's up to you.'

Gracie's eyebrows had elevated. 'He usually uses a researcher for the prelim. Why is he giving you his personal attention?'

Celia had pretended to be uninterested, but she had to admit she too was curious. 'I'll answer him tomorrow.'

She was crossing the foyer when she saw the woman. A security man was attempting to hold her in the doorway, but the woman's eyes, looking past him, were fixed on her, imploring. 'Sorry, Mrs Aitken,' the security man said. 'We tried telling her you'd gone home, but she wouldn't be put off. She's been lurking outside since just after lunch. Never left the pavement.'

'Who is she?' Celia said, but she knew the answer. '*You are my last resort*' was written on the woman's face.

She walked across to the door. 'It's OK, I know now who she is.' For a moment, as the security man relaxed his hold, she panicked. What was the woman's name? She could see the letter, could remember every word except the name at the end. And then it came. 'Mrs Blenkiron? It's you, isn't it?'

She took the woman's arm and drew her towards a waiting taxi. She ought to take her somewhere and buy her a coffee, a meal even, but Gavin was waiting at home. 'Get in,' she said, and gave her address to the driver.

They didn't speak much on the way. 'I'm sorry,' the woman said, but Celia put a finger to her lips.

'Let's get home,' she said. 'You look all in.'

Sean was hovering in the doorway. 'You're here,' he said, with relief.

'Sean, I'm sorry.' She hesitated. 'This is Mrs Blenkiron. Sean Duffy, my tenant and guardian angel.' She could see Sean was curious. What should she say? 'She has a bit of a problem. We're going to have a cup of tea and sort things out.' Sean was still looking hopeful of being let into the secret, but she wasn't having it. 'We'll be fine; don't let us keep you.'

He gave her one of his wounded looks, but made for the stairs. 'OK, but shout if I can do anything. Gavin's with me, playing on his Xbox.'

'I'm home,' she called up the stairs, and got a distracted 'OK. Fine.'

In the end she poured two brandy and gingers, and handed one to the woman. 'You look frozen. Get that down you. When did you last eat?'

'I'm not hungry,' Sandra said, but when Celia came back with cheese and crackers she wolfed them down.

'I'm going to make a phone call, and then we'll talk. Take your coat off, and get comfortable.'

On the other end of the line, Gracie listened in silence as Celia told her of the meeting, but news that she had brought the woman home produced an instant reaction. 'Are you mad? I give up, I bloody give up. And what were Security thinking of, letting her hang around like that? I'll have words tomorrow. Now, put her in a cab and send her packing.'

'She lives in Norfolk,' Celia said drily, and held the phone away from her ear as Gracie erupted. When she put down the phone, she went back to the sitting-room. 'Sandra ... I think that's your name? ... you live in Norfolk.'

The girl was looking increasingly tearful, but she nodded her head. 'How are you going to get home?'

'On the train, I suppose.' This time her head was shaking and a tear rolled down the thin cheek.

'OK,' Celia said, trying to keep desperation out of her voice. 'Let's have this drink, and then I'll get you a cup of tea, and we'll sort it.' She left the girl in the sitting-room and went into the kitchen, followed by Sean, downstairs again and now with eyes the size of saucers.

'Who is she?' he asked, nodding back at the room behind them as she filled the kettle.

'I don't know ... I mean, I do, she's someone who's written to me. But I don't know what she's doing here. She lives in Norfolk.'

Sean's eyes widened further. 'She could be an axe murderer?' Seeing her eyebrows raised in mockery, he retracted. 'You know me, I'm a drama queen. She doesn't look as though she could knock the skin off a rice pudding at the moment. Anyway, if there's nothing I can help with I've got to go. Gavin's got homework.'

She tried to thank him, but he shushed her. 'Don't mention it. I like the kid.'

Back in the sitting-room, she tried to appear calm as she poured the tea. 'Now, tell me how you got here, what you want, and how you're getting home. I'm really worried about that. Take this tea. Will someone be missing you?' She searched her mind again for the name on the end of the letter before adding, 'Sandra'.

The girl took a gulp of tea, wiped her mouth with the back of her hand, and began. 'They've had a report done. Another report, it's the third one. They all say the same thing.'

'Go on,' Celia said gently. 'They all say what?'

'That we hurt our baby. Darren, that's his name. Non-accidental injury, they call it. They say me or Stuart did it, but we didn't. We love the baby, we love all three of them.'

The letter flashed up into Celia's mind's eye. '*You are my last resort. I could go to prison for contacting you, but I can't just sit here while they take my children.*'

They went through the details, stopping now and then when emotion overcame Sandra. As Celia watched the girl, she realised how flawed the system was. This was no more than a child; the father probably wasn't much older; and they were up against the massed ranks of authority and all its weaponry. Multi-disciplinary assessments; reports from Cafcass, which represented the children in Family Courts; foster-carers who, if they said the parents were good with their children, would lose their lucrative payments; Children's Guardians who were dependent on the local authority for their next job; the whole incestuous paraphernalia of child protection. If the parents didn't have a crusading solicitor – and they were as scarce as hen's teeth – they'd had it.

At some stage Gavin looked in, averting his eyes from the visitor. 'I'm off to bed. Had some of that ham in the fridge and a Hobnob. Night.' She closed her eyes briefly at the thought of Hobnobs and boiled ham as a balanced diet, and then she got on with the job in hand.

'Go on, Sandra. I need as much detail as you can give me.'

And so the sorry tale of hospitals and courts and accusations continued. The baby had been fretful, they had tried to get an appointment with their doctor, but the receptionist had been unhelpful. So they had taken Darren to A and E, expecting to be soothed and sent home because, by now, the baby had cheered up and was sleeping peacefully. Celia had heard it all before, but that had been on paper. Hearing it now, in her sitting-room, it took on a Kafkaesqe note.

'All right,' she said at last. 'It's half-past nine. I don't honestly think we can get you home. You might catch the last train, but I don't think you're in any fit state to travel alone. Can you telephone your husband?'

Sandra nodded. 'Yes. I told him where I was, when I was waiting for you. I told him I just had to come, because I couldn't think of anything else to do.'

Celia's heart sank. If they were regarding her as some magic solution to the problem, they were going to be sorely disappointed.

'He'll be getting worried now,' she said, and once more Sandra's eyes filled.

'I'll go. I don't want to be any trouble. There'll be a bus, or something ...'

'OK,' Celia said firmly. 'Here's what we do. I want you to ring him and tell him where you are. Tell him you're staying here tonight, and you're quite safe. Tomorrow, I want you to meet someone. Maybe one or two people, people who might help. Then we'll put you on the train home in the early afternoon. And you'll ring him in the morning, too, just to set his mind at rest.'

Sandra was nodding but the movement was apathetic. 'She's stressed out,' Celia thought. Stressed out and beaten down. On an impulse she held out her arms, and the girl came to her. 'I can't promise to make it all come right, Sandra, but I promise you I'll try.'

She left her alone to ring her husband, and went in search of bedclothes. She deliberated over inviting Sandra to share her bed and decided against it. The couch was comfy, and the girl so exhausted she could sleep on a pin. She made Ovaltine for them both, and placed a lamp beside the couch. 'You know where the bathroom is. Leave the light on all night if you want to. I know what it's like in a strange place.'

She went into Gavin's room, hoping to find him asleep. The room was in darkness, but in the light from the window she saw him raising himself on one elbow. She gave him a brief explanation, tucked him in, kissed the top of his head, and left the room. Safe in her bedroom, she sat down and contemplated what she had done. The girl would expect something now: a solution. And so would the husband.

In bed, she went over and over the details of the story to which she had just listened. It was chilling. Sandra and Stuart had met in a dance hall, when he was in the army. He was from mining stock, a Northerner. She had been brought up in care, and it was obvious that Stuart had provided her with the first security she had known. He had left the army after they were married, held a steady job, and three children had followed in quick succession. That they were innocent she had no doubt, even without meeting the husband. He didn't sound like a baby-batterer. And the other two children were thriving, or had been when they were taken.

The night sky was lightening before sleep overtook her. She had thought of thousands of things she could do – well, at least a dozen – but whether or not any of them would pay off was another matter.

CHAPTER 7

Celia

It was an odd breakfast-time. Normally, if Sean was going in to work, he didn't surface until two minutes before he needed to leave the house, and he seldom called in on Celia before he did. Today, he was wide awake and in her kitchen as soon as she was up and about, on the pretext of running out of bread. 'Brown or white?' she asked, raising her eyebrows.

His expression was deadpan. 'A slice of anything will do. I'll eat it here, no time to go back upstairs.' She mouthed the word 'Shameless' at him, and received an angelic smile in return. He had come to get an update on the mystery visitor, and they both knew it.

Gavin didn't say much but, to her delight, he was polite and helpful to their guest, handing her bread and butter. 'He knows something is up,' Celia thought. Sandra toyed with her scrambled eggs, but ate little. At times her eyes seemed tearful, but she kept a smile on her lips and tried to make conversation.

When it was time for Gavin to leave, he moved to Sandra's side. 'I hope things work out for you. My mum will help. She's good at fixing things.'

Last night in his bedroom she had tried to explain. 'They've taken her children away and she wants them back.'

'Did she hurt them?'

'She says she didn't.'

'Do you believe her?'

'I think I do. I don't know for sure, but I'm trying to find out!'

'Have they got a dad?'

'Yes. I haven't met him, but she says he didn't hurt them, either.'

'Why isn't he sticking up for them, then?'

Celia had felt her eyes prick when he said that. So that's what he thought dads were for: to stick up for you. To make sure authority didn't take you away. Did he feel vulnerable now that he had no dad to stick up for him? She had felt the familiar cloud of fear at the responsibility that had fallen upon her as she kissed him goodnight.

'I hope you get home safely,' Gavin was saying now, and holding out his hand. For a moment she thought Sandra was going to reach out and clutch him, and panic flared at what his reaction might be. But Sandra simply nodded her head in thanks, shook his hand and smiled at him, and the next moment he was heading out of the kitchen.

Sean was harder to dislodge. In desperation she went into the hall and called out to him. 'Sean, I need a hand.' He came unwillingly, looking back over his shoulder. 'You are unbelievable,' she hissed.

'*Moi?*'

'Forget the wide-eyed innocence. You're terrified you'll miss something. Go to work. There isn't going to be anything to miss. I'm taking her into the office, then I'm putting her on a train.'

'Poor bitch,' Sean said in tones of doom. 'Do what you can for her but they never give up, the SS. Once they've got you marked ...'

'Go to work.' He went back into the kitchen, and bade Sandra a dignified farewell, before Celia shooed him out of the door.

'Fill me in tonight,' he mouthed as she closed the door on him. She had to wipe the smile from her face before she went back into the kitchen.

'Your house is nice,' Sandra said. She was trying to make conversation again, and Celia responded.

'I like it. I did think about moving when my husband died, but in the end I stayed. And Sean came here as a lodger, so it doesn't seem so empty.'

'I didn't know you'd lost your husband ... I'm sorry.'

'He died last year, late last year. He was a musician, a clarionettist. He played with Purple Shades years ago ... you probably haven't heard of them. But jazz was really his thing, he was a session player.' Sandra was trying to look as though she understood, but Celia could see it was foreign territory. 'He had cancer. It was quite swift in the end.'

'That must have been awful ... watching him, and knowing you couldn't do anything.' Looking at her, Celia knew what Sandra was thinking as she spoke: that she, too, had been powerless to keep the one she loved.

Aloud she said: 'Well, I'm never sure which is worse: a sudden shock, or to watch someone suffering. Anyway, time we were moving. Are you sure you've had enough to eat?'

Sandra got to her feet, but there was no suggestion of haste about her. 'She doesn't want to move on,' Celia thought, 'because she wants me to produce a magic wand.' The thought filled her with a fear that lasted all through the journey into London and to *The Globe* building.

When they got to the office, she left Sandra with Gracie, whose face resembled thunder, and went in search of Charley. 'Ten minutes, in five minutes' time,' he said. 'Sorry, but they say the Opposition's coming out with some bombshell, so I can't be late for morning conference.'

When she got back to Anxious Alley, she found Gracie had thawed somewhat and was plying Sandra with coffee and biscuits. 'Couldn't knock the skin off a rice pudding,' she said to Celia, in a soft voice.

'That's what I value about you, Gracie. Your scientific judgements. Still, Sean said just the same thing.'

Sandra was concentrating on her coffee, but from time to time she glanced down the vastness of the newsroom like someone encountering Sodom and Gomorrah. 'It's big, isn't it?' she said, seeing Celia's eye on her. There was a note in her voice now that was almost cheery. 'Oh God,' Celia thought, 'she thinks the might of the press is on her side'. But press intervention was a two-edged sword. It could save, but more often it would smite.

Charley's spectacles were atop his head when at last she entered his office, which meant he was thinking. 'Yes?'

She moved to the desk and sat down facing him. 'I need something.'

'That's not an uncommon occurrence. Why the drama?'

'It's big. Well, it could be big.'

'Big as in expensive? If so, no.'

'Well, it would cost ... but it could make great copy.' She waited a few seconds. 'Eventually.'

'Now we're getting somewhere. You want me to finance some crazy charity project which ...'

She cut in. 'No, it's not charity. Well, it is in a way, but not like that.' And, before he could chide her for muddled thinking, 'I got this letter. It said I was its ... her ... last resort.'

She had his interest now, and the story rolled out.

'So you see why I want you to explore the whole forced-adoption thing. We can't use Sandra's own story, because she's gagged, but we can still tell it by telling all the other stories.' He didn't say anything and she plunged on. 'I've got her outside. There's huge mileage in it, Charley. There was a *File on Four* programme a few weeks ago, about hundreds of parents who've fled the UK to avoid having their children forcibly adopted by Social Services. Clandestine support-networks are helping them – providing shelter, food, advice, and money; all the things that are necessary for a new life. And really high-profile case studies, like that Italian woman who was forced into giving birth and had her child put up for adoption. That was huge! And there's that judge, Munby, who's trying to reform things ...'

But Charley was holding up his hand. 'Don't go over the top. I'll grant you there might be something in it. Where's this waif and stray of yours?'

'She's with Gracie. You'll like her, Charley, I promise you.'

He took his spectacles from his head and laid them on the desk. 'Wheel her in. I'm feeling weak today, and I know what you're like when you're thwarted.'

Before she took Sandra in to see him she explained who Charley was. 'He's very powerful ... and nice. Kind. You'll need to be very honest, as he'll know if you're holding anything back. But he can make things happen, Sandra. Far more than I can.'

As she had expected, Charley was kind and sympathetic, but probing. After half an hour he had two pages of notes, and Sandra was gazing at him as though he was God Incarnate. Eventually he stood up and held out his hand. 'I think we can help you. We'll certainly try.'

He escorted Sandra to the door, and handed her over to his PA. 'Celia will be with you in two minutes.' Back at his desk, he put both hands together in a pyramid. 'OK. She's patently innocent, but you need to meet the husband,' he told Celia. 'Make sure it isn't him. Second thoughts, tell Trevor to interview the husband – you're too gullible. If Trevor's sure, then we'll pay some legals. An investigator, if necessary. Get a paediatrician ... and a radiologist, if we can lay hands on the X-rays. See how far we can take it. Tell Features. We haven't had a crusade for a while, and it'll make a change from banker-bashing.'

'I could love you, Charles Lewin,' she said.

'Don't waste your time. Just give me some worthwhile stuff.'

They parked Sandra in the canteen with more coffee while they tied up some loose ends. 'You've got to give Fenton a date,'

Gracie said at last. 'Or tell him to get stuffed. I can't fend him off for ever. His PA's rung twice. We're on first-name terms now.'

'OK, tomorrow night, or Thursday. And if Sean can't sit in for me, you'll have to come over for Gavin.'

'Not part of my job description. I don't do children or animals.'

'No heart, that's your trouble.'

'Well, seeing yours is bleeding all the time, that's probably just as well.'

Eventually Celia and Sandra were in a cab, and speeding towards Liverpool Street station. 'Have you got a return ticket? Are you sure it's valid?' Sandra produced the ticket from the depths of her shoulder bag: an Anytime return. 'OK, well let's get the platform number.'

As she helped Sandra into the carriage, Celia gave her a hug. 'Try not to worry. I know that's not easy, but things are moving now. You've got Gracie's number and mine. We'll be in touch. Someone is coming down tomorrow or the next day to talk to Stuart.'

'Will it be you?'

'Probably not ... but they'll be on your side, whoever it is.'

She stood waving as the train glided out of the station. Sandra's face, pressed to the window, stayed with her until she was in the cab, and speeding back to the office.

That afternoon there was a meeting with Features, so she filled them in on the story, and answered their questions.

'How can you be so sure the parents didn't harm the children?' That was Emily, who would write the initial feature because she was good on facts and figures, and they needed to attract attention with startling details.

'Wait till you meet her, you'll see for yourself. And Trevor is going down to interview the father. He sounds OK from what she says, but I'll wait for Trev's take on him.' In the corner Trevor was nodding agreement. Celia liked him. Not young, but not old enough to be full of cynicism. If the father was kosher, he'd be all right with Trev.

At the end, it was agreed. The first feature, written by Emily, would outline the steep rise in the number of children taken into care since the Baby P. case. Later they'd outline some of the known cases of miscarriage of justice, such as that of the Websters, whose tragic case had been portrayed on *Panorama*. The next day, dependent on Trevor's visit to Norfolk, they would outline Sandra's story, minus any details that might identify them or the local authority. Subsequent articles would deal with the forensic side of child protection, a view from Social Services, fostering, the secret Family Courts ... 'It could run and run,' Emily said, almost licking her lips.

'They'll do a good job,' Celia thought, 'but I wonder if they'll give a shit for the poor sods involved?'

Back at her desk, Celia arranged for Gracie to ring Sandra the next morning, and give her the exact time of Trevor's visit. 'I'm going home now,' she said defiantly. 'I feel as if I've worked an 18-hour shift.'

When Gavin let himself in, she was ready with juice and biscuits.

'You're home!' he said.

'I'm home, and I'm not going out, so you have me for the whole night.'

'I'll be watching *Sherlock*,' he said warily.

'*Sherlock* it is.' She felt suddenly overcome with love for him, but she didn't reach out. There had been enough emotion for one day.

CHAPTER 8

Sandra

She settled into a corner seat and tried to clear her mind. The past 24 hours had been hectic, with so many things to think about, and Stuart would want to know every little detail. That was what she had loved about him from the start, the way he wanted to know everything that was going on. 'Nosey,' she had called him on that first date. He had taken her to Shoeburyness, where he was stationed, and pointed out the massive barracks. She had been disappointed that he didn't turn up in uniform but he had told her that no one wore uniform on their time off. She hadn't known he was a soldier when he had asked her for that first dance. In Southend, on her first holiday. Her and Mary Armstrong, a week in a B and B near the seafront. 'He's a bit of all right,' Mary had whispered, and then he was walking towards her, and something had told her, even then, that this was important. When he'd turned up at Marks's the next week, she'd thought her heart would burst.

She realised she had a foolish smile on her face, and looked around the carriage, terrified lest anyone was staring. But no one was interested. They were all buried in their newspapers or gazing at their Kindles as though afraid they might miss something. It was raining now, and the raindrops ran in crazy zigzags down the carriage windows. She watched for a few moments, suspending worry, not thinking about all the things that editor had told her, and all the explanations she would have to give when she got home. But even the rain deserted her at last, and the dull misery of thinking of a house without children returned.

The train was due into Norwich at 3.45. She bought tea from the trolley when it came round, and drank the strong, dark liquid with a grimace. The events of the past few hours were still coursing round her brain. How had it happened? One moment she had been sitting at the breakfast table, trying to get up the energy to do the washing-up, and the next minute she was putting on her coat, taking money from the savings jar, and getting on a train. But it had been worth it. For the first time in a long time she had looked into someone's eyes and not seen suspicion there.

What must Stuart have thought when he got back and found the house empty, though? He hadn't sounded angry when she rang him from Celia's, he'd just sounded flat. As though nothing surprised him any more. As though your wife ringing you from a strange house miles and miles away happened every day of the week. It was all because of the bloody social worker's visit that morning: the effect on him had been what triggered her off. They had had a letter, and opened it straight away, knowing it was important; but it was just about the next court date and a lot of legal jargon. And then the social worker had arrived unexpectedly, raising her eyebrows at the sight of Sandra still in her pyjamas. 'I thought I'd pop in, as I was in the neighbourhood. I want to make sure you know we only have your welfare at heart.' The woman's voice had oozed sincerity, but her eyes were like flint.

'How do you mean?' Stuart had said it politely. Different words had been forming on her own tongue, but suddenly he beat her to it. His voice was rising. 'What do you mean, our welfare? You've taken our children, you threaten and scare us, you never keep your word – where's the bloody welfare in that?'

'Now, now, Mr Blenkiron.' A tinge of pink had come into Mrs Harker's cheeks. 'That's been one of our worries. Your temper. We know the stress you're under ...'

Sandra had felt the fury rising in him, felt it through the hand she clasped between her own. She willed him to keep his mouth shut, but it was useless.

'Don't speak to me about fucking stress, when it's all of your making.'

That was the excuse Mrs Harker had needed. 'I'm afraid we'll have to leave it now. I need to talk to my line manager. We'll be in touch. You know where I am if you need anything.'

Sandra had wanted to say, 'What about seeing the children ... will it be this week?' But the words wouldn't come. There wasn't any point.

And so she had got dressed and left the house as soon as Stuart went to work; and at least her trip hadn't made things worse. She tried to tell herself it had made things better, but it probably hadn't. The rain had started again, the train was chugging into the station, and she gathered up her things to leave.

She had expected the house to be empty, but as soon as she turned the key in the lock she heard the radio in the kitchen.

'You're home!'

Stuart was rinsing a cup in the sink, and he turned at the sound of her voice. 'I didn't go in today.'

Sandra felt her heart sink at the despair in his voice. 'Why not?'

'It just felt wrong, somehow. You not here, wondering what time you'd be back. Wondering if you'd be back ... I mean why should you? There's nothing left to come home for. No reason to go to work. Don't look like that, Sandra. I know we need the money, but sometimes ...'

She moved to his side and put her arms around him. 'I know, love, I know. But the journalist's going to help, Stu. And the paper. People listen to newspapers.'

'We're not allowed to talk to them, Sandra. You know that. You could go to prison.'

'That's why I didn't tell you – so you're not involved. So you'll still be there for them, whatever they do to me.' He was shaking his head, and she felt the tension go out of him, till all she was holding was a lifeless bulk. 'I'll tell you what! We're going out for a drink. It's ages …'

He was interrupting, his voice flat and lifeless. 'We can't afford it.'

'We can, and we are.' To hell with the rent and the money for the gas. Right now they needed to get out of the house. And anyway, half the rent and the gas had gone on the rail ticket. 'Get your coat on. I'm not arguing.'

They walked hand in hand to the pub, but it was like holding the hand of a child. 'He's lost his nerve,' she thought, and felt fear clutch at her throat – until she remembered that she could be brave enough for both of them, if she had to. In the pub, she ordered him a pint, and cranberry juice for herself. She felt heady already, what with one thing and another. No point in making things worse.

'Now,' she said at last, 'let me tell you what happened. I got a ticket at the station …'

She saw he was getting ready to ask how much. 'Never mind what it cost, it needed to be done. Anyway, I got to London and I got in a taxi – I'd never have found the right bus. When I got there, there was a man on the door, who wouldn't let me in. Wouldn't even send a message upstairs. So I just stood there, a bit round the corner, and I waited. There were people coming and going all the time, but not her.'

'How did you know what she looked like? And she might not have been there that day.'

'Her picture's at the top of her column. And I just had a feeling she was in there. She came out at half-past five. There was another woman with her, but she went through a door. I thought the doorman was going to see me off, but Celia wouldn't let him.'

'Celia?'

'That's her name. Celia Aitken. She's lovely, Stuart. Anyroad, she said to get in a taxi with her and she took me home. She's got a boy, and she dotes on him, you can see that. And there's a lodger. I think he's gay, and he was nice, too. We talked. She really listened, and she knows all about social workers. We're not the only ones, not by a long chalk. Anyway, in the end she said it was too late to get the train, and that's when I rang you.'

'What's she like? Looks, I mean. Old?'

'Not really. She's got dark hair, and she's a widow. Quite pretty. A bit like Olivia Colman. You know, *Broadchurch*. She told me about her husband dying. He was only 37. A musician.'

'Cancer?'

'Yes. She's being brave about it, but she's very sad. I could see it in her eyes.'

She told him about Celia's house, then, and everything Celia had told her about the way the system worked, and about all the other people who'd written in to her. 'Then, this morning, I went with her to the newspaper and met the editor. He was a bit fierce, but kind underneath. He says they'll do something ... an exposé, or something like that. It won't actually mention us, but it'll be about us and people like us. And they'll get us a solicitor, a top man. What d'you think about that?'

She had expected Stuart to perk up as she told her tale, but he remained withdrawn. 'What is it?' she said at last. 'I'm sorry I went without telling you, but I'm back now.'

'Another letter's come,' he said flatly. 'They won't let us move the Legal Aid, because they say the solicitor we've got hasn't done anything wrong.'

'Because he hasn't done anything at all,' Sandra said. 'That's the whole point.'

They walked home through pools of lamplight, holding on to one another because clutching anyone, anything, helped. Once inside the house they moved together towards the stairs, not bothering to check kitchen or living-room, wanting only to lie down in the dark and comfort one another.

There was enough light from the street lamps, and they undressed. Not hurriedly. There was no room for fervour here.

She wanted to love him, to give him relief from the fear that oppressed him. He kissed her gently, touched her breast. She put up a hand to his face and felt his cheek wet. 'I love you Stuart.'

'I know.'

They lay on the bed, not bothering with sheets or duvet. She put out a hand and felt his erection. Not dominant as once it was, but still a sign that he desired her. He moved above her, and she kissed his face, his neck, his shoulder. Felt him enter her and hugged him tight with every muscle. But it was no use.

'I can't Sandra.' He was wilting inside her.

'It doesn't matter. I love you, Stuart.' She felt his tears on her shoulder, and all she could do was hold him like a child, and vow vengeance on the people who had rendered him less than a man.

CHAPTER 9

Celia

Gracie was obviously pleased with herself. As Celia advanced on Anxious Alley she could see her assistant was getting ready to emote. 'I've done it,' she said, as Celia divested herself of coat and bag. 'Don't ask me how ... well, do ask me, because it was bloody hard work.'

'How did you do it?' Celia knew better than try to hurry things along. She had no idea what Gracie was talking about, but it was obviously important.

'I've found her,' Gracie said. 'Her ... the forced-adoption woman. Glenda Forbes. I told you all about her. No, don't look vacant, I told you yesterday.'

'You tell me so much,' Celia said faintly, but Gracie was oblivious of sarcasm when she had something vital to impart.

'And ...' She paused for dramatic effect. 'And she's here in London for two days, speaking at a conference. You're seeing her today at four p. m. at her hotel. You can put it on expenses. Tea, I mean, or whatever she drinks. You should get a good interview out of her. They say she's won hundreds of cases. Well, not exactly won them, because she's not properly qualified or anything like that ...'

Gracie paused for breath, and Celia stepped in. 'What do we know about her ... actually *know* as opposed to "they say"? Do me a brief, anything you can get. Oh, and well done.'

'Don't stop.' Gracie rolled her eyes. 'It's not often I get a word of praise. Coffee or tea?'

After that they worked steadily for more than two hours, Celia on letters, Gracie on the Glenda Forbes brief.

'It doesn't stop, does it?' Celia said at last, putting another Social Services letter in its pile.

'It's got worse since Baby P.' Gracie tapped her teeth with her pen. 'In a way, you can't blame the social workers. They're damned if they do, damned if they don't.'

'And the Government's adoption tsar urging them on, suggesting the splitting-up of siblings! Doesn't he realise the bonds children have?' Celia paused, then, thinking of Gavin who had no siblings to bond with, and never would, now.

'You're right,' Gracie said, as she returned to her desk. 'Remember that letter, the one from the man who said his social worker keeping him and his brother together had made all the difference to his growing up?'

Charley summoned Celia at lunch-time. 'I've sent out for sandwiches. Sit down, and tell me how far you've got.'

He listened carefully as Celia explained to him about Glenda Forbes. 'So she's a sort of knight errant, riding to the rescue in cases like these?'

'I suppose she is. No qualification, just a lot of experience.'
'Background?'
'I don't know. But I will after this afternoon.'
'What motivates her? You need to be sure she's not preying on families in trouble. Or after money.'

'I will, but Gracie is sure she's kosher and ...'
'... Gracie is never fooled,' he finished for her.

They talked about other things, then. Gavin; and whether or not she needed a holiday. Celia liked it when Charley's face softened. Actually – and she'd never thought of this before – he was handsome, in a craggy sort of way. But it hadn't saved his marriage. His wife had gone off with the children, and had then taken him to the cleaners financially, or so the story went. Of course, everyone's sympathy had been with Charley, but you never knew exactly what went on in anyone else's marriage. Perhaps it was handsome is as handsome does – though she couldn't imagine him being unkind. Forceful; relentless in pursuit of a goal; but not unkind.

'I feel quite mellow,' she told Gracie, when she got back to her desk.

'Stay like that,' Gracie said tersely. 'Here's the brief on the Forbes woman, and there's a cab booked for 3.45.'

Celia finished wading through the letters, signed off the week's copy, and saved the brief to read in the cab. Glenda Forbes's hotel was in Camden, so she obviously watched the pennies, but the brief made fascinating reading. Glenda Forbes was 38, unmarried – though she had a young son from a long-standing relationship – and had once held an executive post with a High Street retailer. So how had she become a champion of those mistreated by the Family Courts?

Gracie would have checked every avenue, but there was no explanation: Glenda Forbes had suddenly appeared as a champion of parents deprived of their children, and later as a McKenzie friend, who could stand beside people when they were in court; she was now seen as a beacon of light in the murky world of forced adoption. She had been responsible for several high-profile overturnings of care orders, and was, at present, involved in a dozen or more adoption proceedings. That she had never succeeded in overturning an adoption order was not surprising: that had never happened in Britain.

'Will I like her?' Celia wondered as she put away the brief. If she didn't, she was in for a grim couple of hours. She was approaching the reception desk when she heard a voice behind her. 'Celia?'

She turned to see a tall woman with a rather solemn face and untidy auburn hair prematurely flecked with grey. 'I've seen you on TV,' the woman said. 'That's how I recognised you. Shall we sit down over there?'

She spoke almost reluctantly, and Celia's hopes sank. When someone didn't want to be interviewed, it made for an uphill struggle.

She ordered tea, brushing aside Glenda Forbes's protest that 'There's no need to bother.'

'I'm dying for a cup,' Celia said. 'And I'm grateful to you for making time to see me when you're only in London for a short while.'

If she was hoping to soften the woman's defences, it wasn't working. 'I'm not sure I can help you,' Glenda Forbes went on. 'I can't talk about individual cases.'

'I know that. Actually, this is not so much an interview as a chance to ask your advice. Some of my colleagues will want to interview you later, but I'm really after picking your brains.' Glenda Forbes's eyebrows twitched at that, but she didn't speak. 'I've had a letter ... well, I've had a lot of letters over the years about forced adoption, but for some reason this one really got to me. I've met the mother. She seems a nice woman, and her distress is dreadful to see.'

'Unexplained injury?' Obviously Glenda Forbes didn't believe in wasting words or time.

'Yes. How did you know?'

'It's one of the commonest excuses, rapidly being overtaken by "risk of emotional harm", whatever that means. Are the children in care?'

'At the moment, yes, but there's an order of some sort coming up.'

'So the parents are allowed contact, but the contact is becoming less frequent, and sometimes the kids aren't there, or the contact centre is further away?' Celia nodded. 'It's the usual pattern. Designed to weaken the parent-child bond.'

She knows her stuff, Celia thought, and sat back as a torrent of information poured forth. If it was all true, it was dynamite – but someone like Trevor would have to talk with Glenda Forbes, and then check the facts.

According to her, Social Service departments got as much as £27,000 when they placed a child, and £2,000 when a child was fostered, which could be said to constitute a financial inducement to act. One fostering agency, founded a few years ago by two social workers, was making £10 million per year, and had been sold by its founders for a reported £130 million. Celia could hardly believe such astronomical figures, but Glenda seemed sure of her case.

She was defending the right of the state to step in where necessary, now. 'Would I have had Baby P. out of his home? You bet I would. It's what happens afterwards that I take issue with … no proper appeal system, everything being decided by the very people who took the child in the first place. Every year more than 25,000 children are removed from UK parents, most of whom have not committed any crime and who are not addicted to alcohol or drugs. A lot of them are taken for "risk" of future emotional harm; yet an average of 10,000 children in state care go missing every year! What about the emotional harm involved there?'

She was warming to her theme, and Celia wondered why she was so impassioned. 'I care,' she thought, 'but this woman burns with her cause.'

Now Glenda was on to the secrecy of the Family Court. 'They refuse to admit relatives, or allow parents to call witnesses; they refuse a second expert opinion; they quote parents' previous offences committed 20 years before; and they often forbid parents to contact their own children. One mother was jailed for three years for meeting her daughter against court orders; and a father was jailed for waving at his children in care as they passed by in the street.'

She looked quizzically at Celia. 'You're wondering if I'm making this up. I wish I were. As for gagging orders, they would stop people appealing to their MPs if they could. How's that for democracy? At some parents' contact visits, the children are not allowed to discuss their cases, say they want to go home, or complain of sexual or physical abuse by fosterers or social workers. If they do any of these things, contact with the parents can be stopped. Foster-carers can make £590 per week per child; care homes cost an average £4,000 per week per child; and the whole system costs over £2 billion a year! It's become a cash cow for some people, and it's causing misery for others.'

'You make it sound horrendous,' Celia said faintly.

'It is horrendous!' said Glenda. 'You should Google Professor Jane Ireland's report on expert witnesses. She was commissioned by the Family Justice Council to look into reports submitted by psychologists to the Family Courts. She found most of them incompetent. They were simply "professional experts", making a fat living from the Court. And as courts usually rely on a single expert, you can imagine what that means.'

She smiled at Celia's look of disbelief. 'Don't take my word for it: read the report. Professor Ireland found that a fifth of them weren't even properly qualified, and yet a report could easily bring them £4,000. One "expert" claimed to write 200 reports a year. Do the maths.'

They talked for the next hour – or rather Glenda questioned Celia about the Blenkirons, and Celia answered as best she could. The words 'flow charts' and 'Guardians' and 'orders' and 'proceedings' rolled smoothly off Glenda's tongue: she obviously lived for her self-appointed task. Suddenly, she looked up from the notepad she had filled with scrawled scraps of information. A young woman was approaching them, and it was obvious that this was Glenda's daughter. The resemblance was marked. 'My daughter,' she said shortly. 'And the reason I do this.'

After the girl had chatted for a few moments and then left, Glenda said, 'I was 22.' Her voice was flat but Celia could sense the intensity of the emotion underneath. 'She was born when I was 17, but her father stood by me. We were happy, even though money was tight. When she was four, I noticed her leg was swollen, so I took her to the Welfare. They knew me there, and I felt safe. Anyway, I won't bore you with detail. They put her in care, and then they rang rings round me. I had a solicitor, but he was in the local authority's pocket. He went to work for them, eventually – a reward for being their creature, no doubt. In the end, they decided on adoption. Her father and I split up after that. It often happens, parents turn on one another.

'I didn't see Sue for 14 years, and then she sought me out. She'd had good adoptive parents. She's still in touch with them, but as soon as she could she came looking for me. She knew I had loved her, and that I would never have hurt her. She begrudges those years we were apart. I also have a son of seven. They're not at ease with one another, even two years on, but we're working on it. That's why I do this: to try and save other people from what happened to me and Sue.'

They parted, shaking hands and promising to meet again. 'Next time I'll bring some of my clients with me,' Glenda promised.

Sean didn't seem inclined to talk when Celia got home, and she was glad. He could be sensitive when he sensed she was upset. 'The boy went off somewhere, that boy he's pally with. He said he'd be back at seven.'

She thanked him, and then went into the kitchen and poured herself a Scotch. Her head was swimming with facts and scraps of information. Above all, she was remembering the passion in the woman's voice, and the young woman who was the reason behind it. Would Sandra's children need to seek her out in 20 years' time? 'Not if I can help it,' Celia vowed, and poured herself another drink.

She found the Ireland report without difficulty. It was scathing. Of the expert-witness reports they had examined, 65 per cent were rated as 'poor' or 'very poor'. Some 'experts' had not even thought it important to interview the people they had been asked to assess, and some of the intelligence tests they had used were 20 years out of date. Some reports failed to answer vital questions. 'Simply hopelessly confused' had been one verdict.

But the most damning section was the one on fees. On average, experts charged £120 an hour, which was higher than the rate for working in psychological practice. The report condemned experts for making their living by writing such reports alone. And it highlighted the fact that the secrecy of the Family Courts allowed experts to avoid the scrutiny that their work would receive in other courts.

Lady Gaga's sudden warbling from above was a welcome diversion. Celia switched off the computer, and went to start making the supper.

CHAPTER 10

Sandra

The reporter arrived at 11.30, fresh off the train. Stuart and Sandra had been up, washed and dressed, for hours, even though Gracie had given them an exact arrival time. He was younger than Sandra had expected, with a smile that crinkled up his face. 'Sandra?' he asked, and held out his hand, when she opened the door. 'I'm Trevor ... and don't look so scared. I don't bite.'

Sandra stammered out something, but even to her own ears it sounded like mumbo-jumbo. Stuart appeared behind her, then, and Trevor re-introduced himself, allowing her time to compose herself.

'I'm forgetting my manners,' she said, 'keeping you on the step. Come in. Can I get you tea, or a sandwich, or anything?' She could hear the ingratiating tone of her voice, and it sickened her, but she kept it there just the same. 'Or coffee?' She would have offered him anything just to get him on-side. Just to get him to go back to the newspaper and say they were all right.

'That's very kind, but I've got a hell of a thirst on me. And I haven't got the car like a millstone round my neck. God bless trains. So why don't I take you two down the pub? There's one just around the corner, I saw it from the taxi.'

They hadn't been to that pub since the children were taken. '*Too ashamed*,' people would say; and, in a way, it was true. They were ashamed: no one else round here had ever had their children taken into care. Sandra had seen the sly looks in the Co-op, the crossing the street to avoid meeting. '*As though we had the clap!*' Stuart had said. His boss at work had backed him, had tackled the talk head on and said he didn't believe it.

But others had been different: she had seen the hurt in Stuart's eyes, so she knew it was so.

For one wild minute, she considered saying no to the reporter. 'Not that pub. Somewhere out of the area, maybe, but not the one round the corner.'

But the reporter, who said his name was Trevor, was too much for them, sweeping them up and into the Pollard Arms, and ordering drinks all round, and sausage and chips three times.

'The paper is paying,' he said, when Stuart reached for his wallet. Sandra felt a flush of relief, because three drinks and three meals would have cleared them out for the rest of the week. And they couldn't touch the money they'd put aside for an appeal, if one was necessary. Not that you'd get much justice for a couple of hundred pounds, but the way it was dragging on they might yet manage a bit more. So they chewed sausage and moved the chips around on their plates, all the while answering his questions.

'Tell me about your everyday routine, when the children were at home, before it all began.' That was fairly easy, spelling out the day, hour by hour.

'So Dad sometimes bathed them?'

'Yes, if he was in the right shift. But he was very careful with them ...'

He held up a hand. 'I'm not trying to trap you, Sandra. We're on your side.'

She tried to relax then, and answer truthfully. Who had fed the children? Put them to bed? Were they good kids? What part did Dad play in discipline? The questions came thick and fast, although Trevor gobbled his food like there was no tomorrow. She saw Stuart relax after a while, become more talkative as the beer got inside him. Was this all part of a plan? Fill him with ale and start with everyday questions, and then the killer punch: *Did you hurt your baby?* But that question never came. Trevor made notes, wiped his mouth with a paper napkin, and pressed on.

'Tell me about the day it all went wrong.'

There was silence for a moment, while Sandra waited for Stuart to speak, and then tried to marshal her own thoughts. Where had it gone wrong? She felt the usual confusion, the moment when she wondered if perhaps they were to blame ... and then reason re-asserted itself and she knew what she had to say.

'It was just an ordinary day. We were thinking about Christmas, and the kids were getting excited. The night before I'd been showing them how we made paper lanterns ... you know, you fold the paper and then cut it ...'

Trevor was nodding reassurance. 'Anyway, they went to bed eventually. A bit excited. Even the baby knew something was going on. They knew Christmas meant a lot to me, always has. Even when I was in care.'

Trevor was raising inquisitive eyebrows. 'Care?' he said. And then she had to tell him about that, and how they were always nice to you at Christmas, even the foster parents who were only in it for the money. When she was with the Clarks they had bought her presents with their own money. Little things, but it had meant more than the big present the council always sent.

'We were going to have a real tree for the first time. We'd always had artificial ones up till then. I mean, we were all happy. I went to wake up the kids, and Ann Marie ... she's the oldest ... she said the baby had been been grizzling all night. I didn't think anything of it until I touched his leg, and he cried out.' Suddenly her mouth was dry. How did you explain a nightmare?

'Go on,' Trevor said, and there was such sympathy in his voice that she could go on, telling how they had gone to the hospital A and E, and everyone's eyes had been on them, accusing. After that it had been meetings, and forms to fill and sign. Everyone else having a lot to say, and them not allowed to speak. No one meeting your eyes any more, and trying to remember who was who, like the woman called a Guardian who they had hardly ever seen, although she had written reports on them. How many reports had there been? 'Enough to stretch from here to Portsmouth,' Stuart had said once, and it was true.

'If only we hadn't gone to A and E,' she said, when the tale was finished. 'He's fine now, so it can't have been much. Metaphyseal fractures, the solicitor said. Anyway, they wouldn't have anything other than that we'd injured him. One of us.'

Trevor was nodding. 'I read up on them after Celia explained. Apparently, they're controversial – they can be the result of trauma, that's violence, but not necessarily.'

'They tried to get me to shop Sandra.' Stuart was entering the fray now, indignation making his voice more high-pitched than usual. He mustn't lose his temper, not in front of someone from the paper. But Trevor was nodding understanding, and gathering up his things.

'I'd like to see the kids' bedroom, if I may. Readers like that sort of thing, and we want them to get interested in you, in getting you back together as a family.'

As they walked back to the house, Sandra thanked her lucky stars that she had bottomed the rooms a few days ago. As she led him upstairs, sunlight was streaming through the window. She stood back as they entered the room, and he turned and smiled at her when he saw Ann Marie's animals piled high on the pillow. She stood by, as he moved round, making notes as he went. He smiled at her again when he came to the board with Ann Marie's drawings pinned to it. 'You've got a little Rembrandt here,' he said, and the kindness in his voice was too much.

'I'm sorry, I'm ...' But he was shushing her, tucking his pad under his arm to lay both hands on the arms she had raised to shield her face.

'Listen, you cry if you want to. It's a good release. But then you've got to go downstairs and let that man of yours think everything's all right. He can't let go because he's a man, God help him, and we're not supposed to feel things. But I can see the misery in his guts. I know how I'd feel if it was my lot, though the times I've wished them in Nova Scotia don't bear counting. Now that's a good girl; dry your eyes, and trust *The Globe*.'

He motioned for her to lead the way downstairs, and they left the sunlit bedroom that was now silent and once had throbbed with the chatter of children.

'We're going to go all out,' Trevor said, as he gathered up his things before departing. 'A campaign. Not just on you ... the gagging order bars that ... but on the whole Family Court thing. Celia will keep you in touch. You liked her, didn't you? She won't let you down.'

That was the trouble, though. No one ever let you down deliberately. They just did.

When they were left alone in the silent house, they subsided into chairs. 'We're worn out,' Sandra thought. Worn out with trying to look like people who would never hurt their children. Had Trevor believed them? He had shaken their hands when he left. Could he have done that if he didn't believe them? Yes. Because people lied.

'What do you think?'

She knew Stuart had been waiting to ask her that ever since they'd got home, but she still couldn't give a direct answer. Instead she said, 'What about?'

'You know. Him.' What should she say? That she had liked Trevor, and was hopeful – or that, like him, she was beginning to believe that they would never get their kids back again. She didn't want to say anything because, in the mood he was in, he would twist it.

As if he read her thoughts, Stuart spoke. 'What do you think he'll say when he gets back to London? "The bastards deserved to lose their kids"?' He was trying to sound jovial, but his voice cracked on the last sentence.

'Now stop that. He liked us. You heard what he said about the campaign, and everything. They wouldn't be doing that if they didn't believe us.'

She was trying to think of something else to say when the phone rang.

'Stuart?' The woman on the other end of the line sounded agitated.

'No, it's his wife. I'll get him for you.' She held out the phone, but he didn't reach for it. Instead he wrinkled his brow and mouthed, 'Who is it?' Sandra shook her head, mouthing back. 'She asked for you.' And then, understanding his reluctance, 'It's not the Social.'

He took the phone, then, saying his name gruffly, as though already scenting trouble. Sandra saw his brow darken as he listened, and occasionally uttered an 'uh-huh' or a 'yes' or a 'no'. When he put the phone back in its cradle she could see that he was struggling to hold back tears.

'What's the matter?'

'It's Granddad. A stroke, they think.'

'Is it bad?'

'Bad enough. He's in the Infirmary. She's going to keep us posted. It's the woman who lives two doors up.'

'You ought to go and see him, Stuart. You're all he's got.'

'I know … but how can I, with all this going on?'

She put her arms round him, then, feeling the frustration in him. 'I know, love. I know.' In the end they decided to leave discussion until the morning.

There was an old movie on one of the funny channels, and they sat side by side watching it without really taking it in. After that it was the news, and then *Emmerdale*, but for once the soap failed to hold their interest. It was only eight o'clock, still light outside, but they mounted the stairs to bed. Too tired to think, too tired to get washed or brush their teeth, too tired to make love, and, in the end, too tired to sleep.

CHAPTER 11

Celia

It began as a low-pitched whine, but by the time she was awake enough to sit up in bed it had developed into a full-bodied howl. It was an animal of some sort, but how the hell had it got in the house? Gavin was on the landing when she emerged from the bedroom, pulling on her dressing-gown. 'In God's name, what is that?'

He was trying to sound nonchalant as he replied, 'It's only the dog. It's got post-traumatic stress disorder, Sean says.'

'Dog? Sean's got a dog? Since when?'

She saw Gavin's expression change into 'Have I said too much?' mode, and then his brow corrugate as he sought for the least damaging reply.

'Since when?' she repeated.

'Since ... ages. I thought you knew.'

Now he was definitely lying. Celia crossed to the stairs, and called up, 'Sean! Here, now!' Whether he could hear her above the dog's caterwauling, or was being deliberately deaf, was another matter. It took yelling his name twice more to produce an answer.

'Yes?' he said. So it was going to be injured innocence.

'Gavin says you've got a dog.'

Gavin's protestation was heartfelt. 'I didn't ... well, I didn't *tell* her. She just heard.'

From behind Sean's jeans-clad legs the dog had emerged. It was large, hairy, and stick-thin. It looked at her defiantly, but its tail and ears were down, and she felt a stir of compassion.

'It's got nowhere to go ...' Her son was doing the pleading, and Sean was letting him.

'How long?' she asked.

'Only since yesterday ... Monday ... well ...'

'Get your stories straight. We'll talk about this later.' She needed time to think. One more mouth to feed – it didn't make sense. And yet, everything she knew about child bereavement screamed, 'Get them an animal.' Perhaps it was what Gavin needed? Besides, the dog looked as though it had had a hell of a life up to now.

All the same, she couldn't let them get away with it too easily. They would take over completely if she gave them half a chance. In the kitchen she filled the kettle and turned on the radio. Nigel Farage was exuding bonhomie, as usual. She put bread in the toaster and waited for the kettle to boil. At seven tonight she would be seated opposite Paul Fenton on a TV sofa, facing an audience of 2.5 million. She had taken the day off to ensure that she was calm and collected by evening. She had even contemplated a long lie-in and a leisurely brunch. Instead she was working out how you evict a dog without causing your only son life-long trauma ... and possibly losing your lodger into the bargain.

'Well,' she said, when they were settled around the table, the dog at Gavin's feet. 'Who's going to start? And the truth, please. No fairy stories about it just wandering in half an hour ago.'

'As if!' Sean said, in injured tones. So that was the format: '*You baddie, me goodie.*'

Once or twice, Gavin pleaded the dog's cause, but Sean's hand-wringing was more effective. The dog had been beaten, abused, neglected, thrown out ... any minute now he would say he'd found it hanging from a tree! If he ever wanted to leave IT, Celia reflected, he could find a permanent niche in TV drama.

'OK,' she said, at last. 'I can't settle this now, so it can stay for two days. Two days max. Now I'm off to regain my composure before, what I might remind you, is going to be an ordeal.'

'You'll be a smash,' Sean said, smiling now he'd got his

own way. 'Everyone loves agony aunts, anyway. It'll be easy-peasy!'

She contented herself with giving him an old-fashioned look, but he just smiled back.

'You've done telly before. You do it all the time,' Gavin said, trying to be helpful.

'Not like this,' she said and made for the safety of her bedroom.

She spent the afternoon in and out of the shower, peering at herself in mirrors, rehearsing possible responses in her head. What was Paul likely to ask her? He could be a swine with guests who were not forthcoming, that was well known. More than one guest had got up and flounced out – but she wouldn't give him that satisfaction, no matter how hard he probed. She tried lying down with her feet up, hoping to quell the tumult within her, but gazing at the ceiling only made it worse. Why the hell had she agreed to do it? It was Gracie's fault: she should have put her foot down. She'd done that before, with other invitations to Celia of which she disapproved.

Occasionally laughter drifted up from below, interspersed with the occasional bark. They were having fun, and, in spite of herself, her lips curled with pleasure. She could cope with the dog, as long as it settled down. She'd certainly fatten it up. Its ribs were a bit too prominent for comfort.

Gracie rang at 4.30. 'So?'

Celia could imagine Gracie gazing over her spectacles as she waited for the answer. 'So what?'

'Don't be obtuse. Glenda Forbes – how did it go? I thought you might have rung me this morning, after all the trouble I took!'

'It was good. Well, productive. But gut-wrenching, as well. If half of what she told me was true, it's a national scandal.'

She outlined the course of yesterday's visit, and then played her trump card. 'I know now why she does it.'

She had Gracie's interest. 'They took her daughter from her. An "unexplained injury" when she was four. She was adopted by nice people, but she had no contact with her mother – not for years. And then, when she was old enough, the girl sought her out. She's back with Glenda now. I met her yesterday.'

'And the poor adoptive parents have been dumped, I suppose?'

'No, she's still in contact with them. Very fond of them, and grateful, but just wanted her Mum.'

'Poor sods. Fifteen years of investment, and then given the bum's rush.'

'Something like that ... which is an aspect I'd never thought of.'

'It's stolen goods, Ceely.'

'I suppose it is.'

Gracie's call had been a temporary relief from thinking about what lay ahead. But the call ceased at five p. m. when Gracie went home, and there was still an hour to fill. Celia put her dress on at 5.30. In the mirror she looked gaunt without make-up. Perhaps the dark dress was a mistake? She was halfway out of it when she realised that she had nothing else nearly as suitable. It would have to do, and, anyway, she hadn't been invited because she was a fashion plate. If they did a half-way decent make-up, and sorted her hair, she'd get by.

It was a relief when the studio car drew up at the door, and there was no escape. She sank back into its depths, and tried not to think about what lay ahead. In two hours ... three at the most ... she'd be in another car, speeding home. And she would never, ever, agree to do another chat show.

The make-up room was long and brightly lit, with rows of chairs facing a long mirror. The man in the first chair was a politician. A Tory. The man at the other end of the line was a trade-union leader, which meant there might be a punch-up on air, and the make-up artists had diplomatically placed the future combatants as far away from one another as possible.

She sat back in the chair as a pink wrap was placed around her, and tried not to think of the ordeal ahead. The political opponents were the heavy item. The giggly comedienne she had seen in the green room was the light relief. She must be the 'get your hanky out' moment that every good chat-show needed. She tried to occupy her thoughts as a mist of foundation drifted across her face and throat. The dog would have to go. Sean was prone to taking off from time to time, and her hands were much too full to baby-sit an animal … especially one with PTSD. On the other hand, Sean and Gavin were a powerful combination. She realised she was smiling inwardly at the thought of two reproachful faces if the dog got the chop.

'Smile,' said the make-up artist, and she dutifully pouched her cheeks for blusher.

When they were finished with her, the face that looked back from the mirror was that of a stranger, but a good-looking stranger. 'Thank you,' she said with fervour, and scuttled back to the green room to wait her turn.

'You're the last item,' the researcher told her. 'He's given you 17 minutes!' Her tone said that 17 minutes was a privilege rarely accorded, and Celia's heart sank even further. What the hell could they talk about for 17 minutes?

In the event, it seemed to pass in a flash. Paul Fenton was by turns probing and sympathetic. So adept was he that she soon forgot the cameras, and the studio audience beyond. She told him about her early life, her first steps in journalism. He was looking at her intently now. What was coming?

'I get the feeling, Celia, that you've never quite been part of the Fleet Street scenario. Oh, geographically it isn't Fleet Street any more, but the cut and thrust, dog eat dog, hasn't changed. If anything, it's got worse. Women columnists are not called the bitches of Fleet Street for no reason.'

'Ah, but I'm not a columnist, I'm an agony aunt. And besides ...' She couldn't resist a riposte. 'You could say the bitchiness is more apparent on television now than in print.'

He was grinning, so it was all right. '*Touché*!' he said, and then moved on to her marriage and Michael's death. 'What was it like to sit there on that television couch, comforting other people. Didn't you want to lean in to the camera and say, "What about me? What about my pain?"'

She heard a voice answering, calmly and coherently, and could scarcely believe it was her own. 'Yes, it was painful. If I hadn't had my son, I think I might not have made it. It's nearly a year now. It gets easier with time, but I still have my moments. However, it gave me a new understanding of what other people go through. Obviously, bereavement is part of my postbag – well, I've been there now, so I'm better equipped to deal with it; more empathetic if you like, I think that's the word.'

They were over the hurdle, then, and it was suddenly easy to talk about her job, the thousands of letters and phone calls, so many of them about age-old problems, but different because every person is unique, and must solve their problems in their own way. And then he was leaning forward to lay his hand on hers.

'Thank you for being a wonderful guest.' He was making his goodbyes to camera now, thanking his guests, promising treats in store for tomorrow, ending with his catchphrase: 'I'll be back!' Someone was ushering her towards the studio doors, and the audience was applauding. 'In here,' someone else said. Drinks were waiting in the green room, and trays of tiny sandwiches.

'You were marvellous!' The producer looked and sounded relieved, and Celia was tempted to say, 'Did you think I'd be dreadful?' Instead she smiled and reached for a glass of wine.

A few moments later Fenton was there, his face cleansed of make-up. He moved among the people in the green room, thanking his guests, patting the backs of his crew, generating the feel-good factor.

'He's good at what he does,' Celia thought; and then he was at her side. 'Thank you,' he said.

'So I did all right?' '

'You know you did. It was wonderful, warm, and funny and, at times, very emotional. You couldn't hear the comments in the gallery. Neither could I, even though I wore an earpiece. Because there weren't any comments. They were spellbound.'

She laughed to show she didn't believe a word he was saying, but a little knot of pleasure had formed in her chest.

He leaned towards her to whisper, 'Two more minutes, and then we can get out of here.' She wanted to say, 'I must go straight home,' but the words wouldn't come – and, anyway, he had already moved away.

CHAPTER 12

Sandra

The visit seemed to have lasted for ever. The same old exhortations, promises, refusals, as usual, and more and more of the jargon Sandra never understood. But at least the woman was now gathering up her papers. 'I'll see you out,' she said as politely as she could.

As she closed the door on the departing social worker, she thought of Mrs Harker's last visit. Stuart had been at work, and the social worker had settled in a chair, for all the world like a family friend. She'd even accepted a cup of tea, and had talked about the progress Bobby was making at his new nursery. Then she had got down to the real business of the day.

'I've been talking with the Children's Guardian – you know, Mrs Brooks, she represents the children's interests?' Sandra had barely seen the woman, but she knew who she was, so she nodded.

'Well, we've been talking and we both think ... and you know we're on your side, yours and the children's, that is ... we both think that you should be honest about what happened. We know how it can be – no real intention to hurt, just stress, a troubled night, perhaps, and things boil over. We both understand your loyalty to your husband, but it would be better all round if you were honest with us about what really happened. Then we could begin to sort things out, and you could all get back to normal.'

'They've decided Stuart's the bogeyman, and they want me to shop him,' Sandra thought again.

Mrs Harker was continuing: 'The children are doing very well in their new environments, but they miss one another. They miss you. They could all be back here in a few days if we could draw a line under it all.' She looked beseechingly at Sandra, and smiled. But only with her mouth.

Inside Sandra, a sigh grew, grew so big it threatened to choke her. 'We've been down this road already. I've told you … we've both told you: we put him to bed and he was fine, and in the morning he was whingey and his leg was swollen. So we took him to A and E. Why would we have done that, if one of us had hurt him?'

'But that's just it! You're basically good parents, so you did the responsible thing. And now the responsible thing would be to tell us the truth, so it can all be cleared up.'

She had wanted to shout: 'So you can fucking take the kids away for good!' But she didn't. If she did it, would go down in the book, one more nail in the coffin of their family life. She had looked Mrs Harker in the eye, and repeated her story.

Suddenly Sandra realised she was standing with one hand on the door, lost in contemplation. She turned back into the room.

Stuart was putting on his coat. 'I've got to get off, love. I'll just make it, as it is.'

She smiled and nodded. His shift started at 12, and there might be traffic. The social worker had arrived just as they were getting breakfast, both of them still in their night-clothes. Did they make these surprise visits in the hope they would catch you at a disadvantage? She wouldn't put it past them, Sandra thought.

'I'm sorry I lost me rag a bit there, Sands. It's just that you know it's all bloody futile. She comes and she gloats over us. It works me up. I try not to rise to it, but it just gets me.'

'I know,' Sandra said. 'I know.' They were the only words that would come.

After he had gone, she looked at the squalor of the breakfast table, fat congealing on the plates, drips of milk on the cloth, crumbs, even a line of salt from an over-enthusiastic shake. She ought to clear it up. Instead she stood up, and stripped off her nightie. If they couldn't get the Legal Aid changed to a new solicitor, they would have to get the money elsewhere and pay for proper representation themselves. She had been thinking about it for ages; now she was going to do it.

Half an hour later she was on the bus into town, her bag clutched against her chest. Everything they had of value was in there, apart from her engagement ring. That was still on her finger, but it could go if necessary. There was the case of silver spoons that had been a wedding present from her workmates; the gold bracelet Stuart had bought her as an engagement present; the carriage clock that his works had given them, the little silver rattle that had been passed down through Stuart's family and given to Ann Marie when she was born. She would pawn that rather than sell it: it was a family heirloom. And there was her ring. That should fetch good money.

There were two possible places. One she had always known about, the back shop behind the jewellers, the one no one liked to be seen going in and out of. The pawnbroker's. A bell jangled when she pushed at the door, and she felt as though the whole street outside must have stopped to stare. The place was dark and small, with a counter at one end. A woman appeared from behind a screen, and that was a shock: you always imagined pawnbrokers would be men.

Sandra pulled the ring off her finger and held it out. 'I want to pledge this. Just for a while.'

The woman was examining it closely. 'We don't usually do dress rings.'

'It's not a dress ring. They're diamonds.'

The woman was screwing an eyeglass against her eye, and squinting at the ring as she held it aloft. 'The most I could do would be fifteen.'

Fifteen pounds! They had saved for months to raise the £300 the ring had cost, and the jeweller had said it would appreciate in value with time. She could hear the woman laughing as she fled the shop, the ring, snatched back, in her hand.

She sat in the park for a while to collect herself. Beyond the railings she could hear traffic whizzing by, sometimes people talking and laughing as they walked on the pavement. The sound was somehow calming: ordinary life, people getting on with things, some of them people with problems like her own. Well, not quite like hers but still – hills to climb.

She got to her feet and made her way back into the town centre. She had seen the notice in the evening paper: '*Jewellery and silverware bought. Good prices.*' The notice had named a local hotel, and given times. Today it was 12 o'clock ... five minutes to go.

A porter in the hotel lobby gave her a room number on the second floor, and she mounted the stairs. The door to the room was ajar, and when Sandra entered she saw a table over by the window. Behind it sat a man, a huge man. Flesh lay in rolls around his neck and quivered beneath the wool sweater he wore. There were three other women in the room, sitting on chairs, obviously a queue; and a fourth woman was sitting opposite the man at the table. He was taking notes from a tin box, and as he handed them over she saw his pudgy hands were festooned with rings.

He didn't speak, and neither did his customer. She thrust the notes into her handbag, closed it, got up, and left the room, without meeting the eyes of anyone else. The woman who took her place was tiny and ancient, so fragile that she made an incongruous picture as she sat opposite the gigantic man. Sandra felt a giggle rise up inside her, and hastily subdued it.

The old lady was opening her shabby handbag and upending it over the table. Jewellery was cascading from it ... gold, silver, here and there the flash of coloured stones. Sandra felt a stab of pity: the old woman must be desperate to bring her all to such a place. Except that there was a king's ransom on that table ... As the man's pudgy fingers began to sort through it, pushing gold here, silver there, stones to yet another place, Sandra suddenly realised what was happening. The old woman was a go-between, a fence. The pile on the table was the haul of more than one burglary, and the woman had been here before. Many times before. That was why there was no conversation: they had no need of it.

She thought of the time when an elderly woman down the street had been burgled. It had taken her months to get over it. In some ways, she never had. '*I'd wring the bugger's neck if I laid hands on him,*' Stuart had said, witnessing the old lady's distress. What would he think of her, sitting here in what was little more than a thieves' kitchen? She got to her feet and left the room.

On the bus going home, she clutched the bag, feeling at first relief that she still had their treasures, and then despair at one more avenue now closed to them.

CHAPTER 13

Celia

Trevor was jubilant. 'We're getting there. The web is alive with talk about our feature yesterday. Wait till they see tomorrow!' Seeing Celia's raised brows, he amplified: 'We're doing the Websters. You remember ... *Panorama*? John Sweeney?'

She remembered the Websters well. Sandra's story had echoes of theirs: three children removed because one child had metaphyseal fractures. Barely six months later, the children had been removed and put up for adoption to separate homes. By the time it emerged that the child in question had an underlying bone fragility caused by lactose intolerance, it was too late.

'Are you interviewing them?' she asked.

'No. Just recapping and adding comments. The story speaks for itself. It's now acknowledged as a gross miscarriage of justice ... according to the judge, the adoption proceedings took only one day, and he described them as "cursory".'

'They ran away, didn't they ... when she got pregnant?'

'They went to Ireland. Social workers followed them, and when the parents came back they slapped a gagging order on them. It was the *Mail* and the Beeb who got it lifted, and kept the baby for them, but it was too late to get the other kids back. Come to think of it, I'm fairly sure it was Judge Munby's decision to lift the gagging order, and allow the Websters to instruct new experts. So he was aware of what was going on, even then.'

'The council didn't get to take the new baby?'

'No. The new experts exposed the truth, they kept the baby ...'

'... and without that new baby, none of the truth about the others would have come out?'

'Exactly.'

Celia thought about it as the taxi carried her to her dinner with Paul Fenton. A gross miscarriage of justice, and not a blind thing anyone could do about it. What if that happened to the Blenkirons? It didn't bear thinking about.

Once again, Paul seemed to be well known. They were shown to a table that was clearly reserved for the cognoscenti, and the restaurateur clasped Paul like a brother.

'He's a bit OTT,' Paul said, when they were at last alone. 'But wait until you taste the food. And I'm told you like Viognier – tell me what you think of this.'

Celia was still wondering how he knew about her taste in wine when their first course arrived. The food was indeed good. She had not been hungry until the scallops appeared, dressed and arranged to create maximum temptation.

'Um,' she said, when it was eaten. 'I see what you mean about the food.' On Paul's recommendation, she had ordered a sausage and red onion hot-pot to follow. It came with a potato and beetroot gratin that melted in the mouth. Sitting across the table from him, she found it hard to believe all the stories about Paul Fenton – the stitchings-up, the ruthless exploitations of friends and workmates alike. Tonight he looked relaxed, almost boyish, and he was certainly being the perfect host.

It was confusing to be fussed over. Michael had always made her feel safe, but he'd never fussed. She had missed his calmness. Now she winced a little at the thought that she was comparing Paul Fenton with him. The hand refilling her glass was brown and slim, with elegantly manicured nails, but it was still forceful. And he had a knack of making you feel like confiding in him.

From the start, she had been determined not to let him get to know her too well, but he held her gaze as she talked, prompting her here and there but gently. 'I'm saying too much,' she thought, but she went on talking, just the same. He smiled at her feeble jokes, his eyes crinkling at the corners, and he seemed really interested in Gavin. She would have to find out more about his own background. Was there a woman somewhere? Children, even? He looked like someone who had an interesting back story. She refused pudding on the grounds that she was already full, but did accept a spoonful of his banana tarte tatin.

'Wicked isn't it?'

She resisted a second proffered spoonful, and agreed that it was indeed wicked. 'I'm enjoying this,' she thought, and felt surprised, and then again a little guilty. She was wiping her lips with her napkin when she saw Jane O'Neil coming through the door. Christ! It would be all round the office tomorrow. Jane might work for a rival paper, but the jungle drums had a wide range. She felt her skin prickle with embarrassment. Why had she dolled herself up, put on lipstick, even eyeliner?

'Something wrong?' Paul's tone was sympathetic, but he had put out a hand. She snatched hers away.

'No, nothing. It was … it's just someone I know.'

'And you're embarrassed to be seen with me?' His tone was amused, but his eyes were kind. He half turned to see where she had been looking, but mercifully Jane O'Neil was now seated and out of sight.

'No. Yes … not you, anyone.'

'This isn't India, Celia. We don't require widows to mount the funeral pyre.'

'I know, it's silly, but it's just hard. You're suddenly someone you never expected to be. Never imagined you would be. And you don't know how to behave.' Why was she saying all that, to him of all people?

He was smiling. 'You sound about 17 and very, very scared.'

'I'm 38, but the scared part is true. Nothing prepares you for this. If you ever think about being widowed, you imagine being noble, stoic, a monument to your dead husband. When it comes down to it, you just stagger from one crisis to the next.'

She had a sudden and frightening desire to have his arms around her. She reached for her glass, and then pushed it away – she had had too much already. 'I want to be held,' she thought. 'I just want someone to hold me.' Aloud she said, 'I ought to be going. I'm outrageous in the way I rely on Sean. I don't know what I'd do without him.'

'You must have coffee ... and I want to hear more about your work.'

The waiter approached at that moment, giving her time to pull herself together. When the man had retreated, Fenton smiled. 'You're thinking deeply?' It was a question, and his eyes were on her, demanding an answer.

'Work,' she said quickly. 'That case I was telling you about.'

'The children taken into care? How's it going?'

'Getting murkier by the minute. I met an amazing woman the other day, a crusader called Glenda Forbes. She says that agencies get as much as £27,000 when they place a child for adoption, and £2,000 when a child is fostered. I can hardly believe those figures, but she swears they're kosher. However, she defends the right for the state to step in where necessary.'

'Surely no one denies that; but, on the other hand, if you're correct, justice is not always done.'

'True – and it's the scale of it that scares me. I had 450 letters on the subject last year.'

'Four hundred and fifty! That sounds like *Empty Cradles*,' Paul said.

'Empty cradles?'

'You haven't heard about the big scandal, about thousands of children taken from their families and shipped out to the colonies? The woman who uncovered it wrote a book about it, called *Empty Cradles*. There was a film, too, called *Oranges* something. Not as good as the book. It was after the war. And it all went on into the 1970s, I believe. Something like 4,000 children were shipped to Australia, New Zealand, Rhodesia, Canada, and God knows where else.'

'Orphans?'

'Not necessarily. Although some of the children were told their parents were dead, when they weren't. All the children's charities were involved in it.'

'How old were the children? Teenagers?'

'No, I think some of them were pre-school age, poor little buggers. Just plucked from their homes and scattered to the four corners of the earth. This social worker ... the woman who wrote the book ... found many of them had been abused in the very places where they'd been sent for sanctuary. Some Canadian farmers were even charged with manslaughter: they'd used the kids as slave labour. And the ones sent to the Christian Brotherhood fared even worse.' Paul had obviously been affected by the book, for he spoke with passion.

'I think I heard from one of them, then,' said Celia, 'one who was left behind. He and his brother were taken into care, and then one day his big brother vanished from the sort of camp they were in. He was told he'd been sent overseas to somewhere marvellous, but the kid had been grieving ever since – and he was 50 when he wrote to me.'

'They never met again?'

'No. I gave him what help I could, but I suppose too much time had elapsed.'

'And all in the name of making things better.' Again there was what seemed like real passion in Paul's voice, and she warmed to it. She made a mental note to get Gracie to Google the book they'd been talking about, and began to gather up her things.

Suddenly he put out a hand and laid it over hers. 'Slow down. You're supposed to be relaxing, not fretting over the world's woes. Take that anxious look off your face.'

She told him about Anxious Alley, then, and he laughed.

After that, it was music, and books, and who and what she approved of in politics.

'You're remarkably right-wing for someone who lost their parents so young, and must have had to rough it a bit.'

'I don't think it was that bad. I had the aunts, and a good education.' She sounded surprised, and indeed she was. She had never considered herself right-wing. More a very wet liberal.

'I'm winding you up,' Paul said, smiling. 'But you did have a lot to contend with. It must have been a bit of an up-and-down existence.'

'I went to good schools. I never wanted for anything.'

'Not materially. But there are other things in life. And then there was losing your husband. I can only imagine what that was like.'

She gave what she hoped was a broad smile. 'You're very thorough, Mr Fenton. You seem to know every little thing about me. Are you always so thorough with your former guests?'

'Oh, tonight is not about interrogating you, Celia. I've already done that. Tonight is purely for the pleasure of your company. And yes, I did a little research. You interest me.'

She felt at once elated and out of her depth; and, as if he realised her confusion, Paul changed the subject completely, telling her a funny story about a guest on his last programme, and encouraging her to reciprocate.

They didn't speak much in the taxi, and he behaved impeccably when they reached the house, handing her out of the cab and waiting while she fished for the key.

'Thank you for tonight.' He was smiling down at her as he continued: 'Can I give you dinner to say thank you?'

'You've already given me dinner. The next one should be on me ... the gratitude, and the dinner.' Celia winced as she realised she had implied there would be a second meeting. She turned away then, to avoid anything like a farewell kiss.

Once inside, she sat down at her computer and Googled his name. There were several Paul Fentons listed, but it was easy to pick out the right one. 'Paul Alexander Fenton (born 30 March 1971), British journalist, television host, and winner of a Junior Wimbledon title in 1987.' She was surprised to see that he had written a book, *Musings on Fame*, and made a mental note to order it from Amazon.

His parents were Stanley Morgan Fenton, a civil engineer, and Elizabeth Anne Fenton (née Cresswell). Stanley had died in 1999, and Elizabeth two years later. There was no mention of siblings, so he really was a wolf who walked alone. He had been educated at Oundle and at Trinity College, Cambridge. His degree was second class, but that hadn't stopped him rising through the ranks of Fleet Street like a rocket, to become editor of the *Mirror*'s showbiz page; then a columnist on the *Mail*, for which he still wrote occasionally. He now had his own chat-show on Channel 4, and a weekly column in a Sunday supplement. There were details of previous girlfriends, but none listed as current; an impressive list of his 'friends', which included almost everyone who was anyone in show-business; and details of a previous series in which he had visited major cities and given his take on them. There were hints about politics, and a suggestion that Tony Blair had wanted him to stand for Labour in the 1997 election. So he was a man of many parts – which made it all the more extraordinary that he had been sitting with her in a London restaurant.

She made cocoa, and carried it through to her bedroom, then she went to Gavin's room. He was sound asleep, a book discarded on the coverlet. She lay down beside him and put an arm over him. It was amazing how good it was to hold her child. She felt the stress begin to leave her, and reached to turn out the lamp. So she would sleep in her clothes tonight? So what!

She was drifting off when Sandra's words floated into her

mind: '*You don't know where to put your arms. They just feel empty all the time.*'

'I've got to help her.' She had spoken aloud, and Gavin stirred slightly. She tightened her arm around him, and closed her eyes. But sleep wouldn't come. Besides, she ought to be in her own bed. In the end she got up and returned to her own room.

CHAPTER 14

Sandra

She had fried the last two eggs for breakfast in an attempt to give the day a good start. Tomorrow's visit at the contact centre was not mentioned, but the thought of it hung in the air like smog. They ought to feel glad about going, seeing their children again, keeping the bond alive ... but it didn't work like that. It felt more like a trip to the condemned cell. All the same, it had to be coped with, and they would be devastated if it was cancelled.

Before that, though, they had to go to London and face the solicitor that *The Globe* had found for them. Celia had said he was lovely, but Celia seemed to think that of everyone. All the same, if he was nice, it might do Stuart good. At the moment he didn't seem to want to discuss their trip to London – or anything else, for that matter. She tried to engage him in chat about the football match spread across the back page of the morning paper, but a 'yes' or a 'no' was as much as she got. At last she took the bull by the horns. 'Are you going to ring about your Granddad? We'll be leaving soon?'

'I might.'

'You should. You're not shirking it, are you?'

'No. Well, a bit. And I know I'm letting him down ...' Stuart's face crumpled, and she got to her feet to comfort him.

'Don't take on, love.' He was putting her away, and clearing his throat. He was the one taking on, but he'd die before admitting it. The most she got was a half-smile, and 'Let's get today over. Then I'll think about going home.'

'*Going home!*' So he still thought of County Durham as home, although they had been here for seven years. Maybe they should move north when it was all sorted? When they had the kids back. There was nowhere she thought of as home: that was what being in care did to you. You were moved about so much you lost any sense of a place you could call your own. How many placements had she had? Eleven? Twelve?

She took pains with her hair, and put on mascara and lipstick. Must try to look her best. Making an impression on this solicitor was important. 'One of the best in London,' Celia had called him. She closed her eyes briefly on a plea that Celia had not exaggerated.

They were silent as they drove to the station. In her handbag were the two standard rail tickets Celia had sent, along with a set of instructions. They were to make their way to the solicitor's chambers in Lincoln's Inn Fields, and she would meet them there. '*We'll have a bite of lunch after, and discuss what he's told you,*' the note said. After that it would be up to them to go straight back to Liverpool Street or stay in London for a while. '*You've got Anytime tickets so why not have a bit of a break?*'

Sandra had smiled when she read that, but it was a wry smile. She could only hope they had enough money to see them safely home. A wave of misery swept over her at the unfairness of it all. They hadn't done anything to anyone, and yet here they were, strapped for cash ... and it would be worse next week, with the stoppages for Stuart's absence today. They were broken, and childless; there was an old man probably dying at the other end of the country, and God knows when they could afford to get to him. They were on their way to be grilled by a solicitor, who might or might not take their case; and their neighbours thought them little better than paedophiles. In spite of herself, a little moan escaped her.

'Come on, we're going on the choo-choo,' Stuart said. He was trying to jolly her along, but his tone was so filled with misery that it was almost made her smile. And the baby language reminded her of him giving Bobby rides on his back as they played choo-choos. She put her hand on his knee and squeezed it. She loved his limbs, strong and muscular. She had thought them capable of defending her and the children against anything. But they were useless against the state. Against Cafcass and the Guardians, and the massed forces of Social Services.

They sat opposite one another on the train, knees touching, his feet either side of hers or sometimes in between them. It felt strangely intimate, in spite of the full carriage. Sometimes their eyes met and they half-smiled. Mostly they looked out of the window at fields and houses, factories and car-parks whizzing by. She wondered if Stuart was thinking what she was thinking – or, rather, wondering. What was going on behind the curtained windows of houses big and small? Were they having peaceful breakfasts, or had they already left for work or the school run?

They were going through the outskirts of London when she realised that he was probably thinking about the place he called home. About his Granddad in a hospital bed. He ought to go to him, once they got today over. Thinking about the day ahead suddenly dimmed the sunshine outside the window. What if the solicitor didn't like them? What if they didn't like him? He was important, Celia had said. He didn't need business the way their old solicitor did, anxious not to upset the council, kow-towing to anyone with an official position. 'And doing bugger all for us,' she thought, and then looked guiltily around in case she had spoken aloud.

Stuart took her hand as they walked through the station. 'We're getting a taxi,' he said, and took no notice of her intake of breath.

Lincoln's Inn Fields was certainly not countryside; and the solicitor's was an imposing building with brass door-furnishings that could have graced a cathedral. They were offered coffee while they waited, and then Celia was there, reaching out to hug Sandra, and shaking hands with Stuart. 'He won't keep us long,' Celia said; and the next moment they were being ushered into the great man's office.

Laurence Cohen was smaller than Sandra had imagined, and almost boyish. For a moment her heart sank: he didn't look old enough to impress a policeman, let alone a judge. But as he began to talk, she felt herself relax. There was no soft soap about him. He warned them that the only way was to be truthful and hold nothing back. 'Now, begin at the beginning,' he said, 'and leave nothing out. I've seen the paperwork. Now I want the real story.'

Sandra looked at Stuart, and saw he was expecting her to begin. 'Well,' she said – and then it came tumbling out.

Mr Cohen was nodding, as though in agreement. Once or twice he held up a hand to halt her, and asked a question, which she answered as best she could. When she began to falter, Stuart took over, suddenly more vocal than usual. 'We've told them and told them. I've offered to take a lie-detector test. Bring it on, I said, that'll settle it. But they don't listen. From that first minute they've decided: you're a child abuser, plain and simple.'

It was Mr Cohen's turn, now. What had the social worker said … her exact words? What had their solicitor said to that? The questions went on until, at last, the tale was told and he sat back in his chair, fingertips together like the spire of a church.

'Right!' he said. 'You may not know that it is now proposed that a 26-week timetable will apply to care proceedings, and that currently pilot schemes are operating under the proposed framework. The pilot ends soon, but I have no doubt that it will become the norm, since the whole thrust of reform has been to speed up proceedings. Part of this process is to force parties to agree things, to restrict the use of competing experts, and so on. All in all, it's a recipe for injustice.'

He held up a sheet of paper, coloured here and there in different inks and crammed with typescript.

'This is the Justice Ministry flow-chart for public-law proceedings under the pilot. I won't give it to you to read, as it's clear as mud. The first steps are usually where Social Services are in ongoing involvement with a family, which results in their deciding that formal proceedings are required. In your case, it seems that these preliminary steps were missed out, and Social Services got an Emergency Protection Order, which only lasts eight days, to remove the children, or get the parents to agree that the children should go voluntarily into care. Thereafter, reference to the flow-chart shows how quickly things happen.

'Especially in emergency cases, parents like you, who have had no previous contact with Social Services, haven't a clue about the system. I can remember two people telling me that it was only after the final hearing, when they lost the children, that the horror of it all really hit them. Innocent people naturally assume that the system will protect them, and that the truth will out. Sadly, too often they're wrong! There is so much jargon, and manoeuvring, and lack of communication and explanation, that the parents often do not understand what is happening. If their legal advisers don't make things crystal clear, they're lost.

'I don't totally blame the lawyers, as they themselves are put under so much pressure by the system. The trouble is that too few are prepared to rock the boat. But I am! So here's what we do.'

Sandra tried to take it all in, but a little bubble of hope was springing up in her chest, distracting her from his words. It went on swelling as they made their goodbyes, and emerged into the street. Celia jumped into a taxi almost straight away, offering profuse apologies that she had too much work to stay for the suggested lunch, and promising to ring them from home in the evening. She offered to take them with her, and drop them off, but they shook their heads in unison. 'We want to walk a bit, get some fresh air.'

There was a park ahead and they made for it. It was a

mistake. It was full of children, laughing, running, clutching at mums and dads, and here and there a uniformed nanny.

'What do you think?' Sandra asked, as they walked down a tree-lined path.

'He talks the talk,' Stuart said. 'But they all do that.'

As if in league with his sombre tone, the sun went behind a cloud, and the day darkened. At that moment the phone in her handbag rang. Who would be phoning her at this time? She fumbled for it. 'Hello?'

'Sandra, it's me, Mary.' They paused by a bench, and subsided on to it. Mary was Sandra's best ... her only ... friend. They had worked together, danced together, fallen in love at the same time. Best of all, she was one of the few people who knew what was happening now. 'How's things? Have they seen sense yet?'

It was a relief to talk freely and know she was believed. Beside her, Stuart was smiling encouragement. 'Not yet,' she said. 'But we've made some progress.'

CHAPTER 15

Celia

She woke before dawn, after a fitful night, the things she had heard from Glenda Forbes going round and round in her head. *'It's all over in the first week ... they won't go back on their original decision.'*

'Then why ...?'

'Why do I bother? Because you have to. You're doing it now, because of the sheer despair you see in your letter woman. You can't walk away.'

Celia raised herself on her elbow and looked at the clock. Ten minutes to six. By the time she had put the kettle on, the *Today* programme would be starting, and she could use it to shut down the uncomfortable thoughts in her head. She had an hour to herself before it was time to lay out Gavin's school clothes and pack his lunch-box.

She usually enjoyed the task, but today images kept intruding. And Glenda's voice was in her head. *'At the last contact, the parents are warned not to cry. That's emotional abuse, in their book, and they'll terminate the visit. So the parents must not cry aloud.'*

Her desk was piled high when she reached Anxious Alley. Letters, columns in preparation, the schedule for the following month. 'And don't forget you're seeing Paul Fenton again tomorrow tonight,' Gracie said. 'He's been on the phone. He'll pick you up at 7.30, so get out of here on time. You could do with a bit of a scrub.'

'You're such a treasure,' Celia replied, baring her teeth in mock gratitude. She had forgotten about Fenton, which didn't explain why being reminded of him made her so uncomfortable.

There was more mail than usual, and they worked in silence for most of the morning. At 11, Gracie brought coffee to their desks, and they sat back for a moment, letting the chatter of the newsroom wash over them.

'Something up?' Celia enquired. There was more of a buzz than usual, and no groups were chatting round the water cooler.

'It's the Milibands: someone has said David didn't really back Ed's defence of their father after that attack in the *Daily Mail*. It's not true, but someone has said it, so they're all having the vapours.'

Celia went back to her letters. Most of them came from the 20-30-year age group. Older generations were slower to share their problems with anyone outside the family, but the younger generation had no such reservations.

At 12.15 she received an invitation to lunch with Charley in his office. 'He's ordered Thai,' the message-bearer said enviously.

Charley waved her to a seat when she entered his office. 'Sit down. I ordered Pad Thai. I know it's your favourite.'

She slipped into a chair and smiled at him. 'You're being extra nice. Are you softening me up for bad news?'

When he grinned, the years seemed to fall away from him. Celia knew he was 48, but today he could have passed for 40.

'Your job's safe ... at least for this week. The way things are going, we might all be out of a job by Christmas. Anyway, the reason I asked you to lunch was to give you some good news. Laurence Cohen phoned me this morning to say he'll take on the Blenkirons as clients. Apparently he's discussed the medical evidence, and he has a guy who'll supply rebuttal.'

They discussed the day's article for the campaign; then a profile of an amazing man called Ian Joseph, a millionaire who lived in France and devoted himself to people he saw as victims of injustice at the hands of social-services departments. According to Charley, it would make a good page. Celia murmured her satisfaction.

'We've fired the opening salvo,' Charley said, and she felt a glow. That meant it would be an ongoing battle. 'On the whole, it's not a bad start,' he said, 'but now we have to keep it up. This French guy is kosher: Trevor's checked him out. He funds it all out of his own pocket; he's totally altruistic.'

'So there's more than enough for a campaign?'

'Looks like it. Did you see that piece by Christopher Booker on Sunday? He reminded the Party leaders that they'd all stood up in Parliament to apologise over what happened to the poor little buggers we wrenched from their parents and sent to the Commonwealth, and accused them of refusing to see what's going on under their noses right now!'

'I did see it. He's been brilliant throughout.'

'And now, with our efforts, something may just begin to happen.'

'Do you really think so?' It seemed almost too good to be true.

Charley was wiping his mouth with a napkin, only to grin again. 'I may be a journo, Celia, but I don't lie all the time. Anyway, let's get another meet in the diary. And it's a long time since we had a drink together. Must remedy that.'

She smiled, remembering, as she ate, how attentive to her he had been after Michael's death: sympathising, but also spurring her on. He had been good with Gavin, too. 'You must come to dinner one night,' she said. 'It won't be up to this standard, but you can bring a good bottle. Gavin would be pleased to see you again.'

They talked about families, then, her one child, his three, whom he saw infrequently since his ex had remarried and moved to America.

'Thanks,' she said, when it was time to go back to Anxious Alley. 'I don't know why, but I just want to do this campaign.

He was nodding. 'Laurence is a good man – maybe he'll swing it. But we need to put the other side as well.'

She nodded. Charley was reaching for a card. 'This woman

did child-protection for years, in Hackney. She's working for a charity now, but apparently she's fair-minded, and is willing to discuss the whole system. Trevor is interviewing her, but if you want to sit in, do.'

Celia took the proffered card, and turned in the doorway. 'Thanks for helping them, Charley. I owe you.'

She rang Sandra as soon as she settled at her desk, but she reached only voice-mail. Deciding against giving the good news about the rebuttal expert, she just asked for a return call asap. She rang again an hour later; but still there was only the recorded voice. After the third call, she decided the phone must be out of order. It would have to wait.

Suddenly Gracie appeared, toting a parcel. 'Couriered! Must be important.'

'So you want me to open it?' Celia replied.

'Of course I do. It might be a bomb. I don't do mystery parcels.'

Inside the padded envelope was a copy of *Empty Cradles*, and a note that said, '*Hope this helps. Paul.*'

She put it in her bag, and tried to concentrate. She had a lot to think about, including what she would wear for her date with Paul tomorrow. She felt her cheeks redden: why was she thinking of it as a date? It was a friendly meeting, nothing more. She put it in her bag and tried to concentrate.

Trevor paused by her desk a moment later. 'Seen today's copy? We're describing the recent history of forced adoption, with the emphasis on the Blair years.' A moment later he had the piece on her screen.

The facts were staggering. In 2000, the Blair government had raised targets so as to increase the number of children being adopted. He had promised millions of pounds to councils that achieved their targets. Some had received more than £2 million each. The money was supposed to be spent on finding homes for hard-to-place children, but it had had a different consequence. Encouraged by the promise of extra cash, social workers had begun to earmark 'adoptable' children – the kind that would-be adopters wanted. The number of older children adopted had fallen, and social workers were accused of selecting babies for adoption, even before their birth, in order to win bonuses.

'It sounds Orwellian,' Celia said.

Trevor nodded. 'I remember Sue Reid did a stonking piece on it in the *Mail*, at the time. I only half-believed it, then. Now I know better.

She was home in time to make Gavin's tea, and listen to his tale of woe about a football match that had ended in his best friend's being sent off. 'It wasn't fair, Mum! I said so, and he said he'd report me for cheek.'

Celia wanted to hug him for his loyalty to a friend, but she had to toe the line. 'You can't argue with teachers, darling.'

'Even when it's true?' She hugged him then, enjoying the feel of him at first resisting and then giving way, glad to nestle against her. Sandra must have done this with her children – and now she would be sitting in a silent house, without them.

'Why are you crying?' Gavin had broken free and was looking at her, puzzled.

'Because I love you so much. Now, go and do your homework.'

When he had gone, she turned on her radio, lowered the sound, and picked up *Empty Cradles*. It began as the story of an ordinary woman, a social worker, stumbling across what seemed like a single injustice – and turned out to be a huge scandal. As she read on, it had eerie resonances with her own case. Was Sandra's story a one-off, or part of something much bigger and ultimately scandalous? The children in *Empty Cradles* had been generally aged between three and 14, most being between seven and ten. They had been sent away to a foreign land, never to return, always without their families, and often to cold, unwelcoming homes, or equally cold institutions.

Well-known national charities such as Barnardo's had played a prominent part in this, along with the Church of England, the Methodist Church, the Salvation Army, and the Catholic Church. What had possessed them to exile children in such a way? The book's title was a quote from the Archbishop of Perth, when welcoming British child migrants shipped to Australia in 1938: 'At a time when empty cradles are contributing woefully to empty spaces, it is necessary to look for external sources of supply. And if we do not supply from our own stock, we are leaving ourselves all the more exposed to the menace of the teeming millions of our neighbouring Asiatic races.'

His Grace would be accused of racism if he said that today. Nowadays people often had the same unpleasant ideas: they just knew better than to voice them aloud. She read on.

The desire to poach Britain's children had accelerated in the post-war years. Australia had wanted at least 17,000 children a year. Seventeen thousand children taken away from all they knew, some of them as young as three. She thought of Gavin at three, clutching his Poody Dog and moving closer to her for reassurance if he thought danger threatened. The memory disturbed her so much that she got up and went to the computer.

She found what she wanted under 'Child Migration': 'Only Britain has used child migration as a significant part of its child-care strategy over a period of four centuries, rather than as a policy of last resort during times of war or civil unrest. Many of these children were removed without their parents' knowledge or consent. The final party arrived in Australia in 1970. It is estimated that child-migration programmes were responsible for the removal of over 130,000 children from the United Kingdom to Canada, New Zealand, Zimbabwe (formerly Rhodesia) and Australia. Governments have not been able to provide precise statistics concerning the numbers of children received from the United Kingdom.'

Celia had to put up a hand to wipe her eyes, then. Poor little things, they hadn't even been worth a proper count. She read on. 'Child migrants were sent abroad without passports, social histories, or even the most basic documents, such as a full birth certificate. Brothers and sisters were frequently separated on the docks, or sent to institutions in remote regions, only to be put to work as labourers the next day. Many were injured in building accidents at an age when they would have been in school or playing with their friends if they had remained in the United Kingdom. Many felt an extreme sense of rejection by their family and country of origin or both. Like characters from one of Kafka's novels, they had been sentenced but the nature of their crime was a complete mystery.'

'Throughout its long history, child migration has been punctuated by a series of scandals. The lack of educational provision, the overwork and inadequate pay, the suicides following episodes of ill-treatment, and the appalling evidence of protracted physical and sexual abuse ... '

She switched the computer off at that point, unable to take any more.

CHAPTER 16

Sandra

Once upon a time she had loved Saturday mornings. Sometimes she had carried the breakfast to bed and they had all piled in, Stuart with the baby tucked under one arm, and forking scrambled eggs up with his free hand, Ann Marie and Bobby squabbling over who got the drippiest piece of toast. They had loved Lurpak, would eat anything as long as it was liberally spread with butter. And then there had been the debates over where they should go for the day. It was always the swingy park.

Now she dreaded Saturdays. At least 16 empty hours stretching ahead, hours that made them almost sick of one another's company. The kids had been the yeast in the loaf, the thing that lightened everything and made it magic. They hadn't seen them at weekends for months, now. 'We need our rest time, too,' Mrs Harker had said, when once she asked.

Sandra eased over on to her back and stared at the ceiling. It was looking grubby. They had intended to decorate this year, give everything a lick of paint. But that would have to wait now. Even when they had the kids back, they would be in debt. She owed everyone, especially the Provvy ... and now the Provvy woman was being sniffy about lending more.

Beside her, Stuart stirred. She turned her head to look at him, feeling a little thrill at how handsome he was. To her, anyway. His nose was big, but it went well with a big head on a big man. His eyes were still shut as he spoke: 'What time is it?'

She turned to look at the bedside clock. 'Ten to eight.' She wondered if he might reach out for her. Half of her wanted it, the other half didn't, knowing it would end in failure. 'I'm getting up, anyway. Do you want a cuppa bringing up?' There was nothing much for breakfast, but she could do him some eggy bread if he was hungry.

'No, ta. I'm getting up too.'

They shared the paper over the breakfast table. Stuart had the front and back, she the middle section. She was reading about duck-egg blue being the coming colour when she heard him let out a snort of anger. She looked up. 'What's up?'

He was holding out the paper, showing her a picture of a man and woman trying to hide their faces as they went into court. She took it from him and began to read. Beneath the picture of the pair trying to avoid attention were full-face photographs of them both, together with their names. She searched for what they had done, all the while wondering if one day she and Stuart would be pilloried like that.

The copy was scathing. 'One of this pair inflicted horrific injuries on their newborn baby – but both walked free because it couldn't be proved which of them had inflicted the injuries, a court heard. Their nine-week-old child was left with a fractured skull, fractured ribs, and other disturbing injuries, the court was told. The two admitted a cruelty charge on the basis of not getting earlier medical treatment for one of the injuries, and both walked free from Newcastle Crown Court.

A judge said: "The photographs of the injuries suffered by the child, and the description of the non-accidental injuries are extremely distressing, and would be extremely distressing to anyone. The perpetrator knows who he or she is, and I hope that shame and regret in that person, whoever that person is, is deeply felt and long-term. I cannot sentence either of you on the basis that someone ought to pay for those terrible, non-accidental injuries. Whatever people's views about the injuries suffered are concerned, which are clearly extremely unpleasant, you are to be sentenced only for failure to seek medical attention at an appropriate time in respect of a single injury, without knowledge of how the injury occurred. I am suspending the prison sentences, because there is absolutely no public interest in sending either defendant to custody for a short time."'

Sandra looked up to find Stuart's eyes, filled with anger, fixed on her face. 'They got off,' she said, incredulously.

'They should be bloody horse-whipped.'

'What if they didn't do it, though, Stuart? Think about that. They might be like us ...'

He was looking at her with horror. 'It's there in black and white. They did it. Everyone knows they did it ... and they're getting off scot-free.'

Sandra persisted. 'They believe we did it! You're not thinking straight. I'm not saying these people didn't do it. It says here that he's shown remorse, and she has been devastated by the proceedings. But think on: this could be us one day – and we know *we* didn't do it.'

Stuart had his stubborn face on now, and she knew it was useless to go on arguing. But inside her, conflicting sentiments were raging. If social workers had to deal with cases like that, no wonder they ceased to trust anyone. She would never, ever like Mrs Harker, but at least she could try to understand what made her tick.

They didn't speak again until the tea had cooled in the pot and it was time to leave the table and begin the day.

'What do you want to do?' she asked.

He shrugged. 'Go out. Stay in.'

So that was how it was going to be. The newspaper had upset him, and she was going to suffer for it. She felt a sudden burst of anger. Why take it out on her? But reason prevailed when she looked at his poor, tired face. 'Let's go out,' she said. 'I could just fancy a trip to the seaside.'

They decided to go to Lowestoft, principally because they had never gone there with the children. She didn't know much about Lowestoft, but it was supposed to be all right, and there was bound to be a pub or a café. In fact, the town was a pleasant surprise, with sandy beaches and a variety of seafront attractions. They walked arm in arm towards the pier, and then took refuge on a seat looking out to sea. 'We could get some fish,' she said at last. 'Take it home. It says over there that there's a smokehouse.'

'Can't stand kippers,' he said. She abandoned the idea of a fish supper. When Stuart was in a mood like this, there was no sense in trying to make conversation. He was still burning with outrage at what he had read in the paper, and she couldn't quite work out why. Was it because the abusive parents had walked free? Or was it because anyone could think that he had any kind of kinship with people like that? She sat on in silence until at last he suggested they find a café.

'Yes,' she said, 'I could murder a coffee.'

As they walked back along the promenade she thought of the one time she had been taken to the seaside in childhood. It was when she had been placed with the Fosters. They had taken a picnic to the beach, and she could still taste the sand in the sandwiches. Brenda Foster had had a nice little bathing costume: red and white elasticated cotton with bows on the shoulders. She hadn't got a costume, so Mrs Foster had tucked her dress into her knickers and warned her not to get it wet. They had looked for shells and tiny little pieces of coloured glass called boody. She had kept her bits in an envelope for years and years. For all she knew, they might be somewhere in the house still, for she couldn't imagine ever having thrown them away. She had been with the Fosters for 18 months, her longest placement but one. Brenda would be 28, now, married probably, and living in a nice house.

While Stuart queued for the coffee, she thought about the children. If they had to go into long-term care, she would ask for them to be kept together. Except that fosterers never wanted to take a family. 'Too difficult to handle,' Mrs Briggs had said once, when she'd turned away twins.

'Penny for them,' Stuart said when he returned with the

coffee. It was in big cups with froth on the top, and a wooden stick to stir; and she could tell that he was regretting his offhandness earlier, and wanting to make amends.

'Nice,' she said, cupping her hands round the warmth. 'I was just thinking about when I went to the beach once, years ago.'

'We lived there,' he said, his face lighting up. 'At Seaham beach. It was a fantastic place. And the Blast – that was where the coal used to come down from the pit. It looked like the surface of the moon. Film companies used to come and film it. All gone now, of course, thanks to Thatcher.'

A child had toddled over from the next table, and was holding out a stuffed toy. 'That's nice,' Stuart said and held out a hand. The child was trusting, and the toy was transferred. The next minute he had hoisted the little boy on to his knee and was deep in a three-way conversation with toy and child. Sandra looked apologetically at the mother, but she was smiling, pleased that someone liked her child, and glad to have it amused for a while. She nodded towards Stuart. 'He's a dab hand. Got bairns of his own?'

'Three,' Sandra said, and was suddenly seized by terror. The woman might ask questions, wonder why the children weren't with them. 'They're with my Mum and Dad,' she said quickly. 'We've just escaped for half an hour.'

The woman edged closer. 'Live in Lowestoft, do they?'

Inside Sandra panic grew. 'No, Great Yarmouth. We just decided to come down the coast.' She looked at her watch. 'And we should be getting back. They can be a handful. '

'You don't need to tell me.' The woman edged closer still.

Stuart was looking puzzled. 'We should be getting back,' Sandra said brightly. 'You know how me Mam goes on if they get stroppy.'

He was handing back the child and getting to his feet. 'What was all that about?' he asked when they were outside.

'She was asking questions. About the kids.'

'You didn't need to answer them. Anyway, we've got nothing to be ashamed of. We haven't done anything, Sands. You're taking on as though we were guilty.'

She shook her head. She couldn't explain. And, anyway, all she wanted now was to get home, get inside, and lock the door on the world.

Chapter 17

Celia

She asked for Glenda Forbes at the hotel reception, and was told she was expected. Five women were in the room with Glenda, all of them gazing expectantly at Celia as she walked through the door.

'Hallo,' Celia said. She didn't know what else to say. It felt like intruding on a wake, and it was a relief when Glenda took charge. 'This is Celia. I've told you all about her. She's definitely on our side, but she needs to know your stories before she can be of any help. So, please talk freely to her, everyone.'

She turned towards Celia. 'I suggest you talk to them one at a time. It'll just be a muddle if everyone talks at once. So go and sit over there, and I'll sort it out.'

Celia took a seat by the window, and got out her recorder as Glenda brought the first woman towards her. Except that this wasn't a woman, she looked like a girl. 'This is Kathy,' Glenda said. And then, to the girl, 'Tell Celia your story. You can trust her, and she needs to know.'

'I don't know where to begin,' the girl said falteringly. Her fair hair was streaked with grey, but she couldn't be more than 19 or 20. She had the pallor of someone who doesn't eat or sleep much, and the nails on her thin fingers were bitten to the quick.

'Well,' Celia said encouragingly. 'Tell me about your mum and dad, and when you were small.' She soon realised that was a mistake, for the girl's eyes filled with tears.

'Not much to tell,' she said, drawing the sides of her cardigan around her bony frame.

'She's girding up for what she thinks is going to be a struggle,' Celia thought, and put out a hand. 'OK. Shall I ask you some questions, and then you can answer them?'

The girl nodded, relieved.

'Right! Well, how old are you?'

She was 22. 'I lived with my mother till I was three then we ... me and my brother ... were taken into care. I don't know why, really. They said me Mam was poorly, when I asked. We were going to be adopted, I think, because they talked about an "all-time mummy and daddy"'. She fell silent then.

'Did it happen?' Celia asked eventually.

'Billy was adopted. No one wanted me. Well, a couple of times there were people, but it never came off.'

'So you were fostered?'

'Yes. A lot of times. One time I went into a Barnardo's.'

'With your brother?'

'No, I never saw him again after he was adopted, except the once. We did meet then, but I don't think his new mam and dad were keen.'

'So you were in fostering until you grew up?' She looked as though she should still be in fostering now. A babe in the woods.

'Yes. When I was 16 I went into a B and B. I had a job in a factory, and the Social gave me loads of things to set me up. I asked about our Billy, but they said it was all confidential, but I could go on a list somewhere. I asked about me Mam as well, but she had died a long time before.'

'So you worked, and you had a place of your own. What happened then?'

The girl's glance dropped. 'I fell wrong. He worked at the same place. He said we'd get married, but his Mam put her foot down. The social worker said she'd back me up, but she never. They said I had to go on a parenting course, only there wasn't a place ... it was on account of I'd never had a mother, or mothering, or whatever they call it. They said the baby would be deprived, but it wouldn't have. I loved that baby.'

'Was it boy or girl?'

'A boy. I called him William, after our Billy. They said it was only temporary care, but I knew they were lying. You could see it in their faces. "Be brave," they said.' She was angry now, too angry for tears.

'How long ago was this?'

'Three years ago. I'm still fighting. Glenda says there's a chance ... but that's all.' There was despair in her voice.

'She knows,' Celia thought. 'She's had it, and she knows it.'

The second woman was called Jenny, and she was older, with a different story. Her daughter had abandoned her four children, and had gone off with a Pole. Jenny, who had virtually been in charge of the children for years, had applied for guardianship. It had been granted in the case of the three older children, but the youngest, an 18-month-old whom she had cared for from birth, was put up for adoption. Inside Celia, unease grew. This was a carbon copy of another case, last year, and that had not ended well.

'I'm going to fight it every inch of the way. I love that little girl. We all do. The other kids are lost without her. Glenda's helping me, and I'll win in the end because I've got to.'

'How old are you?' Celia asked.

'Forty-eight. I had a good job as a teaching assistant. My husband's a joiner. We both wanted to keep the family together. He's beside himself about it, because she was a grandpa's little girl. But we're hopeful. She's been placed for adoption, but it's not over yet. Not by a long chalk.'

While she waited for the third woman to join her, Celia tried to make sense of the story she had just heard. If Jenny was fit to look after three of the children, why not all four? Surely it couldn't be because an 18-month-old baby was eminently adoptable? Her successful adoption would allow the Social Services to tick a box – and pick up a fee. Had some small children indeed become merely commercial transactions?

The third woman's case was reminiscent of Sandra's. An

unexplained injury, a suspicious doctor, and now the same merry-go-round of hearings and accusations. She was disinclined to meet Celia's eye, and vague about circumstances, but adamant that she and her partner were innocent. Celia took dutiful notes, but if there was a question-mark over any of them, this was the one.

The next could scarcely contain her agony. She had put up with an abusive marriage for the sake of the children. 'I wanted them to have a dad like other kids.' In the end he had broken her arm, and Social Services had swooped. 'The police got involved, and they must've brought the SS in. I knew he'd never touch the kids: that's the one good thing I can say about him, he loved his kids. But they wouldn't hear it. They said it was emotional abuse, and I'd let them see violence in the house – only I didn't. I used to hide the bruises, and I never cried out. I didn't want them to know.'

'Are you with him now?'

'No, that's the point. I've left him, and the council have rehoused me. I've got a home together ... he let me have all the stuff. He doesn't want them adopted any more than I do. I've told them and told them I'll never see him again, never let him near the kids, but it makes no difference. It's as though it was me that was in the wrong. It's certainly me that's paying the price. And the kids – what must be going through their minds?'

'Do you still see them?'

'Once in a blue moon, now. They're phasing it out, Glenda says. Making it so they won't miss me when they don't see me any more.'

The tears came then, until she lifted a defiant head. 'I won't give up, though. Not while I've got breath.'

The fifth woman was young, and smartly dressed. 'Thank you for what you're doing,' she said as she took her seat.

'Thank you for talking to me. I don't know anything about your case, so give me as much detail as you can.'

This case was certainly different, Celia thought, as detail

emerged. 'I was 17 when I had Louise. Her father was a student, and he just ran away. I'll never forget the look of horror on his face when I told him. Anyway, my Mum and Dad stood by me. I had the baby, a little girl. We didn't even let him know, and he never asked. My Dad wanted to seek his parents out, and tell them but I didn't want that. I went back to college, and got a qualification, and I did my best for my baby.'

'You still lived at home?'

'Yes. I couldn't have done anything without Mam and Dad. Anyway, time went on. Louise is eight now, but when she was six and a half her father turned up. Out of the blue. "Bloody cheek," Dad said, but I was torn. After all, Louise was bound to ask questions eventually. Everyone has a dad. So I let him see her. He was really nice about it – apologised, the lot. Then he asked if he could take Louise to meet his parents. That got my Mam's rag out. She said no: Louise already had a grandma who cared about her. Who'd done all the dirty work at the beginning. That was enough.'

'How did you feel?'

The woman considered for a moment. 'Left to my own devices, I'd probably have said OK, but my Mam was right: she had done all the hard work. So I wasn't going to cross her.'

'What happened then?'

'They went to court for access. Had a top-flight barrister, the lot. They got access, and that's when it all went pear-shaped.' Her hands had begun to pluck at her skirt. She's not as calm as she seems, Celia thought.

'To cut a long story short, they kept pushing and pushing for more access, overnights, weekends, the lot. And that caused more trouble at home. Mam persuaded me that we should take Louise away. We have family in Ireland, so we went there. Mam thought ... and I hoped ... that they'd get fed up with fighting. They'd never been interested before, so why should they be now.'

'And you were wrong?'

'They had us brought back. They had the law on their side. I asked my MP for help, and he said they could buy better legal help than we could.'

'Did he mean that you should give up?'

'I suppose so. He wasn't much help, anyway. The court gave Louise's father residential rights, and I would get access. Not my Mam. But he moved right away, so I couldn't afford to see her. And when I did manage to rake up the fare, he was always ready with an excuse. We're still going for access but ...' She shook her head to indicate hopelessness.

Celia tried to murmur encouragement but she had an awful feeling that all these women were doomed to disappointment. She gathered up her things, thanked them all, paid tribute to Glenda and her efforts, promised to keep in touch, and made her goodbyes.

In the car, on the way back to the office, she thought through what she had heard, and jotted down some notes. They might be of use to Features, along with the tape, and Glenda's contact details.

CHAPTER 18

Sandra

'I've been thinking,' Sandra said. 'When we get them back, we'll go somewhere for a real break.'

'Paris Disneyland?' At least he was grinning. 'I'll have to put in a few extra shifts for that.'

'No, not something daft. Just a nice break. We could go to see your Granddad. Make sure he's getting better. Let him see everything is all right again.' She shouldn't have said that. It would remind him of the night he had cried at the humiliation of telling his beloved grandfather that his kids had been taken into care. 'Well, a little B and B somewhere, just for a weekend. Before Ann Marie goes back to school.'

He was wiping his mouth. 'Yes, well, we'll talk about it when the time comes.' She didn't reply. He hadn't said it but it lurked in the room just the same: '*If the time comes.*' The contact centre was not mentioned, but it was the elephant in the room.

They didn't speak much in the car. They were always tense before contact, wondering if all three of the children would be there. Nine times out of ten, there was an excuse for at least one absence. Ann Marie and Bobby were there when they arrived. The little girl ran to them with a shriek of 'Mummy', but Bobby stayed by his foster-mother's knee until Stuart went to him. 'He's only three,' she reminded herself. 'He's bound to be confused.' As she cuddled her daughter, she thought about what a job it would be to settle them all when they did come back. If they came back. She felt fear tremble in her chest, and then come up into her throat like bile. But the baby was coming through the door in the social worker's arms, and the sweet familiar smell of his neck when she buried her face there banished every emotion but love.

They settled in a corner with all three children.

The social workers had gone into the kitchen. She could hear them talking and laughing over the clink of coffee cups. The contact-centre woman stayed at her desk, watching. They watched every move, and sometimes made notes, so your heart was in your mouth all the time in case one of the children slipped, or fell, or cried for no reason at all, and it was held against you.

Outside the window there was suddenly the faint sound of cheering. The contact-centre woman got to her feet and crossed to the window. 'It's Peter Andre!' she said excitedly. 'He's out there in the street, outside the theatre.' She turned and scurried towards the kitchen, obviously to call the others to see the celebrity.

Stuart was looking puzzled. 'He's a singer,' Sandra said. 'Used to be married to Jordan.'

'Oh,' he said, but she could see it hadn't meant much to him.

Ann Marie had grown tired of examining the pattern on her dress, and looked up at her daddy. 'Can we go home?' she said. Sandra waited to see if he would answer, but suddenly Stuart was rising to his feet, handing her the baby, scooping Bobby into his arms, and taking his daughter by the hand. 'Come on,' he said, 'while we've got the chance.'

Sandra didn't take it in for a moment, and then terror gripped her. The women had emerged from the kitchen but were clustered at the window, staring out and pointing, wild with excitement. She shook her head, imploring Stuart with her eyes, but then they were out in the street and making for the car.

All the way to the car she waited for shouting behind them, but it never came ... or else she didn't hear it above the noise of the crowd outside the theatre. There wasn't time to strap anyone in. She huddled in the back seat, all three children held to her, as Stuart put the car into gear and then let out the clutch.

'This is madness,' she said, but he was storming ahead and

gave no sign of hearing her. Bobby began to cry, a thin wail of anxiety.

'Are we going home?' Ann Marie asked, and her voice was hopeful.

'We can't go home. That's the first place they'll look.' Sandra's voice was unnaturally calm.

'I know,' Stuart said. 'But we need to get some things. I'll park round the back. You go in and get them, but don't attract attention. And don't take more than five minutes. We need to be on our way.'

'Where to?' She said it faintly, but she already knew. They were going north.

He pulled up in the back lane, and handed her his keys.

'Are we going home?' Ann Marie asked again, joyful at the prospect.

'No, pet, not yet. Soon.'

Inside, Sandra packed hurriedly. Nappies, clean clothes, biscuits, orange juice, baby formula, and a bottle – anything that might be useful – plus all the money tucked away for bills and the legal aid. It was strange to leave your own house like a thief, but she did it, slinking down the yard and closing the back gate with extra care in case it banged and a head appeared in a neighbouring window.

When she got back to the car, Stuart had put the baby in its car seat, and strapped the other two in. At least that was a relief. But the children were unnaturally quiet. They know something's up, she thought.

'Where are we going?' she asked again when the car was moving, but he didn't answer. Instead he drove like a man possessed until they were out of Norwich, and on the motorway. Once a police car passed them, lights flashing, siren blaring, but it was soon out of sight, and Sandra's heart could go back from her throat to its place beneath her ribs.

He was threading through the outskirts of Dereham when he suddenly slowed and put the car into reverse. A moment later she realised why. A battered Ford Fiesta stood outside a terraced house, a For Sale sign taped to its grimy rear window.

'How much money have we got?' She started to add it up as he drove a few hundred yards away and parked. Between them they had £220.

'Stay here,' he said, and left the car. Twenty minutes later, the Fiesta drew up alongside them. 'You'll have to drive our car for a little bit,' he said leaning in at the window. 'I'll go first. You follow me.'

'What about the baby?'

'He'll be all right in the seat. Get going!'

'How much?'

'Everything,' he said. 'And this.' He held up his wrist, and she saw his watch was gone. The watch she had bought him when they married, with all the dials and fiddly bits he had loved.

She hated driving, but there was no option. She started the car and fell in behind. They drove into the service station west of Wisbech, and threaded through the vans. She knew what he was doing: looking for a place where a car could stay, undetected, for as long as possible. At last she had parked, and then he was beside her.

'We need to move the kids and all the gear.' Ann Marie and Bobby were sleeping, and they carried them tenderly to the new car. Two trips each, and everything was transferred. 'Let's go,' he said, and slipped back behind the wheel.

After that she dozed as they headed on towards the motorway north. She began to breathe again once they reached Boston. When they got on to the A1, they would be anonymous in the Fiesta. Police would be looking for their old car, and it would be ages before they found it, if they ever did now that it was a needle in a haystack.

They pulled into another service station just before Leeds, and got the children a meal. They were still sleepy, but at least they ate something. 'Are we going home?' Ann Marie asked again, but she didn't seem to expect an answer.

Sandra knew they were on the last stretch when she saw Scotch Corner on the signposts. She remembered it from their last trip north. In an hour, or little more, they were turning off the motorway and following the signs for Seaham. His grand-father's house was in a narrow terrace. She had been here a few times before, but never to stay. Previously they had stayed in a cheap hotel, but now this place was to be their sanctuary. They reached it at 7.30, and by eight o'clock the children were fed and tucked up, side by side, in the double bed. She cried, then, sitting at the kitchen table, crying with relief and fear, and because she was not used to the whisky Stuart had ladled into her.

'We've broken in,' she said, wiping her nose with the back of her hand.

He grinned, like a schoolboy. 'It's all you can do if you have no key.'

He could make light of it as much as he chose, she thought. But however you looked at it, they were in deep, deep trouble.

CHAPTER 19

Celia

This time the restaurant was small and intimate, booths rather than tables, and subdued lighting. 'I've decided you're bad for my figure,' she said, eyeing the menu. 'It's all irresistible, and deadly.'

'I'm a great believer in deadly,' he said, without lifting his eyes from the menu. 'Try the whitebait.'

She took his advice on every course, and tried to quell the unease inside her. 'I shouldn't have said yes,' she thought, and was suddenly mortified, remembering how she had giggled when he phoned. Like a stupid kid, she thought, recalling Gracie's eyes on her. And yet they had all been urging her to go out – wasn't that the usual advice for the bereft? Start again. Fill the empty space. You can't dwell on the past.

As if he sensed her discomfort, Paul spoke. 'Now, tell me about your letter from the woman ... the last resort thing. Any developments?'

He listened patiently, sometimes pausing fork half-way to mouth to pose a question, as she told him all she had learned from Sandra. 'They have no one in the world except the old grandfather, and he's miles away. County Durham. Some ex-mining village by the sea. Honestly, if you met Sandra, you'd realise she couldn't hurt her children. She's really gentle, Paul. She had a lousy upbringing, passed from one foster home to another.'

'Parents?'

'Her mother seems to have been unstable ... anyway, she vanished at some point. And the father was a GI.'

His eyes widened. 'A GI? When was she born?'

'Not a wartime GI, one of the corps still stationed here ...

Lakenheath, I think. How her mother met him I don't know, but she did, and he was smoke as soon as the pregnancy was announced.'

'So Sandra never knew her father?'

'No. And that's one of the things that goes against her: the lack of a normal upbringing. They say that about almost everyone who grew up in care, suggesting they're emotionally deprived, and therefore incapable of passing on emotional warmth to their children.'

'So they take them away and put them into care – so that they, in turn, can be emotionally deprived. Clever!'

'I'm just beginning to realise the extent of it – children removed from loving parents, "just in case" they're hurt.'

'But mothers do hurt their children, Celia. Think of Baby P.'

'No one seems to think of anything else. That was a disgrace, a total dereliction of duty on the part of a local authority. This is different.'

'So you say. OK, OK, I'm being deliberately provocative, but I don't want to see you getting in too deep, and then getting your fingers burned.'

She wanted to argue, but actually it was nice that he cared, that he wanted to protect her. Instead she smiled, and got on with eating her food until he asked about Glenda Forbes.

'That woman you were going to see, the crusader. Any more from her?'

'I'm seeing her again soon, and I've met some of her clients. I'm calling them clients … I don't mean they pay her, she just takes them under her wing. She does it because she herself had her daughter taken away, for no reason, as far as I can make out. Anyway, the girl sought her out as soon as she was 18.'

'So she hadn't forgotten her Mum?'

'I don't think they do, if they were loved. You might want to blot out early memories if they were painful, but if all your memories are of warmth and security, I think they probably stay with you.'

'Which means curtains for the poor bastards who adopted them.'

'I'm afraid it does, and that's criminally unfair, too.'

He was covering her hand with his own. 'Remember what I've said: sometimes people lie, sometimes they let you down.'

'You've turned cynical in your old age!'

She laughed as he pretended to wince. 'And me thinking I'm just coming into my prime.'

'Seriously, though, I take your point,' she said. 'Some people are not fit to rear children, and then the state must step in. But we have to get it right, because it's so important. I must give you a book that Charley Lewin gave to me – it's a cardinal example of how things can get out of hand. It's a story of a mother who lost her children because they said she had injured one of them. In fact, the child had cancer. But it was years before it all came to light, and now it will take a lifetime to mend her relationships with her children.' As she spoke she heard her voice thickening with emotion.

'Hey,' he said. 'This is off-duty time.'

'I'm sorry, I'm talking shop.'

'You're not. You're talking about something that obviously means a great deal to you. But you need a break. What chance have you of getting away for a few days?'

'Well, I've got leave to take, but I can't go now, not with …' She stopped short. 'Well, not just yet.' Mustn't start talking about the Blenkirons again.

'Where do you relax? Spain? Or somewhere more exotic?'

'France, usually. That was before Gavin was born. Since then we've usually gone to places with facilities for children.' She winced inwardly at the word 'we'. There wasn't a 'we' any more, just a single parent and a lone child. She sought desperately for a change of subject. 'I'm planning to take Gavin to the theatre soon. I suggested it the other day, but he wasn't enthusiastic.'

They talked of theatre, then, and she felt her composure returning; but the ache remained.

They were about to start on dessert when she looked at her watch. Ten past ten: Sandra would be sitting at home thinking of her absent children; Gavin would be in bed, or on his way there. Sean would be saying goodnight, going back upstairs, leaving her son alone in the silent downstairs flat. She reminded herself that he would be surrounded by paraphernalia, his Xbox and WiFi and God knows what else, focused on whatever was engaging his attention at the time. It didn't matter that he would be contented: she had left him alone. Other women were fighting for the right to be with their children, and she was neglecting hers.

'I'm sorry, but I really have to get home. I've just remembered … I should have …'

'Hey!' He was looking at her sternly. 'Eat your pudding.' He was signalling for the bill as she felt her panic subside, to be replaced by embarrassment. A few minutes later they were out on the pavement, and a cab was gliding to a halt beside them. '

'It's all right,' he said, when they were inside it. 'Panic over.'

'I'm sorry. I just …'

'You just wanted to go home. I understand.'

She was filled with sudden gratitude. He didn't think her stupid; he understood. When they reached the house, he got out of the cab with her, and waited while she fumbled for keys. 'Thank you, it was lovely,' she said.

'So are you,' he said, and kissed her cheek.

A moment later the taxi was gliding away, and she was safe in the hall, wondering why her legs suddenly threatened to fail her. The light on the answerphone was flashing. She checked the number: Gracie. Too late now for ringing back; it would have to wait until morning.

The rest of the house was in darkness. She mustn't wake them. Sean didn't usually go to bed this early, but perhaps he had a guest tonight. She crept into Gavin's room and listened to his even breathing. She could see the shape of his head on the pillow, and she smiled in the darkness. Michael's son. Michael.

The tears started as she made her way back to the living-room. She knew what she wanted, and it was there, where she had hidden it. The wine she had drunk was making her maudlin, but she could do nothing about it. She had to do what she had been trying hard not to do for the past year. It was there, covered with a pile of others: *Music of the Night,* the last CD Michael had made.

She stood until the first notes of 'Something' filtered into the silent room. '*Something in the way you walk attracts me like no other lover.*' She could see Michael now, standing erect, his instrument raised skywards, putting his heart and soul into his music. She had never realised that the clarinet sobbed ... like a human voice, crying out, begging and pleading. That was why they called it a misery stick! She had often wondered. She stood in the middle of the room, her arms wrapped around her body, her feet moving in time with the music. It was 'The last time ever I saw your face' now. '*And felt your heart beat ...*'

The first time she had seen Michael, he had been laughing at something someone had just said, and then their eyes had met, and his face had changed. He knew the moment was important. She had felt it, too. Like coming home. Her nose was running now, but she let it run, unwilling to move the arms that were holding her, even though they were her own. The music filled the room, filled her mind with pictures ... Michel smiling down at his new-born son, the lover's face across a crowded room, holding promise of intimacy to come, that same face faintly smiling in death. 'Don't cry out loud' ... that was his solo. '*Don't cry out loud. Just keep it inside and learn how to hide your feelings. Fly high and proud, and if you should fall, remember you almost had it all.*' She had had it all, and she wasn't sure she could live without it.

The last notes of 'Don't cry out loud' were hanging in the air when the telephone rang. Who could be ringing on the landline at this time of night? For one moment she imagined it might be Michael, ringing to say he was coming home ... She picked up the receiver.

'Celia? Hope I haven't got you out of bed.' It was Charley. 'Gracie's been trying to get hold of you. I told her to get to bed, and I'd keep phoning. There's been a development ...'

She tried to say something, but words wouldn't come, and then he was shushing her, telling her not to worry. 'I'll be with you in five minutes. Hang in there!'

She sat in Michael's chair, the music all around her, until Charley was at the door, demanding entry, wrapping his coat around her, forcing her back into the chair. He switched off the CD player, and held a coffee cup to lips that were trembling, because she was cold and tired. His arms around her were balm.

CHAPTER 20

Sandra

For a moment, after waking, she thought she was at home, and then the unfamiliar furniture swam into view. They had put clean sheets on the bed last night but it still smelled musty, probably because they had lain folded in a drawer since Adam was a boy. And this was the spare room so, in all probability, no one had slept in this room since Stuart left. It was a narrow room, with a tall window covered by paper-thin curtains. There was a faint patina of dust on the furniture, and a general air of stillness, of not having been disturbed until they had invaded it last night.

Beside her, Stuart was snoring gently. She raised herself on her elbow and looked at him, sleeping like a baby. What have we done, she thought. And where will it end? Should she wake him and demand a plan of action? Instead, she eased herself from the bed and went next door to check on the children.

She had forgotten how beautiful they looked in sleep. Eyelashes fanning plump cheeks, fingers hovering near mouths, hair mere wisps on the pillow, but beautiful nevertheless. She slid back into her own bed eventually, watching waking light dappled on the ceiling, taking in the pattern of the curtains, the faded splendour of the wallpaper. But she couldn't sleep. It was easier to get up and dressed, and face the unfamiliar house.

Downstairs, in the kitchen-cum-living-room, there was evidence that a woman had reigned here once: artificial flowers in a vase on the sideboard, standing on an embroidered runner. Runners! She hadn't seen them since childhood. Come to think of it, no one did embroidery any more. Not by hand, anyway. There were photographs, too. She picked up one: Stuart in a sailor suit, plump arms and legs shooting out from too-short legs and sleeves. She would kid him about that when he got up.

She moved across to the fireside. Obviously, this was where Granddad lived and reigned. Everything was grouped around his chair – pipe, slippers, an opened book laid on its face: *Stars of Sunderland A.F.C.* So he was a football supporter. There was a radio, too, and her fingers hovered over the knobs. Should she turn it on? If she did, she might hear an appeal for sightings of runaway parents who had abducted their children. Better leave it silent.

Suddenly there was a soft plop in the passage. Sandra moved into the hall and picked up the *Daily Mirror* from the mat. Last night they had moved a pile of papers and post from the same mat. Perhaps they should let the shop know, and stop the paper?

She carried it to the living-room and sat down to peruse it, but she wasn't interested in the news it contained. She searched each page column by column, terrified that she would come across a news item in which she herself featured. But there was nothing, and she laid it aside with a sigh of relief.

She made the best breakfast she could from the provisions she had brought from home. There was milk in the fridge, but it was solid in the bottle. Later on, one of them would have to do a shop. She thought of what they had agreed the night before: they could never go out as a family, nor could one of them go out with all three children.

'They'll be looking for us together,' Stuart said. 'So if we go in ones and twos, we'll get by.'

She took him a cup of tea with a teaspoon of condensed milk in it from a tin she had found in the pantry. 'Ta,' he said, sitting up in the bed, and sipping eagerly. After that it was time to wake the children, luxuriating in the smell of them, the softness of neck and cheek. 'I love you, Mummy,' Ann Marie said, and she had to blink back tears. Bobby was more reticent, and the baby only wanted to nuzzle someone, anyone.

When they were all seated round the table, she felt a faint

flush of pleasure. This was how it used to be. She was about to signal her contentment to Stuart when Bobby spoke. 'Where's Mamie?' he asked. 'I want Mamie.'

She tried to tell herself it was only natural. He had been with his foster mother for three months now, and he was only three. Of course she had become the centre of his world, but that would change once everything went back to normal. Except that this was not normal. This was criminal. It could only end in tears.

'I want to visit Granddad,' Stuart said as she cleared the table.

Sandra nodded, but added a cautionary note. 'We'll need shopping. But we haven't much money, not after the car.'

Stuart was tapping his nose. 'That's what you think.' The jar was in the cupboard, hidden behind tins. 'He's never trusted banks,' Stuart said. There were notes packed tightly inside, £10s and £20s, and at the bottom, pound coins and 50-pence pieces.

'There's a fortune there,' she said.

'Not a fortune, but enough for now.'

She wanted to say 'What then?' but the words wouldn't come. There was no point in discussing the future. They didn't have one.

They embraced before he went out, the children watching them curiously. 'They're not sure what's happening,' Sandra thought, and was filled with compassion. She stood behind the curtain to watch him go, exiting nonchalantly as though he had a right to be there. Which he did, in a way. She checked her phone, then. There were seven messages, all from Celia.

She tried to maintain an outward calm, for fear of upsetting the children, but her thoughts were racing. Celia knew. The messages were all begging her to make contact, to come back. And if Celia knew, so did her newspaper. Sooner or later there would be photographs. Trevor had taken a pile away with him, so there would be pictures in the papers with their names underneath, and it would only be a matter of time before they were apprehended. 'We've ruined everything,' she thought. 'If we ever had a chance, we've thrown it away now.'

The children were getting restive, but there was nothing for them to play with. 'Can we go down the swingies?' Ann Marie asked, and all Sandra could do was shake her head. Eventually, a search of the sideboard produced a box of dominoes. She tried to teach them the rudiments of the game, but at last she gave up and left them contentedly playing swaps.

It seemed an age before Stuart returned, and when he did his face was sombre. 'Granddad's changed, Sands. I walked right down the ward and back before I recognised him. He's shrivelled.'

'But he knew you?'

'Yes, he's still got his marbles.'

'Then that's the main thing. You can go back tonight and take him some stuff. He'll need a change of pyjamas.'

They found underwear and night clothes in a drawer in the main bedroom. 'They stink,' Stuart said, and looked pleadingly at her.

'I'll wash them.' she said. 'Don't worry.'

A search of the house revealed no signs of a washer. There was a big tub in the outhouse and something Stuart identified as a 'poss stick'. 'They pounded the clothes with it,' he said tentatively.

'No.' Sandra said firmly. 'We'll have to find a laundrette.'

Now she sat in the laundrette, the baby on her knee, watching the clothes go round and round in the washer. Stuart had dropped her off at the corner, but only after they had made sure no one was observing them. It was dangerous to have all three children in the car, but impossible to leave any of them behind in the empty house. The Madeleine McCann affair had seen to that.

'Lovely baby!' The woman was in her forties, and looked harassed, but she was beaming at Darren, and Sandra felt a glow of pride. 'Only one?'

The woman was obviously in the mood to talk, and Sandra felt a prickle of alarm. What if she said yes, and the woman saw her getting into the car with the other children? But if she said no, more questions would follow. She nodded in what she hoped was a dismissive manner, and fixed her eyes on her churning wash load. But the woman was not prepared to be deterred.

'Washer bust?' she asked sympathetically.

'Yes. It'll be fixed tomorrow but this lot couldn't wait.' They would have to find another laundrette to go to ... except that there would be friendly women there, too. Suddenly she was filled with terror at the thought of their isolation.

It was a relief when the washing began to spin, and she knew she was almost ready to escape. The baby was whingeing, and she reached in her pocket for his dummy, before she realised there hadn't been a dummy there for months. Not since they had wrenched him from her arms, and she had put it in his mouth to still his sobs.

She was glad to be back in the car with Stuart. They parked at the back of a big supermarket, and she went in alone. She brought groceries, some sweets, plenty of fruit and milk. At least she could feed them, cherish them until the authorities came to take them away.

'Are you all right pet?' The man was grizzled and a bit unkempt; but his eyes were kind.

'Yes,' she said. 'Thank you, I'm just a bit fluey. You know what it's like.'

He nodded sympathy and moved on, and Sandra scurried towards the check-out. He could not have known that her tears were the result of realising she was spending an old man's money, which was theft.

Back at the house, she made fish fingers and chips in a

huge black chip pan that obviously had seen much use. Ann Marie and Bobby were quiet while they were eating, but as soon as the meal was over they began to whinge and then to quarrel.

'I'll take them out,' Stuart said. 'There used to be swings in the Welfare Park, or I'll find something else.' Their eyes met, and she knew what he was thinking. She couldn't come with them, because people would be looking for a family of five.

'Put the telly on,' he said. 'We won't be long. When I bring them back I'll go up the hospital again, and see how Granddad is.'

When they had gone, Sandra put the baby down to sleep, and then turned on the TV. It was a cookery programme, and she tried to take an interest in it, but it was impossible. A voice in her head kept asking the unanswerable question: 'What are we going to do?'

CHAPTER 21

Celia

It was 9.15 when she entered the office. Gracie's eyes were wide with alarm. 'Where've you been? I've rung you till I was blue in the face.'

'I haven't checked my messages,' Celia admitted. 'Last night was ... well ... fraught.'

'The police have been here.' Gracie's tone was full of foreboding. 'Your precious Sandra has only taken off with her kids. There's a nationwide warning out, and the police want to interview you. And you've got a meeting at 11.30. This is more important though, them running off.'

'I know.'

Gracie's eye's widened. 'You don't mean ...?'

'No, they're not with me. And I didn't aid and abet. Charley told me about it last night.'

'Charley?' Gracie was all agog.

'Yes. He rang, and then he came round. It's a mess.'

'Well, they've blown it now,' Gracie said. 'They didn't have much chance before, but now they've got zilch.'

Charley had been equally downbeat: 'Whatever chance we had of introducing new evidence is gone. They are child abductors. End of story.'

'It's their own children,' Celia had said, but she said it without conviction.

'You'd better ring Laurence Cohen tomorrow. If there's any way round this, he'll know.'

At her desk now, she rang the solicitor.

'Damn,' he said, taking in her words. 'That's very bad news.'

'Surely there's something we can do?'

'If we can get them back, get them voluntarily to hand back the children, I might, just might, be able to sort it. But there'll be a countrywide alert for them now. They'll be picked up within 24 hours – and when that happens, they've had it.'

The police came back at 10.30, courteous but steely. They had found papers with her name and address on it in the Blenkiron home, so they knew that there was a connection. 'We have to remind you that withholding information is an offence. It's in the Blenkirons' best interests to come forward, so if you're in touch with them ...'

She answered, then, that she had no idea of the Blenkirons' whereabouts, and promised to call the minute she heard from them.

After they'd left, Gracie said, 'If you ask me, they must be guilty. Why run if they're innocent?'

'Because no one will believe them?' Celia asked, and received no reply. She could understand the torrent of emotion that might engulf a parent, a torrent huge enough to make them do the one thing that would scupper their case. 'I wouldn't let anyone take Gavin,' she thought. 'Not while I had breath in my body.'

She had been ringing Sandra at intervals since the night before, getting only the answerphone. This morning was no different.

'We'll have to abort the campaign if they're charged,' Charley told her when she went to his office.

'I hope I can get them back. I don't know how, because she's not returning my calls. But I'm not giving up.' She looked at him, wondering if she should thank him for last night. Would it embarrass him to remember how he had simply held her for what seemed like hours, until her sobbing ceased, and she regained her composure. She would never risk that happening again. In the end, she simply smiled and said, 'OK,' and left his room.

An hour later they gathered in Charley's office, all of them weighed down by indecision. 'We've planned the campaign ahead on the basis of a successful conclusion to the Blenkirons' case.' Trevor sounded morose. 'Now … ?'

'It could still work out,' Celia said, doubtfully.

'There's plenty of content, even without them,' Trevor agreed. 'But it makes all the effort seem pointless. Where's the climax? It was going to be a victory for justice … or common sense, if you like. That's gone.'

'Giving readers facts is never pointless, Trev. But let's not prejudge the issue.' This was Charley at his best, pulling them all together. 'Celia, have you any idea where they might be? Will they get in touch, or can you raise them on the phone?'

'I've tried, Charley, non-stop. As for where they are … I hardly know them. There's a faint possibility they've gone north …' She would have explained why, but Charley held up a hand.

'If we're asked, we must tell the police all we know, so the less we know the better. Let's just say that if they can be persuaded to return the children of their own accord, we're still in with a chance.'

'So I should try and get them back here?'

'That's up to you. We also have to discuss the issue of when and what we publish. For now, let's all carry on as normal. Celia, could you give me a moment.'

When they were alone, he motioned her to a chair. 'If you have any ideas, pursue them. Anything you need, just ask. If you can deliver the family to Laurence Cohen, we're still in business. I'll keep a lid on the story for now, but you understand that I'll have to print it if any other paper does. We can't sit on it for long, Ceely. One of the others will come out with it soon, and then we'll be left high and dry.'

There was apology in his voice, but there was finality, too. He was a newspaperman to his fingertips, and the Blenkirons were a story. He would hang on, because he was a decent man, but there was a limit.

She nodded. 'I do have an idea where they might be, just a vague one, but it's worth a try. I'm seeing that retired social worker of yours this morning. After that, I'll take off after them.'

Charley rose to his feet. 'Be careful.'

She nodded and went back to her desk.

'So?' Gracie was looking at her expectantly.'

'I'm going to try to find them, Gracie. Needle in haystack isn't the word for it, but I have to try. The last time we spoke, Sandra told me that Stuart's grandfather had been taken ill. He lives in the north-east, and that may be where they've gone, to see the old man. Can you hold the fort here? I should only be gone for 48 hours. And can you ring the car pool for me? I need a biggish vehicle, but one that's not hard to drive. They'll know.'

The social worker, Maddie Simpson, arrived promptly. Gracie brought coffee to an interview room, and she and Celia settled opposite one another.

'Charley tells me you have huge experience in the field of child-protection. I really appreciate your giving me some time. I just want to get the whole picture, but if you'd also talk to one of our feature writers ...?'

The woman nodded. 'No problem. What do you want to know?'

'Obviously, most of the letters I get come from people who have a grievance ...'

'... so they see social workers as ogres? I'm told we're called the SS. When I mentioned what I did, people treated me as though I were Cruella de Vil.'

'That's about it. Does it upset you?'

'It used to. But I really contacted Charles Lewin, whom I've known for many years, because I was disturbed by some of the things the social worker your paper quoted in a recent article had to say. I'm an Independent Social Worker and Children's Guardian, with more than 20 years' experience of working in the Family Courts in various roles. I did not agree with the assertion that children are removed "very, very, very rarely". Time and again, particularly over recent years, I have seen children removed from their families on the basis of incomplete, inadequate, or frankly inaccurate evidence. I've seen them removed when the correct procedures have not been followed.'

This was dynamite, and Celia didn't interrupt.

'Last week, I witnessed a social worker giving evidence in a Family Court towards removing two children from their mother, to whom they are extremely attached, that afternoon. The social worker in question had been allocated the case the previous day. She had not met the children, she had not met the mother, and she had not read the file.'

'That's very scary.'

'Government changes in the Family Courts, together with changes with regard to the arrangements for Guardians, have led to children and families getting a far worse deal than they did in the not-too-distant past. I became an Independent Social Worker around seven years ago, after 13 years with the local authority. I could no longer work within an emerging culture whereby cases were supervised and decisions made by managers who held the purse strings, and who had no relationship whatsoever with the families in question. Back then, Independent Social Workers were used as expert witnesses, so that if a family felt that they had not been treated fairly by a local authority, an ISW would be instructed to conduct an assessment of the family for the benefit of the Court. This would usually be a very full assessment, conducted by some of the most experienced social workers in the country. A recent survey showed that most had in excess of 20 years' experience.

'Unfortunately, changes to legal aid and within the Family Courts meant that, first, ISW fees, already by far the lowest in the court hierarchy, were halved. After that, insults were piled on top of injuries: not only were ISWs no longer deemed "experts", but the hours allocated to assessments were set, with an astonishing lack of consistency, by administrators in Legal Aid Agency – and were, in most cases, completely inadequate. There have also been cases where the Legal Aid Agency tried to reclaim fees retrospectively, some two years after cases closed.'

'So you're saying the system is getting worse?'

'Much worse. Since the inception of Cafcass, the role of the Children's Guardian has been eroded to the extent that in some cases they do not even see the child, and their reports have been reduced to a series of bullet points. In the past, the Guardian was an extremely experienced professional with a long history as a social-work practitioner. Now add into the mix inexperienced, often very young, and inadequately supervised social workers, Guardians who have as little as three years' post-qualifying experience, and courts being forced to limit the length of proceedings – and it is little wonder that mistakes are made, and injustices done. I have seen some quite astonishing abuses of power, and it is not surprising that so many of our most experienced social workers, ISWs and Children's Guardians are getting out.'

A bell was ringing for Celia. What had Sandra said? *'The kids are supposed to have a Guardian, but we've hardly ever seen her.'*

Maddie Simpson was continuing, obviously letting out anger that had been festering. 'I came into social work full of good will. I wanted to bind up wounds. But nothing, nothing at all in my training, had prepared me for the lies I was told by the people I dealt with. I soon found that some could look like angels and act like devils. But I learned to deal with that, and to pick out the decent people, victims of misfortune or mistake, from the others. Now, it's officialdom that poses the biggest problem.'

Gracie was waiting with more coffee when she got back to

Anxious Alley. 'What did you make of her?'

'I liked her. And she was certainly vocal. But the wonderful thing about her was her willingness to accept that sometimes social workers get things wrong. I've left her with Trevor, now; he'll probably pass her on, because he's got his hands full, but she's a page in herself. Still, I've got to get going now. Cross your fingers I get somewhere … I don't fancy a wild-goose chase.'

It was 2.30 when she got home, driving the people carrier the car pool had provided. To her surprise, she found Sean and Gavin in the kitchen, playing with a dog frantic with pleasure at having company.

'What are you two doing here?'

Sean answered first. 'I'm skiving. He's just broken up.' Celia had forgotten it was the last day of term. 'More to the point, what are you doing here at …' he looked at his watch, '3.15?'

It took Sean 20 minutes to winkle the story out of her. 'That's crazy,' he said when she finished. 'The family will be picked up before they can blink. Poor buggers.'

'Will it go against them?' Gavin asked. His tone was serious, his brows drawn together in concentration.

'I'm afraid so.' She was about to tell him it wasn't his worry when he spoke.

'You've got to find them, Mum. We've got to get them back, before it's too late.'

Sean took control. 'You need to eat before you go. And you need something to work on.' Gavin was dispatched to the pizzeria round the corner, and Sean proceeded to extract the little information Celia possessed.

'They have no family and precious few friends, as far as I can make out. There's only an old grandfather on Stuart's side of the family, who lives in a former pit village on the coast in Durham.'

'What else?'

'That's about it. He lives in a terraced house. Near a railway line. I don't know anything else, really. It's not much, is it? I thought I'd get up there, perhaps talk with our stringer there, try pot luck.'

'Don't stop thinking, and I'll start a search. Tell me their surname again – Stuart's, that is. If the grandfather is on his dad's side, that's a start.'

'It's Blenkiron ... and I think Sandra did say he was brought up by his father's parents.' Sean was half-way out of the door when she remembered. 'There's a church there, St John's, I think that was the name. Yes ... St John's.' That was enough to get him going and he was out of the door, calling over his shoulder as he went. 'Keep my pizza. And get your packing done.'

When Gavin came back she saw from his expression that he was ready for an argument. 'I want to come with you. You need company on a journey like that, so I'm coming.'

'OK,' she said meekly, and laughed out loud at his surprised expression.

They had eaten their pizza when Sean came back triumphant. There were several former pit towns in the north-east that had a coastline, but only one of them with a St John's church. Seaham Harbour.

Sean snatched a slice of pizza and vanished again. They ate their pizza, and then went to pack. They emerged with their bags at 4.30, by which time Sean was waiting, waving aloft several sheets of A4.

'I am only a genius. According to the last census, there are five Blenkirons in Seaham. Well, three, 'cos two are couples: Ada and Samuel in Ranksborough Street – that's in Dawdon. There's an Albert Ernest in Strangway Street, and there's Elizabeth and Walter in Foundry Road. Odd names they have up there.'

'It's still Britain, Sean. You make it sound like Outer

Mongolia. You've done a terrific job though. Remind me I owe you.'

'Oh, I will, darling. I certainly will. And I've done you an auto-route into the bargain.'

He came with them to the people carrier, and helped them load the bags, the dog_padding along behind. Gavin bent to embrace it and murmur words of love. Sean let out a theatrical sigh. 'Best to say your goodbyes. If a good home comes up while you're away ... well, I'll just have to let the dog go. Seeing as it can't stay here.'

Celia leaned forward and whispered in his ear: 'You are a devious bastard, and I will see my day.' Aloud she said, 'OK, the dog can stay. Providing it behaves itself.'

Gavin's look of joy was all she needed by way of thanks. Sean contended himself with one of his martyred expressions. 'Well, we haven't been able to name him, poor little sod, seeing as he couldn't stay. Is it all right if we call him Frasier?'

She was about to nod when Gavin interrupted. 'Let's call him Quijibo.'

Sean snorted. 'That's one of the invented words he uses to beat me at Scrabbble. Quijibo! I'm not calling that out in the park!'

'What does it mean?' Celia was bemused.

'Ask your son. It isn't in the dictionary.'

'It should be.' Gavin was looking smug. 'It's in *The Simpsons*. Bart says it.'

'We're calling the dog Frasier,' Celia said firmly. And the next moment they were on their way.

They stopped only once, at Leicester Services where they took on coffee and sandwiches and chocolate bars. They didn't speak much on the way, but Gavin issued instructions from Sean's auto-route from time to time. As the miles slipped away, Celia realised she felt strangely contented. She was on a mission with her son beside her. They were in cahoots, and it was lovely.

It was ten past ten when they arrived at the hotel that Gracie had booked them into. They ate their sandwiches, and drank Coke sitting on one of the twin beds.

'I'm glad you're here,' she said. 'It's good to have someone to help.'

'Will we find them, Mum? We have to, don't we?'

'Pretty much. If they're to have any chance of staying together.'

Suddenly he crossed to her bed and hugged her, a rare occurrence. 'Me in the bathroom first,' he said when they disengaged, and was gone.

While she had the chance, she phoned Paul Fenton.

'You must be crazy,' he said. 'You have nothing to go on.'

'I have the name of the town in County Durham, and the church where they married – St John's. So, fingers crossed.'

They said their goodnights just as Gavin emerged from the bathroom. Ten minutes later they were both in bed, with the alarm set for 7.30.

CHAPTER 22

Sandra

Tension in the house was rising. Sandra could feel it in Stuart's furrowed brow, in Bobby's grizzling, in the baby's quiet wail.

'We need to get out,' Stuart said, but he said it despairingly. She wanted to cry out, ask why ever they had done it – but it wouldn't help, so she stayed quiet. At ten o'clock, Stuart rang the hospital. The news was not good: his grandfather was failing fast. 'Quite peaceful,' the sister said, 'but failing, I'm afraid.'

'Are you going to go in?'

'Yes. I want to be with him at the last, if I can.'

'It could go on for a long time, love.'

'I know that. But as long as I can stay there, I will. I owe him that.'

At 11 o'clock she took the baby upstairs for a nap. 'I'll take these two down the Welfare Park,' he said. She could see he needed to get out, so she didn't argue.

Upstairs, she lay on the bed until the baby's breathing deepened, and it slept. It looked the picture of health now. She put out a hand to one of its legs, sturdy and rounded with a dimple at the knee. How could she ever have harmed one of those little limbs? Why were so many people willing to believe she had?

Eventually she slid carefully from the bed, and went over to the dressing-table. There was a comb and brush set there, and a hand mirror with a pattern of flowers. They must have belonged to Stuart's grandmother, and yet she had been dead for 20 years or more. It was his grandfather who had brought him up. She pulled open one of the drawers. Handkerchiefs with a crocheted border. She hadn't seen anything like that for years. The next drawer contained jewellery, bright beads and bangles. Vintage, they would call them now. 'He kept her things,' Sandra thought. 'He kept her bedroom just as she left it.'

Half an hour later she closed the last drawer, stroking its contents carefully into place before she did so. The baby was moving, so the nap must be over. She bent over and took him in her arms. 'There now, who's had a nice sleep? What a good boy.'

Stuart was shepherding the children in at the back door when she got downstairs. 'They've been good,' he said, 'both of them. But they'd had enough.'

She gave Darren to his father, and opened two tins of soup. 'We'll have fish and chips tonight,' she promised as they dipped chunks of bread into their mugs and sucked the soup from them.

'I should go now,' Stuart said at last, but he didn't move.

'He's shirking it,' she thought, and leaned to touch his cheek with her hand.

'We'll come with you,' she said suddenly. 'We'll be as careful as we can, but let's get out of here.' She didn't say 'before we all go crazy', but her meaning was plain.

They loaded the children into the car and set off for the hospital, parking at the very edge of the car park. 'Will we be all right here?' Sandra asked nervously.

'I don't know,' he said. His tone implied that it didn't matter much.

'It's only a matter of time,' Sandra thought, and felt a sense of relief. The sooner it was over the better.

'I won't be long,' Stuart said, and went into the hospital on his own.

'Is Daddy going to see Granddad Blenkiron?' Ann Marie asked.

'She's bright as a button,' Sandra thought, glowing with pride. What would become of her when they gave her back to

DENISE ROBERTSON

strangers? Aloud she said, 'Yes, pet. He's poorly, I'm afraid.'

'Can we see him?' Bobby had suddenly brightened. Could it be at the memory of Granddad Blenkiron's sweetie box when he came to visit? Surely not: he had been too young.

She answered their questions as best she could without committing herself. It would be madness to take them in there with CCTV on every corridor. Even now, safe in the car, she was terrified each time a pedestrian approached. It seemed an age before Stuart returned, although the clock on the dashboard said it was only 20 minutes.

He slipped back into the driving seat, shoulders heaving. 'He's going, Sands. I'm losing him. He knows the bairns, though. Wanted to know why I hadn't brought them in with me.'

There was silence for a moment, and then Ann Marie spoke. 'I want to see Granddad.'

'Me, too.' That was Bobby. A few moments later Stuart was unlocking the doors and preparing to get out.

'I want to see Granddad!' Ann Marie said again.

'Have we been fair to her?' Sandra wondered, but then Stuart was taking the baby from her, and helping her out of the car. 'It's the third floor, Ward 3A. He's in the first side-ward.'

Darren's eyes were drooping, but Bobby had taken on a new lease of life at being released from the confines of the car. He chatted away in the lift, and all the way to the ward. And at least he hadn't asked for Mamie in the last hour – that was something.

Walking along the corridor, she felt a prickle of fear. They would never get away with it. As they neared the bed her heart was threatening to leap into her throat. She felt as though everyone they passed was looking at them curiously. Common sense told her this wasn't true, but she couldn't get rid of the feeling. At last they came to the bay that held the old man, and she bent to Bobby. 'You'll have to be very good in here, because Granddad Blenkiron's very poorly.'

She had thought herself prepared for the worst, but she was shocked at the sight of the emaciated figure in the bed. 'Granddad,' she said, holding out her free hand, and the old man's eyes lit up at the sight of the children.

'There's a bonny lad,' he said, smiling at Bobby. The hands plucking at the coverlet were white, the skin almost transparent. Only the eyes in the gaunt face had life. Bobby was tugging at her skirt, suddenly afraid.

'I want Mamie,' he said. The words were a knife in her heart, but Sandra kept her composure.

'What've you been doing with yourself, Granddad? We'll have to get you built up and back home.'

'Aye,' he said. 'Aye, that's right.' It was a game, and they were both playing it.

'Are they treating you all right in here?'

'Aye, fine. Like a king.'

'That's good. No more than you deserve, though.' She lowered the baby until its cheek touched the withered one, then she bent and kissed his brow. 'What do you think of them, Granddad? And Stuart ... he's over the moon at seeing you. We all love you.'

'Why, I know that, pet. I know.' But his eyes were closing, and the hands that had plucked the coverlet were still.

'Say goodbye to Granddad,' she urged the two children, but little Bobby was overcome and hung his head.

'Goodbye, son. Thou's a bonny lad like tha' da, and no mistake.' The old eyes opened again, but they were misting and she knew it was time to go.

She held back her tears until they were out in the corridor, and then she let them run freely. 'I want Mamie,' Bobby said again, and she squeezed his hand because she had no words.

'All right?' Stuart asked when she reached the car.

'Let's get out of here,' she said.

'Where's Mamie?' Bobby said, as she fastened his seatbelt.

'You'll see her soon,' Sandra said, and moved into the

passenger seat as they took the road to Durham.

They parked in a side street below the cathedral. The baby was sound asleep in his baby-chair, and Sandra wiped a hint of dribble from his chin. 'He's teething,' she said. 'Poor little Darren.'

In the end they agreed that Stuart would stay in the car with the baby and Bobby, and she would take Ann Marie into the cathedral. 'And then we'll swap,' she said, trying to sound upbeat. In truth, she felt as though despair would engulf her. They were like hunted animals now.

'Get off, then, and don't hurry back. We'll be fine.'

'Are you sure?' she asked, but he had his determinedly glad face on.

'Yes, off you go,' he said cheerfully. 'We'll be here when you get back.'

She explained the sanctuary knocker on the cathedral door to Ann Marie, just as Stuart had explained it to her the first time he had brought her here. 'Once people who were hunted got inside here, they were safe.'

'No one could hurt them?'

'No, no one.' But as they passed through the door and came into the cool of the cathedral, she knew that sanctuary would not extend to them. If police got wind that they were here, they would come into this sacred place and take them into custody.

They sat in a pew near the front, and she folded Ann Marie's hands together. 'Close your eyes and say a prayer, and God will hear you.' Her daughter obeyed. Sandra's own eyes were fixed now on the rose window that glowed behind the altar. 'Please God, I don't know how, but make it come right some way.'

Afterwards she tried to explain the Miners' Memorial to Ann Marie. 'Granddad was a miner.'

'Under the ground?' The child's eyes were wide.

'Yes. A long way down. See those little figures there, made

of wood. They're all workers, like Granddad was. They were brave.' She looked down at the verse. '*He breaketh open a shaft away from where men sojourn. They are forgotten of the foot that passes by.*' There was a suggestion there of escape, an opening. She took her daughter by the hand and started to retrace her steps.

When she returned to the car, Stuart took Bobby off to see the sights. As he walked away, he hoisted his son on to his shoulders. Sandra watched them. To anyone who didn't know the truth, they looked like a father and son out on a jaunt. She felt a tug on her sleeve and looked down at her daughter's anxious face. Ann Marie didn't speak but her eyes were questioning, and fixed on her mother's face.

'It's all right, pet lamb. Mammy's just got something in her eye.'

CHAPTER 23

Celia

Celia woke as light filtered in through the drawn curtains. In the next bed Gavin slept soundly. He had gone out like a light last night, so he had not heard her take Charley's call.

'We're going with the story tomorrow, Celia,' he had told her. 'We've got no option. The *Record* has got a huge piece by Jane O'Neil, with photographs. God knows where they got them from. So I've had to give the go-ahead, and publish the story, too. I'm sorry, and I've kept it low key. Get a move on, and get them back if you can. It all hinges on that, now.'

'*Get them back*.' How easy that sounded; but it would hardly be easy with every newspaper reader on the lookout for them. She raised herself on her elbow and looked towards the door. The papers had already been slipped underneath. She padded to scoop them up, and carried them back to bed. The *Record* had certainly gone big on the story, and all the detail was there; a County Durham seaside village, an old grandfather, the lot. *The Globe*'s piece was almost as explicit, but Charley had kept the location vaguer.

How the hell had Jane O'Neil found out so much? Only people at *The Globe* had been privy to those details. In fact, she had only told Charley – so how had it got to the *Record*? Unless Charley had spilled his own scoop, in order to be able to appear squeaky clean to her? Newshound that he was, did he care enough to do that? But if it wasn't Charley, then who else? Not Gracie, certainly. And no one else had known. She put the papers aside and made for the shower.

Ever since they had left London, Celia had been conscious of the minutes ticking away. She had thought they would have a day in which to find the Blenkirons: now it was more like hours. For all she knew, someone was already on the phone giving away their whereabouts.

She woke Gavin when she left the shower, and they went down for a hasty breakfast. 'Eat well,' she told him. 'We don't know when we'll get the chance to eat again.'

Sean had provided them with maps and lists of instruction. Gavin had charge of these, and barked orders as they set out for Seaham and the various Blenkirons Sean had listed. She turned dutifully right and left as Gavin ordered, until at last they came in sight of the sea, stretching left and right, with a ship on the far horizon. A sign said 'Dawdon', and they turned towards it.

The first house they tried was a neat semi with a gravelled garden and an assortment of gnomes. 'It's not here,' Celia thought, as they rang the musical bell. The house owner did not have a grandpa, and watched them curiously as they backed down the path. They were no luckier at the next house, terraced and with looped-up curtains and a 'Beware of the dog' sign beside the door.

'One more,' Celia said, as cheerfully as she could. She could see Gavin was excited at the chase, but she was beginning to detect a strong smell of wild goose.

The third address was a narrow street leading down to a railway. Celia's heart was beating as she lifted the knocker. There was a pause, and then the sound of bolts being withdrawn. Her eyes met Gavin's. 'Last chance,' he mouthed. 'If they're not here, that's it.'

'Not necessarily,' Celia said, but she feared he was right. She raised a hand and knocked again. There was silence for a moment, and then the door opened a crack.

'Hallo, Sandra,' Celia said.

They gathered round the kitchen table, Sandra holding the baby, the other children on either side of their father, and gazing wide-eyed at Celia and her son. Gavin took a seat in the corner and began to play with his phone, but Celia could see that he wasn't missing a word.

'You have to come back,' she told Sandra and Stuart flatly. 'It's your only chance. There are police looking for you now all over the country, but especially here in the north. How they found out you were here I'm not sure, but the fact is they know, and so every minute counts.'

'So you think there's a chance ... if we go back?' Stuart sounded hopeless, but his eyes were pleading for an upbeat answer.

'Yes,' Celia said as firmly as she could. 'It's your only chance. Laurence Cohen is working on your case. He has a doctor who's an expert on conditions such as metaphyseal fractures and their origins. And if you've brought the children back voluntarily, that shows you to be responsible parents. It will be a different court, a higher court because you've committed an offence, but we have to get you back to London so that Laurence can hand you over. That way it's voluntary. If the police find you here, or on the way back, you've been captured. It's not voluntary. Do you see the difference?'

Stuart was looking at Sandra. 'What do you think?'

She shrugged. 'It's hopeless, Stuart. Even if they weren't looking for us, how much longer could we hang on here?'

'You could go,' he said suddenly. 'I can't leave Granddad.'

Sandra saw Celia's puzzled expression and explained. 'It's his Granddad, and this is his house. But he's in the Infirmary. He's very poorly; not much hope.'

'Anyway,' Stuart said suddenly, 'how did you find us?'

'Detective work,' Celia said. 'And if I can find you, so can they. Make up your minds.'

'I can't leave Granddad.'

As if on cue, a phone rang. Stuart took out his mobile and put it to his ear. Celia knew it was bad news from the change in his expression.

'He's gone,' he said, looking at Sandra, as he switched off his phone. 'He's gone, and I wasn't there with him.'

She looked at Celia, and then held out Darren. Celia took him, and Sandra crossed to embrace her husband. 'He's better off now, Stu. Nothing can hurt him any more. He'd want us to think of the bairns.'

And so it was settled. A call to Gracie ensured that she would phone the hospital and make all the necessary arrangements with the undertaker. Bags were hastily packed, and stop taps and plugs turned off. Then, for a second, Sandra seemed to waver. Celia took out the *Record*, smoothed it out, and turned it to face them. They were on the front page, mother, father, and the three children whose faces were pixillated to prevent identification. The headline above said: 'Have you seen this family? Hunt moves to north-east.'

Celia felt a surge of fury as she saw the terror on Sandra's face. Charley: it could only have been Charley. He was responsible for this. '*I'll have to go with it if the others get it, Celia. You understand that.*' But he had gone with it anyway, just to get a scoop!

'We can still make it,' she said. 'But not if we stand here talking.'

So it was settled. The children would go with Sandra and Celia in the people carrier. Stuart would follow in the Fiesta.

'I'll go with Stuart,' Gavin volunteered. 'They're not looking for a big boy.'

Stuff was bundled into bags and carried out to the car. Celia had left the people carrier at the top of the street in case anyone linked it to the Blenkiron house. She was counting on the anonymity of that vehicle to get them safely back to London. The Fiesta would surely be described by neighbours, if the police asked; but it was unlikely they would remember the number plate. A Fiesta with a man and a 12-year-old boy in it would not arouse attention.

At last they were packed and ready to go. It was 12.30.

Celia carried the baby out and strapped him into the car seat that Stuart retrieved from the Fiesta. Ann Marie and Bobby climbed into the back. There was none of the chatter of children going on a journey. 'They know something's up,' Celia thought, and damned those responsible for the upheaval in her children's lives.

She hugged Gavin. 'Are you sure you'll be all right?'

'Course I will,' he said, and there was a hint of enjoyment in his tone. So they started out on the 280-mile journey, Celia leading and Stuart following behind. 'Don't look so tense,' she told Sandra. 'We need to look as though we haven't a care in the world. They're not looking for two women with children, or a man with a boy. We'll be OK.' But in her heart she wondered if that were true.

She gave her phone to Sandra. 'Gavin will ring us if necessary,' she said. 'This way we can keep in touch.'

It was a relief to leave Seaham behind and head for the A19. They had decided on taking it as far as Thirsk, where they would join the A1. The sun was high in the sky above them, and soon they were in open country, fields dotted with sheep. The traffic was reasonably heavy, which was all to the good: they didn't want to stick out on an empty road. Celia had never realised how rural the north was. On the left she could see the Cleveland hills, low and rounded. There was a patch of industrial disruption here and there; then suddenly an army base, and a sign that said North Yorkshire. So far, so good. The hills were petering out and they were turning to run up to the A1, with Doncaster 48 miles ahead.

She glanced over her shoulder. 'All quiet?'

'Yes,' Sandra whispered. 'All dozed off.'

They seemed to be in horse country now, but the sky was darkening. The next moment down came the rain. Celia felt panic flutter in her throat. She had entrusted her only son to a man she hardly knew. Was Stuart a safe driver? Suddenly a skein of geese flew across the sky, in perfect formation, and as she looked at them Sandra spoke as if she had read her thoughts. 'Stuart's a good driver. Don't worry about them.'

The sign for the M18 appeared, and Celia signalled a right turn, glancing continually in the rear-view mirror until she saw that the Fiesta too had turned. The M18 was featureless by comparison with the other road, but they could put on speed, and the sun was promising to reappear.

She felt her spirits rise as she drove on. A huge wind farm was twirling away on the right: did they earn their keep? No one seemed sure.

The Fiesta was keeping faith with them, reappearing if ever another car got in between them. Perhaps they were going to make it, after all. Now they were on the M1. A roadside sign was saying 'Derbyshire' when the call came. Sandra listened, and then reported: 'Gavin says they've got trouble, with the exhaust.'

Celia thought wildly. 'There's a service station not far ahead. Tell them to turn in there.' Suddenly 'London' appeared on a sign. What if things went wrong now, when they were more than halfway?

There was a ruined house on the left, and a sign for Chatsworth. In the back, a child began to whimper. Poor little lambs, she thought. They must be thoroughly mixed up after all the upheavals of the past few months. And then there was another sign: 'London 117 miles'. The slip road for the service station came up, and a few moments later she was pulling up and watching the Fiesta approach behind her. Sparks were following it as the broken exhaust trailed on the ground.

They held a hurried conference inside the people carrier, and decided there was no alternative to their all travelling back in it. Gavin and Stuart transferred the bags to the bigger vehicle, while Sandra and Ann Marie went to buy coffee and sandwiches. The children took it in turns to go to the loo, and

15 minutes later they were on their way again. Stuart took the wheel, with Celia beside him and the others crammed in the back.

'Look,' Gavin said, pointing to a sign that said 'National Space Centre'. 'Can we go there?'

'One day,' Celia said, 'but certainly not today.' Another wind farm loomed up. Like Triffids, they were taking over the countryside.

The next sign said Watford Gap, and Celia saw another ruin in a field. Once the building must have throbbed with life; now it was roofless, and it made her shiver.

'There's another Eddie Stobart van,' Gavin said cheerfully. 'That's eight so far.'

London was only 49 miles away now. Celia rang Gracie with a progress report. 'We're all waiting,' Gracie told her. 'Just get here as fast as you can.'

But now an electronic sign across the road was threatening congestion after the next junction, and Celia's heart began to pound again. Where there was congestion, there might be police. But, amazingly, the congestion never materialised, and soon a sign was saying 'Central London 19 miles'. On a flyover above them, three riders were trotting their horses placidly above the traffic below. Celia realised she was smiling at the contrast. How lovely to have all the time in the world to ride.

And then she had to concentrate on directing Stuart towards the area where *The Globe* offices stood. She held her breath as they crawled through the five o'clock traffic, and then the maw of *The Globe*'s underground car-park loomed up; and the next moment they were safe inside. It took only moments to get parents and children out of the car, and then they were all in the lift and ascending.

It was the first time Gracie had seen Sandra and Stuart together. 'Two babes in the wood,' she mouthed at Celia, after she had given them coffee and biscuits. They were using the small meeting-room, and Gracie had done her best to make it look less forbidding.

Laurence Cohen arrived at six o'clock promptly. Charley was already there, shaking hands with Laurence Cohen's sidekick, and exchanging pleasantries with Cohen himself. 'He doesn't really care how this turns out,' Celia thought. 'It's just another story to him; one more front page, if he's lucky.'

But when her glance moved to Sandra and Stuart and the children, she forgot her resentment of her boss. They were getting a chance that was given to few in their position, the chance of justice, and she, at least, should be grateful.

Charley came up to her, and lowered his voice. 'I'm sorry we had to run the story, Celia, but the *Record* was running it anyway. As soon as I heard that, I had no option. We kept the tone down as much as we could.'

She couldn't smile, but she nodded understanding. Except that she didn't understand. Or didn't believe. Had Jane O'Neil really scooped them, and, if so, how? Or had Charley been unable to resist a headline, and was it O'Neil who had come in on their coat-tails?

Charley was turning now. 'Well, I'll leave you in Celia's capable hands. Thanks.' He looked at the Blenkirons. 'I hope today will prove fruitful.'

They were gazing at him with a curious mix of awe and gratitude. If only they knew how quickly he'd sold them out. 'I need to get away,' Celia thought. 'For a few days, anywhere, until this is done. I need some space.'

Two social workers arrived a few moments later. Gracie came in to tell her they were waiting, and Celia went out to meet them. The older woman smiled as she neared, but the younger one's eyes were already flicking round in search of her prey.

'Where are they?' she said.

Before Celia could reply, her colleague intervened. 'Let's

not rush things. We don't want the children upset.' She turned to Celia. 'Could you ask the parents to make their goodbyes and then bring the children out? Don't rush them,' she repeated.

'Thank you,' Celia said, but the social worker shook her head.

'Believe me, we don't like this any more than you do. Let's hope it goes well for all concerned.'

A few moments later the family emerged. Sandra kissed Darren, and then handed him into the social worker's outstretched arms. The older woman held out her hands to Ann Marie and Bobby, but her eyes were on their parents. 'We'll take care of them,' she said.

And then they were led away, only Ann Marie turning for a backward glance.

CHAPTER 24

Celia

Celia slept peacefully, and woke at dawn. She had done it. She had found them and brought them safely back – but to what? It would drag on for weeks, and who could tell how it would end? Had it all been for nothing, that headlong dash towards London? No amount of turning and twisting would give her rest. In the end she got up and sat in the kitchen, nursing a mug of tea and listening to birds wake up in the garden outside.

Of one thing she was certain: she couldn't face seeing Charley. Not until her disgust had abated. She tried telling herself that he had only been doing his job, but it wouldn't wash. He had jeopardised the Blenkirons' one chance of regaining their children, and all for the sake of a pitifully small scoop. Looked at in the great scheme of things, a runaway family was small beer. Certainly not worth selling your soul for.

As soon as she could decently tell herself Gracie would be out of bed, she rang her mobile. She didn't mention Charley, just emphasised her need of a break. 'So that's how I feel ... I just want out of it for a few days. And Gavin is on holiday, so it fits. Can we manage?'

As usual, Gracie was supportive. 'Piece of cake. We've got the back-up column if we need it, but if I give you the likelies, you can email responses ... it'll just be normal working, except you'll be basking in sunshine and I'll be pigging it in the newsroom. *C'est la vie!*'

'Sometimes,' Celia said, 'just sometimes, I know why I haven't had you sacked.'

By the time she rang off, it was all settled.

'Nice,' Gracie had said when she told her the intended destination. 'South of France. Very swish. I've got all the details from your last trip, so leave it to me. You've got a valid passport. What about Gavin?'

Gavin's passport was in the drawer of the desk, along with her own – and Michael's. She opened it and looked at the pages. Music had taken him around the world. He looked back at her from the photo, the mouth unsmiling, as required, but the eyes kind, just as they always had been. She gathered up the passports she needed, and returned the one that would never again be needed to its place.

It was time to ring Charley, then. 'I've sorted everything. There are no problems with copy, so if it's OK with you ...?'

His agreement was immediate, but not effusive. 'He's angry,' she thought as she put down the phone. Well, so be it. It was time to start breakfast, and break the news to Gavin that he was off on a trip.

Sean was enthusiastic about their going. 'Get yourselves away. Do you good.'

'No wild parties here!' she warned, in mock-horror.

He looked at first affronted, and then, when he realised she was joking, a little sheepish.

'As if,' he said. 'As if!'

She was about to call Sandra when her own phone rang. 'Mission accomplished, I suppose?' Paul Fenton said.

'I've got the family back here, and the children have been handed over. Poor devils, you should have seen their faces. One of the social workers was even sympathetic – rather nice, actually. Anyway, I'm glad you rang. I'm going away for a few days with my son.'

'To Nice!' he said, when she told him her destination. 'It's a wonderful place. How would you feel if I popped over for a couple of days?' She knew he was fishing to see how she would take it.

'I'll only be there for a couple of days myself, so there'd hardly be time.' She changed the subject, then, telling him more about her trip north, and the next step in the campaign, before they made their goodbyes.

Then she rang Sandra. 'Are you both OK?'

The voice at the other end was downcast, but determined. They were back at home and making plans to continue the fight. 'I'm sorry for what we did, Celia. Putting you to all that trouble. It was wrong of us.'

'It's over now, Sandra. Put it behind you. I'm ringing because I'm taking my son away for a few days.' As soon as she said it she regretted mentioning Gavin? Sandra had a son, too – two, in fact. Would she get the chance to holiday with them again?

She hurried on. 'I need a break, and I want to be sure to be back for your day in court. I'm going to a place my husband liked very much – Nice, in the South of France. Just for a couple of days. You have my mobile number. And Gracie is there for you, too. Don't hesitate to call either of us, for anything at all.'

Gracie rang a few moments later to say the two of them were on a four o'clock flight out of Heathrow. 'I'll meet you there with all the bumf. Get packing; it's all in hand.'

Gavin spent the afternoon promising Frasier that he would make up for being away, as soon as he got back. 'Will Sean make up to him for missing me?'

'Nothing could make up for you, darling, but Sean will fuss him to death. You know what he's like.'

So it was accomplished. Bags were packed, goodbyes were said, instructions were issued right and left, and they were on their way. Gracie met them at Heathrow, and handed over all the documentation, and a folder full of emails to the column. 'I've included all the possibles, but we only need seven for the column. The rest can wait. You're supposed to be chilling out, not sweating over work.'

Celia embraced Gracie warmly as they parted. 'I couldn't manage without you,' she said.

'Put it in writing,' was the acid reply – exactly what Celia would have expected.

Gavin was quiet during the flight, at times leafing through the magazine he had bought at Heathrow, occasionally glancing out of the window at the cloud forms below, but mostly seeming lost in thought. 'You'll like Nice,' she had told him, when she broke the news about the trip, and he had nodded. He did that a lot nowadays – agreed with her, almost humoured her. 'He's trying to keep me happy,' she thought, and felt her eyes prick.

She closed her eyes, then, trying to pull herself together. This was a holiday, something to lift their spirits. She mustn't spoil it for him. When she opened them a little later, she saw that he was engrossed in a book. She leaned closer to see the title. It was *Empty Cradles*! He looked up and met her eyes.

'I borrowed this. It was on your bedside table, and I read a bit at home. Did it really happen like they say? They took kids away from their mums, and lied to them?'

'I'm afraid it did, but it was a long time ago.' His eyes were on her, questioning. 'I know what you're going to say – that people are still doing bad things in the belief they're doing good.'

The set of his mouth was hostile. 'They can't have thought Sandra and Stuart were bad people. We know them, Mum. They're nice, and they love their kids. If they can split them up, they can split anyone up.'

There was anxiety in his voice now, and it shocked her. 'They couldn't split us up, darling. You and me. It wouldn't be allowed. Besides, the paper wouldn't let it happen. Charley wouldn't … you know what he's like.'

This seemed to mollify him. He returned to the book and, until the order came to fasten seatbelts, he was rapt. And then the plane was beginning its descent, and in a little while the solid heat of the South of France hit them as they emerged from the airport building.

'I want to finish that book later on. It wasn't fair, what happened to those kids,' Gavin said as they moved towards the taxi rank.' He concentrated on their surroundings as the taxi drove into Nice, and their destination came in sight. She could see he was impressed when she pointed out the magnificent pink dome of the hotel further ahead on the Promenade des Anglais. He reacted to the street name too.

'Promenade des Anglais? Does that mean English street?'

'Yes ... except *"promenade"* really means "walk". It's where all the rich English used to go for their morning stroll when they stayed here, I expect.'

His eyes widened at the sight of the porticoed entrance and the liveried porters who seized their luggage. 'It's posh,' he whispered.

She whispered back: 'We might have to wash dishes if the bill's too big.'

But his obvious interest in his surroundings eased the pain she had felt on entering the place where she and his father had been so happy.

Their room overlooked the gardens of the Musée Masséna. Celia went on to the balcony and looked down. Children were playing in the garden, with watchful mothers sitting nearby. A few yards away, beyond the palm-lined street, the sea was deeper blue than the sky beyond. She was about to tell Gavin about the paragliding they would see later on, when he spoke.

'You and Dad came here, didn't you? Were you happy then?'

She nodded, because she couldn't trust herself to speak when she saw his lip was trembling. 'But not as happy as we were when you came along. Now, let's get unpacked, and then we can go downstairs and see everything. Wait till you see the rocking horses in the restaurant.'

They ate in La Ronde, and she felt a frisson of excitement at his appreciation of the décor. 'It's like a fairground,' he said, gazing in wonder at the prancing horses, and the figures poised above them.

'It's an 18th-century carousel, and in a minute you'll get a surprise. Dad liked to eat outside, on the terrace, and tomorrow we will, but tonight I wanted you to see this.' As if on cue it happened: the horses began their rise and fall. The look of pleasure on his face was confirmation that she had been right to bring him here, in spite of her memories. They ate grilled fish and salad, and then a sweet concoction recommended by the waiter. Celia sipped wine, and watched her son, feeling more content than she had done in ages.

Gavin was wiping his mouth with his napkin, and she saw something serious was coming. He was ridiculously like his father when he was in that mood, brow a little furrowed, mouth firm.

'About that book,' he said. 'I just want to say that I'm proud of you ... and the paper. I know it's mostly down to them, but you started it.' She waited, rather lost for words. 'I mean, sometimes it's difficult explaining what you do ... at school, and that sort of thing. Other boys have mums that are ... well, mums, even if they work. But you do things that matter, sometimes. And you know a lot.'

'Well, thank you,' Celia said. 'I'll remind you of that next time you're telling me I don't know what I'm talking about.'

'Well, you don't, sometimes. Anyway, can we ring Sean after this, and find out if Frasier's OK?' They were back to normal, and Celia felt rather relieved.

Later, when he was asleep in the far bed, she stood on the balcony and felt the soft air, faintly smelling of spice and sea, on her face. It was going to be all right. 'Thank you, Michael,' she said softly, and turned back into the room.

CHAPTER 25

Sandra

They had not talked much since they left the police station. The policemen had been nice enough, but the whole thing had been frightening. The magistrates' court had been nothing like the Family Court. For one thing, they had stood in the dock, and had heard the charges read out. 'Abduction' – it sounded like something from a gangster film, not something that happened to ordinary people like them. They had had to answer to their names, and enter a plea, and then they had been bailed.

Trevor had been with them the whole time, and *The Globe* had put up the surety. 'Don't run away,' Trevor had joked, 'that's my pension we've put up for you.' He was trying to cheer them up, but they were beyond jokes. 'You won't go to prison,' Trevor had said consolingly. 'Not when they know all the circumstances. Your solicitor's over the moon about it, getting to a proper court, I mean. He says you'll have a better chance there than in the Family Court.'

They were both clinging on to that, their little bit of hope. But today there were decisions to be made. 'What are we going to do about a car?'

'God knows, Sands. It's not worth getting either of the cars back. They were dropping to bits, anyway. I've still got some of Granddad's money. I could hire one, till we get turned around.'

'It isn't our money, Stuart.'

'He'd want us to have it, I know that for sure. Besides, whose else's is it? There's only me.'

'There'll be a funeral to pay for.' She was sounding downbeat, and she felt ashamed. Stuart didn't deserve any more misery.

'You heard what Celia said yesterday.' He tried to sound

confident. 'That Gracie woman's seeing to everything; and if it comes to it, the undertakers will have to wait for the money till his house is sold.'

There was silence for a while, and then she spoke. 'Are you going to work?'

He shrugged. 'I'll have to go in some time ... to see if I've still got a job. Not today, though. I can't face it.'

She watered the teapot and sat down again. It was 9.15, and the day stretched ahead of them like a wasteland. Neither of them had mentioned the children, although both of them thought of nothing else but the confusion they must feel now, pushed from pillar to post. She was about to say again, 'Did we do right ...?' when the phone rang.

She picked it up and heard a male voice, authoritative and cheerful. 'It's the solicitor,' she mouthed, and then gave the caller her full attention. Halfway through the call she gestured for pen and paper, and began to write furiously. When at last she put down the phone, she smiled for the first time that morning.

'He's got someone ... a doctor ... he says, well, I didn't understand it but it's good news. Good for us. Better than what he told us about before. And he says we've got to get some witnesses. About our parenting – what we were like.'

'Witnesses? Who does he mean?' Stuart was looking sceptical.

'Teachers, the health visitor ... how do I know? Anyone who'll tell the truth.'

'What difference will that make? The Social have already been to the school, you know that. We told the truth, Sands, you and me. And where did it get us? Fucking nowhere.' There were tears in his eyes now, and dumb misery on his face. For once, she felt no sympathy. This was not a time for self-pity.

'Get washed,' she said. 'You may want to sit and let it all go, but I don't. I'm going to the school. Never mind that the social workers went – we should've done it long ago. Someone there will say what Ann Marie was like.' He didn't move, and she crossed to take his face in her hands. 'Come on, love, I can't do it all on me own. We have to fight for them, Stuart. We're all they've got.'

An hour later they were crossing the playground of Amber Park Infants and ringing the bell for admission. The school secretary was lukewarm about their seeing the head: 'He's a very busy man, you know.' But Sandra was in an unstoppable mood, and eventually they were ushered into the head teacher's room.

He came from behind his desk, and held out his hand. 'Mr Blenkiron. Mrs Blenkiron. I'm sorry about what has happened. What can I do for you?'

As Sandra launched into an explanation, the man's face darkened. 'Oh dear, I was half-hoping you'd come to tell me Ann Marie was coming back to us.'

'She will be.' Suddenly Stuart was joining in.

'Yes,' Sandra said. 'But we need you to tell them she was never hurt, that she had a happy home.'

'But I thought it was your son, your baby son ... I can't give evidence about a child I never saw.'

Sandra's heart sank. Nevertheless she pressed on: 'We know that. That's not what the solicitor wants, he's got doctors for that. He wants you to say what you did know about us, as Ann Marie's mother and father. What she was like. You know she was happy!' This last burst out, and it had an effect.

'Yes,' the Head said, 'she was a happy little girl. We all agreed on that. If you want me to testify to that, I will – but I can't vouch for anything outside the parameters of my experience.'

'Parameters?' Stuart said, when they were back in the school yard. 'What planet's he on?'

'Our planet, Stuart. And if he goes in that witness box and tells the truth, he can parameter as much as he likes. Now, it's the nursery next.'

It was painful to be back there, in the place where she had left Bobby so many times. It seemed to be teeming with children, happy children who knew that Mammy would collect them later. But the nursery leader was comforting.

'Will I say he was a happy child? Life and soul of his group, he was. Don't you worry, just leave it to me.' And then her plump arms were round Sandra in a fierce hug. 'I know what I saw, and I'll tell them. You keep your pecker up. We'll sort this.'

But as they walked back from the nursery she noticed that they were attracting attention. People she had never seen before were doing a double take. 'We're famous,' she thought, and it was bitter to think of it. They were turning into their street when she saw a familiar car. 'Stu, that's the health visitor, our health visitor! We can ask her, too.'

The woman was packing a bag into the back seat of her car when they reached her. 'Oh,' she said, when Sandra tapped her on the arm. 'Hello.' She seemed uncomfortable, and started towards the driver's door.

'Look,' Sandra said desperately, taking hold of the health visitor's arm. 'Look, I won't beat about the bush. You've been at our home, twice. Once when Bobby was born, and once for the baby, Darren. Will you tell the court what we were like as parents? How much we loved them?'

But the woman had broken free, and was easing into her car. 'I'm sorry, I can't get involved. It's not allowed. Besides, I don't really know ... I can't judge ...' And the door was shutting and the engine was being gunned into life.

'She can't judge!' Stuart's eyes were sparkling with fury. '*She can't judge?* What else is she doing? She's judged us, Sands, and she's found us guilty.'

They drove home in silence. Stuart was simply beaten down, and Sandra felt increasingly angry. That health visitor had seen her through two births, had visited her at home, had drunk tea with her and complimented her on being a good mother. They had moaned together about the curse, and laughed, and shared experiences. She'd even said she wished all her clients were like her, Sandra. Had she meant any of it, or had she always thought her parenting was rubbish?

Stuart had picked up on her anger. 'It's no good getting worked up, Sands. They've got us by the short and curlies. No one will stick up for us because they're afraid – either that, or they think we are rotten buggers. There's a feller comes in the club, robbed an old lady, did time for it. They'd rather drink with him than me.'

'You never told me you'd been to the club?'

'I tried it, once. Once was enough. They shifted their glasses along the bar, looked at the ceiling, the bar ... the fucking floor. Anywhere rather than look me in the face, because I'm a child abuser.'

'They're not all like that, Stu! There's some who've given us the benefit of the doubt.'

'Even if there were some on our side, there's too many who aren't. We've been judged, Sandra. From the moment they took our bairns, the verdict was in, and the rope round our necks.'

It was useless to try to placate him. He was in a paddy, now, and only time would bring him out of it. The next moment he was standing up and reaching for his jacket. 'I'm off out, and don't ask where because I haven't a bloody clue.'

She sat for a while after he had clashed out, and then she turned on the radio, hoping for some light relief. An item on choral music was coming to an end, and she hoped for something more cheerful. But it was a programme about fostering, and the presenter was praising a couple to the skies for all the good work they had done over the years. 'You gave a stable home life to hundreds of children who had had to be rescued from intolerable conditions. You must be very proud of that.'

The couple were making polite noises about it not being a chore, more of a pleasure. Inside Sandra, anger was growing. The pair were in their 70s, and still fostering. No harm in that if they were fit. But on the way back to London, Celia had told her about some women she'd met, women who'd lost their children just like her. And one of them had been a grandmother of 48 who hadn't been allowed to keep the grandchild she idolised.

'It's a game to them!' Sandra realised she had spoken aloud, and it shocked her. She was talking to herself now! But she had meant what she said: Social Services were plucking kids from one place, and planting them in another, sometimes without rhyme or reason. And there didn't seem to be a thing anyone could do about it.

CHAPTER 26

Celia

There were already people about on the Promenade des Anglais when she stepped through the curtains and on to the balcony. Behind her, in the other bed, Gavin still slept soundly. She had slept well too, which proved she had been right to come away. For a moment guilt threatened to overwhelm her, and then she put it aside. Gracie would hold the fort, and she would make it up to her when she got back. As for the Blenkirons, Gracie had assured her that Trevor had seen them through arrest and charging, and Laurence Cohen was pleased that their day in court would be in what he called a 'proper' court, and not the Family Court. But the taking away of children when a care order was in place was a serious matter. Surely they couldn't send them to jail? That would end any hope of their regaining the children.

She shook her head as though to rid herself of uneasy thoughts, and looked down on the scene below. The paragliders were up and about now, rising from the surface of the blue sea, soaring briefly, only to drop into the sea again. She watched the speedboats criss-crossing the bay, the faint breeze from the sea cooling her morning face.

Michael had teased her about the wind. 'It comes direct from Africa,' he had said, knowing that her geography was hopeless and she wouldn't know whether or not he was telling the truth. She could see him smiling.

'Michael, Michael.'

The name emerged as a little moan, quickly suppressed because Michael's son was sleeping in the room behind her and mustn't be disturbed. She closed her eyes to the wind, remembering. But it seemed less gentle now, less perfumed with the scent of jasmine. Or had she just imagined the perfume because then they had been sitting on the Negresco terrace, and there had been men selling jasmine from little baskets and calling out 'Jas-meen, jas-meen'?

She shivered suddenly, wishing she had put a wrap over her nightdress. The wind seemed suddenly keener. *'Into my heart an air that kills ...'* English Lit., all those years ago, and Miss Pearson yelling at her, 'It's not about the wind, Celia, surely you can see that? He's writing about the past.'

The words were still in her head. *'Into my heart an air that kills from yon far country blows. What are those blue remembered hills ...'* she struggled to remember what came next, but the last verse was clear in her mind: *'That is the land of lost content. I see it shining plain. The happy highways where I went and cannot come again.'* That was the truest line of all. There was no going back. She watched one more paraglider rise and fall, and then she went back into the bedroom to wake her son.

They shared a room-service breakfast, wheeled in on a trolley. 'Lush,' Gavin said, inspecting omelettes fines herbes and fruit, toast and butter, freshly squeezed juice, and coffee. Her spirits lifted as she watched him eat. 'Daddy liked this hotel,' she said as she filled his cup.

There was silence for a moment and then he said, 'We don't talk about Dad much.'

'Would you like to talk about him?'

'Yes, sometimes. I mean, not if ...' He doesn't want to upset me, she thought and was conscience-stricken.

'It doesn't upset me, darling. I thought it might upset you.'

'It did once. In the beginning. Not now. I kind of like to think about him now.'

'Then we will.' They talked of the Negresco, then, and how his father had brought her there. 'We didn't have much money. We weren't poor, like no food and that sort of thing, but we just managed the bills and the mortgage and things like that. And then he got this really posh gig … here, in the South of France. "You're coming, too," he said. And I said, "We can't afford it." Well, you know what he was like when he made up his mind.'

Her son was nodding and smiling, and she warmed to her tale. 'We stayed in a little boarding-house place near the gig, and then he said, "We're going to have two days of luxury," and we moved here. It was madness, because it cost more than he got from the gig, but I'll always remember it and love this place. It's got a tremendous history.' He was wriggling down in his seat the way he always did when something was pleasing him, so she carried on.

'The man who built it was Henri Negresco. He wasn't French, he came from Bucharest. He worked really hard, and became the boss of the Casino here in Nice. But he always wanted to build a grand hotel because his father had been an innkeeper back in Bucharest. That's in Romania.'

'How do you know all this?'

'Dad bought me a book. I don't know where it went. I'll see if I can get one for you, because there's lots more in it There's a crystal chandelier downstairs with sixteen thousand crystals in it, made by Baccarat. It was actually made for the Russian Tsar, but then the Revolution came, so Negresco got it cheap … well, I suppose he did: who else could afford it?' She paused then, but Gavin wanted more.

'Go on,' he said.

'Well, the hotel had hardly opened when the war came. The first World War. The hotel was converted to a hospital, Negresco lost all his money, and then the hotel had to be sold. He died a few years later, a very sad man, I expect.'

'But it's still called after him.'

'Yes, and it's famous all around the world. So he won in the end. I know lots more but let's save it for later on. We need to get out and explore.' It was time to shower and dress, and voyage forth on to the Promenade des Anglais with all its delights.

'There's a lot of shops,' Gavin said as they walked along.

'Nice is a tourist place, darling, and tourists like to buy things. See, it's all things to take home as souvenirs ... or presents. We must buy something for Sean ... and Gracie.'

'And Frasier!'

'Of course.' They bought some English newspapers and settled outside a coffee shop to read them and watch the ceaseless paragliding. There was nothing in any of the papers about the Blenkirons, so the story was dead for the time being. Trevor had a full page on the life chances of children in care, and it made grim reading, but the opening quote, from the judge in charge of Britain's Family Courts, Sir James Munby, was encouraging. 'We have real concerns, shared by other judges, about the recurrent inadequacy of the analysis and reasoning put forward in support of the case for adoption.' That was socking it to them and no mistake. She folded the paper and put it in her bag for reading later.

'What do you want to do now?'

He wrinkled his brow. 'You have a picture on the wall at home. In the dining-room. It's like a hill ... well, a fortress. I think it's here somewhere.'

'Èze,' she said. 'It's a picture of Èze. Dad brought it for me when we were here. Èze it is! We'll need to catch the bus. I think I know where the bus station is, if they haven't moved it.' Michael had rented an open car and they had soared up the Grande Corniche at breakneck speed. Today they would go by bus.

Èze was as magical as she had remembered. A sleepy village 1,400 feet above the sea, with fabulous views over Cap Ferrat and along the coast. They toiled up the slope into the old fortress with its narrow bougainvillea-wrapped passageways. 'There are little shops in there,' Gavin said, excited, and they went into the dim interiors to pore over hand-made jewellery and fabulous hand-printed silk scarves. She chose a brilliantly hued one for Gracie.

'Sean would like that one,' Gavin said firmly, and Celia handed over what felt like a large portion of the euros Gracie had brought her. If the dog proved to be as expensive, they would arrive home penniless.

They ate on the terrace of a rather grand restaurant, overlooking the deep blue ocean. 'Dad said this used to belong to a brother of the Belgian King,' Celia said. 'I can't remember, but it was something sad about him being in love.' The words 'Daddy will know' trembled on her tongue, but mercifully she bit them back.

After lunch they strolled back down to the village and entered the Parfumerie Galimard.

'Pooh, what a pong!" Gavin said, but the smell didn't stop him inspecting the wares.

Celia bought toiletries for Gracie, and a tiny flagon of Canaica Galimard, which promised overtones of vanilla, tuberose, and caramel. 'Smell it,' she said, offering it to Gavin, but he rolled his eyes and uttered Sean's favourite catchphrase.

'As if!'

On the bus on the way back to the hotel, she tried to answer her own question – why was she retracing one of the happiest weeks of her life, that time Michael had brought her to Nice and introduced her to its wonders. Was it a form of masochism, like poking the tooth you know will be sore? Or had she come here seeking solace because she remembered it as a place of pleasure? It was working its magic in a way. She had been happy part of today. Gavin sat beside her now, fiddling with his iPod but looking sun-kissed and contented.

'Happy?' she asked. He didn't speak but the smile he gave her spoke volumes.

'What do you want to do tomorrow?'

His answer was immediate. 'Can we go to Monte Carlo?'

'What d'you know about Monte Carlo?'

'It's a gambling den! Dad told me that. He knew about a lot of things, didn't he?' His voice was suddenly wistful.

'He read a lot, that's why. And he moved around with his music, so he saw a lot of the world.'

She was going to cry, and she mustn't spoil this moment. His next question saved her. 'What does break the bank mean?'

Her explanation took up the rest of the journey.

They trudged a little on the walk from the bus station to the hotel, but at last it came in sight. They mounted the step and went through the doors held open by the immaculate doorman. It was cool in the huge foyer, and they made for the lifts – but a man was rising up from the huge banquette in the middle of the foyer and walking towards them. It was Paul Fenton.

CHAPTER 27

Sandra

On the radio a preacher was talking about God solving problems. 'All that you ask of Him, he gives you,' he was saying. She reached out and switched it off. Stuart would be down any minute, and something like that would set him off. 'There is no God,' he had told her more than once lately. 'If there was, we wouldn't be being tortured like this.'

She picked up the Sunday paper from the doormat, and laid it beside his plate. She was scalding the tea when he came in, stooping a little as he always did in doorways. That was what she had liked about him at first, his height. 'Sit down, love,' she said. 'I've done some toast. And then we need to talk about the funeral.'

'What's to talk about? They've arranged it all, that Gracie and Granddad's solicitor.'

'Well, he is the executor, love. Gracie told you that. It's up to him to make the arrangements. And they've let us pick the hymns, and everything. But I was meaning to talk about getting there. It'll be two trains, so we'll need to be up sharpish.'

'We can drive there. I'm going to hire a car, with Granddad's money.'

'It's not ours, love; we might get wrong. It could go against us.'

'Whose else's could it be, Sands? I'm all he had. I was all he had. Anyway, I'm using it. We'll need a car when we get contact again.'

She didn't tell him that she didn't think they'd get contact again – not unless the newspaper's solicitor managed to sort things. Instead she said, 'More tea?'

They took a bus into town and walked to the car-hire

place. An hour later, Stuart was behind the wheel of a Skoda, and she was fastening the seatbelt in the passenger seat. He drove carefully at first, and then more confidently. 'Nice little car,' he said. 'We might get this model when we buy one.' Eventually he pulled into a pub car-park. 'Let's make a bit of a day of it, Sands. I could murder a pint.'

The pub was full, mostly of families out for Sunday lunch. Sandra tried to close her eyes and ears to the sound of children. Useless to get up and move – children were everywhere. But it was a relief when the family at the next table finished their meal and left. She heard one of the children as they moved away: 'Can we go to the swingy-park, Mummy?' She closed her eyes, trying not to hear Ann Marie's voice saying those same words. When they got them back … if they got them back … she would take them to the swingy-park every bloody day.

Stuart came back with the drinks, and she tried to put a smile on her face. He sipped appreciatively at his pint, and then he noticed that someone had left a paper at the next table. 'I'll have this,' he said. 'It's something to pass the time.' He looked at the front page and then gave a mirthless laugh. 'Just my bloody luck … it's a Tory paper.' But he read on nevertheless.

They sat in silence, Sandra trying to think ahead: what they would eat each day, what she would wear for the funeral, whether or not she dared ring the London solicitor to ask about progress. He was always reassuring when she did ring, but the thought of a possible prison sentence hung over her like a black cloud. Everyone said it wouldn't happen, but with their luck it was almost bound to.

Suddenly Stuart lifted his eyes from the newspaper. 'There's something in here by a chap called Booker. He says the EU's taking an interest in babies being taken away from their parents. On account of twins being taken in Holland. Apparently someone videoed it, and it's on YouTube.' He began to read aloud:

'Last Wednesday in Brussels, this video shown to a

roomful of visibly shocked MEPs and officials was the highlight of a day-long hearing by the European Parliament's committee of petitions into the way thousands of children in EU countries are each year being removed from their families for absurd reasons. Ii …Ilja Anton … Antonovs' … he was struggling with the foreign name … 'told the story of how his brother and sister are being kept miserably in a "living facility" run by a private company, at a cost to Dutch taxpayers of £65,000 a year for each child. Twice the Dutch appeal court has ordered the return of the twins to their family, but each time this has been overruled by a lower "children's court".

'Among the witnesses in Brussels, for 23 petitioners from eight countries, was the Association of McKenzie Friends, led by Sabine McNeill, congratulated by the committee for her "flawless" presentation. The committee has already been angered by the European Commission's refusal to investigate such abuses: EC officials repeated on Wednesday that upholding human rights is solely a matter for national authorities.

'The committee resolved that its members will carry out further inquiries in Britain and Holland, two countries where such abuses are most evident. It will then press for a full European Parliament debate on one of the most disturbing human-rights scandals of our time.'

'Well,' Sandra said, uncertainly. 'At least someone's taking notice.'

They were still discussing it when they reached home, and by then Stuart was impassioned. 'I'd like to see that video. It said in the article that the kids were carried kicking and screaming to a police van.'

'What good would seeing it do? It's not as if it happened in England. And you heard what he said they decided: upholding human rights is a matter for each country.'

'I'd still like to see it.' He sounded like a spoilt kid, and it irritated her.

'Well, you can't. We haven't got YouTube. We haven't even got a computer.'

'I could get one.'

She felt her patience snapping, and struggled to control it. 'I'm going to make some dinner … and don't say you're not hungry. We have to eat, Stuart. Keep our strength up. We're no good to the kids if we get ill.'

She was defrosting some chicken portions when there was a knock at the door.

'Who's that?' Stuart's eyes had widened in alarm. No one ever knocked now, unless it was trouble. But it was the woman across the road standing on the step.

'I've been making pies,' she said. 'And I wondered if you could find a use for one?' Sandra took the covered dish from her, struggling not to break down and sob.

'I know,' the woman said. 'I know. There's folks round here say no smoke without fire, but I saw you with those kids. Both of you. You wouldn't have harmed a hair of their heads. It's only corned beef, but there's onion in it and a bit of potato. I'd have come before, only you don't know what to say. Anyway, I hope you get them back. That's all.'

She was gone before Sandra could stammer out an adequate thank-you.

Coming back into the sitting-room, she was half-laughing, half-crying.

'What's wrong with you?' Stuart was both alarmed and curious.

'There's nothing wrong with me, Stuart. I've just been given a corned-beef pie, and I think it's the nicest present I've ever had in my whole life.'

The pie melted in the mouth, but its effect on them was miraculous. Suddenly, the world seemed a safer place. When he had finished eating, Stuart laid down his knife and fork, and wiped his mouth. 'I'm just nipping out, I won't be long.' She didn't ask him where he was going because she already knew.

He returned, carrying a box that contained a lap-top computer. 'How much?' Sandra asked. 'No, don't tell me. I can't bear to think.'

It took Stuart a while to set it up and get into it, but she marvelled at how much he knew about its workings. 'How do you know all that?'

He tapped the side of his nose. 'I'm talented, that's all. Natural talent.'

'No, seriously. I wouldn't know one end of it from the other.'

'We've got them at work. I mean, I don't use them, but I've been on the odd time. It'll be slower with a dongle. We'll need to get broadband eventually.' She stood back, lost in admiration at his expertise. When at last he tapped out 'Children Taken From Their Parents', a whole new world sprang up before them. 'Which do we read first?' he asked. They settled on a government site called 'If your child is taken into care'. At first they read in silence.

'If your child is taken into care because of a care order, your council will share responsibility for making most of the important decisions about your child's upbringing, including: who looks after them, where they live, how they are educated.'

'Share decisions?' Stuart's tone was sombre. 'When were we allowed to share any decisions? You asked for them not to be split up, and what did they do? Sent them to three separate fosterers. What's sharing about that?'_

They read on, trying not to dwell on mention of adoption, until a sentence made Sandra cry out. It said that the council would listen to the child in question. Ann Marie had asked to come home again and again, and no one had listened to her.

Eventually, she lifted Stuart's hand from the mouse. 'Give it a rest now, love. We've had enough for one day.

CHAPTER 28

Celia

She lay for a while, not moving in case she woke Gavin before she had marshalled her thoughts. Last night she had tried to explain Fenton to him. 'He's just someone from work ... well, not exactly my work ...'

He had interrupted her. 'I know who he is, Mum. He's famous. Well, kind of famous. He has a chat show.'

'That's right. I've been on it.'

'I know that ... but what's he doing here?' That was the 64,000-dollar question, to which she had no proper answer.

'He just wanted a few days away, I suppose.' Even to her own ears, it had sounded weak.

Now she eased from the bed, and tiptoed to the balcony doors. The air outside was warm, but not yet hot. A perfect time of day. But when she put her hand on the balustrade it was full of stored heat: not even the night had cooled it. She stood looking down on the gardens of the Musée Masséna. Already there were people about, children running up and down the pathways just as they had done yesterday. If she had had more children, she might have a child to run to her now. She had Gavin, but, as he had shown on the plane, he was rapidly becoming a man. Perhaps he would go into politics, and crusade against a repeat of *Empty Cradles*. Someone should.

But if he was becoming a man, she would have to be careful of his feelings. He had been polite to Paul Fenton last night, but also wary. She looked around for a diversion, anything to take her mind off the embarrassment of that meeting. The copy of *The Globe* she had bought the day before lay on a rattan chair, and she sat down to read it. Trevor had written a piece on children in care, and the figures that he offered were frightening. The number of children in council care in England had risen by 12 per cent in the previous four years, with overall costs calculated at £3.4bn; and more than 60,000 were now in care, most of whom were said to have suffered abuse or neglect. She read through the figures and the various official pronouncements until she reached the bleak reality. Children in care were more likely to have mental-health problems than their peers, more likely to end up homeless, and also more likely to be excluded from school than other children. So why was authority so hell-bent on increasing their number?

She put the paper aside. Reading such depressing stuff did nothing to assuage her own problems.

Thankfully, when Gavin did wake, he was less concerned with Fenton than with what they were going to do all day. She promised that they would go to Monte Carlo, and then the breakfast trolley arrived, and saved her from further conversation. She rang Gracie as she drank her coffee.

'You're supposed to be chilling,' Gracie said sternly. 'Everything's fine here.' She didn't mention Charley, and neither did Celia. There had been another bust-up in the Coalition and there were rumours about the Cameron marriage. 'Too daft to contemplate,' Gracie said firmly. 'She's the only one I would call a proper wife. The other two are power-hungry. You can see it in their walk.'

That put Mesdames Clegg and Miliband in their place, Celia thought as she put down the phone. Was our Gracie a closet Conservative? She had never given any sign of it before.

Gavin drained his cup, and suggested that getting a move on was a good idea. 'We're only here for two more days. Can't afford to waste time.' He paused on his way to the bathroom. 'Will he be coming?'

'Who's he?' She was stalling for time, and Gavin's look showed he knew it. 'If you mean Paul Fenton, I suppose so. We can hardly tell him to get lost.'

They were almost dressed and ready when Paul Fenton

tapped on their door. 'What are we doing today?' he said, pre-empting any suggestion of their going off on their own.

'We're going to Monte Carlo,' Gavin said firmly.

'Monte Carlo it is, then. The car's outside.'

She might have known he would hire a car, and when they had descended and crossed the grand foyer, the car was exactly what she expected: a long, low, open-topped tourer whose gleaming bodywork dazzled the eye. When they were seated, she in the passenger seat, Gavin behind, Paul turned to the back seat. 'Which of the corniches do you want to take?'

She had thought Gavin would be bemused by mention of the corniches, but she was wrong. 'The one James Bond drove on in that film ... you know, thingy.'

'*Goldeneye*! That was some film! So you want to go on the Grande Corniche? Built first by the Romans, and then updated by Napoleon?'

'Sounds impressive,' Celia said, 'but I hope it's not all hairpin bends, et cetera.'

'I hope it is!' Gavin's tone was fervent, and Fenton hastened to reassure them both. 'It is scary in places, but I know it pretty well.'

They had left Nice, and were climbing, when he gestured to the road below them. 'That's the Moyenne Corniche, the middle one. Grace Kelly was killed when her car went off the cliff there ... 20 years ago?'

'More like 30,' Celia said. The pictures of the tragic princess were still sharp in her mind. Had she been as unhappy as people said, a prisoner in her pink principality, longing always to resume her acting career? And then they were in Monte Carlo, and parking the car to walk down towards the splendour of the casino. There was a café near its entrance, and they sat down to have coffee.

'Are we going inside?' Gavin asked.

'The casino? I don't know whether we can,' Celia said.

Paul was reassuring. 'You can certainly have a look inside.

I'm not sure if there's an age limit, but I'm sure they'll let you have a peek.'

He's good with children, Celia thought, relaxing into her chair.

'Well, let's get cracking.' Gavin was rising to his feet and making for the casino steps, and they hurried to catch up with him.

She let Gavin take the front passenger seat on the return journey. It was good to lean back against the soft leather and gaze down at a cerulean sea dotted with white yachts, and here and there a darker fishing-boat returning to harbour. There was a conversation going on in front, but she didn't strain to hear it. Some things it was better not to know.

They went to their respective rooms when they reached the Negresco, promising to meet at seven for dinner. 'La Rotonde or the terrace? Or do you fancy the Chantecler?'

They settled on the terrace at La Rotonde, and ate delicious seafood. 'That was good,' Gavin said. 'Can we have pudding?'

'You've got to try a Coupe Negresco.' Paul was pointing it out on the menu.

'Looks lush,' Gavin said, and grinned with pleasure when the tall concoction of cream and ice-cream arrived.

They sat and watched him dig into it. 'He'll never finish it,' Celia said.

Fenton laid a note on the table. 'Bets?'

Eventually Gavin laid down his spoon. 'I'm stuffed. It was good, though.'

'Told you!' Fenton said, laughing, picking up his note.

They're getting on, Celia thought, and was both delighted and scared at the idea.

'Can I go up now?' Gavin was already pushing back his chair. 'I want to send some PMs.'

'Can you find your way?'

'Mum!' His indignation was huge.

Fenton chuckled. 'Is the Pope a Catholic? Gavin can probably navigate this place better than you, Mum!'

She watched her son threading his way towards the door, pride swelling up in her throat.

'He's a good lad.' It was as though Paul had read her thoughts.

She met his gaze. 'Why did you come?'

'Did I ever tell you your directness is charming?'

'No. But answer my question.'

'I wanted to see you. Is that so hard to understand?' She felt her cheeks flush, and bit her lip in frustration. He was making her act and feel like a 15-year-old.

'Paul, I'm aware that I have a modicum of charm, but I've never thought it enough to entice a busy man on to an aeroplane.'

'Now that you know it is, what are you going to do about it? Send me home? Don't be silly. You have your son to protect you. And if you have such a delightful ...'

'Don't you dare use the word chaperone. And stop teasing me.'

'OK. Well stop questioning my motives. I was stressed out, I had a window, 48 precious hours, and I chose to spend them with you. Now, drink your Chablis and tell me what's been going on.'

They talked, as the night darkened around them and lights sprang up in adjacent apartments. She talked about the Blenkirons and the dash back from the north, every minute expecting to be apprehended.

'So the lawyer guy thinks he can get them off?'

'It's not "getting them off": they haven't done anything. But he does think he can make sure they keep their children.'

'Good. They sound like nice people.'

They talked of Nice, then, and France in general, and

politics, and showbiz, even whether or not the talk show had had its day. She was about to say something when Paul leaned towards her.

'Come up to my room.'

CHAPTER 29

Sandra

She was awake long before the alarm thrilled at 4.30. In a few hours they would be on the road north to attend the funeral. Her darkest clothes were already laid out on a chair by the window. The car was petrolled up, and at the door. She tried to think of something cheerful to dilute mournful thoughts, but there was nothing she could bring to mind. Yesterday Stuart had pored over the computer all day, even grumbling when she asked him to come and eat.

'It's terrible, Sands ... it's all here. I thought it was only us, but it's hundreds – thousands of people, even. All in the same fucking boat.'

They had switched to another site, then, to an article taken from the *Daily Mail*, and written by a woman called Sue Reid. 'I wonder if Celia knows her?' Sandra asked, but Stuart was already reading aloud.

'"For a mother, there can be no greater horror than having a baby snatched away by the state at birth. The women to whom it has happened say their lives are ruined for ever – and goodness knows what long-term effect it has on the child. Most never recover from this trauma."'

He paused, and looked up at Sandra. 'Cheerful, isn't she?'

'But she's right,' Sandra thought, although she did not say it aloud. No matter how this ended she would never be a whole woman again.

Stuart was reading on: '"The number of babies under one month old being taken into care for adoption is now running at almost four a day (a 300 per cent increase over a decade). In total, 75 children of all ages are being removed from their parents every week, before being handed over to new families.

Some of these may have been willingly given up for adoption, but critics of the Government's policy are convinced that the vast majority are taken by force.'" He turned to look at her. 'It's her you should have written to, not Celia.'

She turned her face into the pillow now, overwhelmed with fear of what might come about, and then she remembered what lay ahead today. Best get on with that.

By the time Stuart was dressed and down, she had scalded tea and buttered toast. The funeral was scheduled for two o'clock. The solicitor had been on the phone for half an hour last night, confirming everything, and filling them in on what had been arranged.

'Gracie will have sorted it all,' Sandra had proclaimed when Stuart put down the phone. 'Celia says she's a slave driver.'

'Well, she's certainly got that solicitor going.' Stuart sounded confused but grateful. 'He's taken care of everything, even the wake. He says not to worry about paying, that it's all in hand.'

'What does he mean by that? Has the paper paid?'

'I don't know; maybe there's insurance. Anyway, he's sorted everything. Flowers from us ... and the bairns. They're all on there.'

'That'll be Gracie. Anyway, drink up love. We should be on our way.'

Ten minutes later they were driving up a street of darkened houses, not a single light to betray someone up and about. They took the A47 west, and then they were on the M1 and heading north. They drove almost in silence for two hours, each busy with their own thoughts, and then Stuart slowed the car.

'Shall we turn in here? I could do with a coffee and a break.' She knew why he wanted to stop here. He was curious about the other car, the Ford Fiesta they had abandoned on the frantic journey south.

They found it where they had left it, looking strangely

forlorn, the broken exhaust clearly visible behind. 'It's not worth reclaiming,' Stuart said. 'They'll notice it's been here for a bit eventually, I suppose, and then they'll tow it away. We never registered it, so they can't trace it to us. He stopped suddenly, and Sandra could see he was pondering.

'What's wrong?'

'If we never registered it, it'll still be in the other feller's name. If they charge for scrapping it, and towing it, he'll be landed with the bill. I don't like that. They didn't look to have much more than us.'

'No. It wouldn't be fair. But we can't worry about that now, Stu. If we get everything sorted, the funeral and everything, we can send him some money. Enough to cover it. Would you be able to find the house again?'

His face cleared. 'Yes. We'll do that.' He turned to the car again and gave the shabby chassis a farewell pat. 'Goodbye, then, bonny lad. You're a heap of scrap, but you were a godsend at the time.'

Sandra nodded. 'Yes, it served its purpose.'

It was noon when they came off the A1, and headed for Seaham Harbour. 'That's a relief,' Stuart said. 'Time to get turned round before the service.'

The cortège was to arrive at the house at 1.30, where they would join it on the journey to St John's. 'Do you think anyone will turn up?' Stuart's voice was sombre.

'I'm sure they will. Your Granddad had a lot of friends.' Privately Sandra feared there would be all too big a funeral. If Seaham people had read the papers and knew about their flight with the children, would they turn out in droves to see parents who were facing a jail sentence, mourning a family member?

They let themselves into the silent house they had left so hurriedly days before. Now it seemed to have taken on the atmosphere of death. She thought of the mementos upstairs in the drawer, relics of two people who had lived and loved, comforted one another in sickness and in health, and now were gone. At least they had a grandson to mourn and remember them. One day she and Stuart would be dust. If they didn't get the children back, who would mourn them? There could be no more children: the internet had made that clear. Once they took your children, they would never allow you to bring forth again – your new baby would be taken as it came, crying, into the world.

'Come on, lass.' Stuart was mistaking her tears for grief. And it was grief in a way.

'I'm OK,' she said, and began to tidy the room.

'Is there time for a cuppa?' Stuart asked eventually.

'No milk,' she said, and then the first stately car passed by the window, and it was time to go.

The funeral director was sombre in formal clothes, but his eyes were kind. 'It's all in hand. Leave everything to me.'

The solicitor had arrived too, in his own car, and came in to introduce himself. 'We've talked on the phone, but it's good to meet properly. I only wish it wasn't on such a sad occasion.' The funeral director was hovering in the background, anxious to usher them out to the waiting car, but the solicitor wasn't to be hurried. 'We have to talk at some stage,' he said. 'I need your instructions. I assume you want the house cleared and put on the market as soon as is practicable?'

Stuart was looking to her for guidance, but the only thing Sandra could think of to say was, 'Is it up to us?'

'Yes. Your husband is sole heir. Your grandfather was a saver, so there'll be money as well as the property. Don't worry about it today. I'll ring you later in the week.'

They were in the car, then, driving past neighbours who bowed their heads in respect as the cortège passed. 'I ought to feel relieved about the money,' Sandra thought. But the house mustn't be torn apart by strangers: there were things there too precious to be touched except by the family. She would think

about it tomorrow. Today she must concentrate on supporting
Stuart, at least knowing their money troubles would be relieved.
But she didn't feel relieved: she felt suddenly numb with the
realisation that the money had come too late. Six months ago it
could have bought them a better solicitor. Now the die was
probably cast.

There might have been a few gawpers among the
congregation, but for the most part the mourners looked
sympathetic, a few of them almost moved to tears as the first
line of 'O Love that will not let me go' rang out.

'They're his mates from the pit,' Stuart whispered, and
then joined in without needing to read from the hymn book.

She pretended to sing, mouthing the words. In reality she
was absorbing the atmosphere of the church. Stuart had
brought her here before, to show her the message dying miners
had scrawled on a piece of wood when they knew no rescue
would come. They were together, and in God's hands, they had
written, or words to that effect; and then there were messages
for their loved ones. Rescue had come too late, but their
rescuers had seen the message and carried it up to the daylight.
She had seen Stuart's throat convulse as they stood there
looking at it, and had known he was thinking of the generations
of men who had hewed coal in the ground underneath their
feet. Men like his grandfather, and his father before him, and
back to the very beginning of mining in this place.

Albert Blenkiron's service in the Korean War was
mentioned, along with his time in the pit. He had been, the
vicar said, a typical Durham miner – a man of few words, but
with a large heart and the courage of a lion. He had loved his
only son, and 'to his grandson, Stuart, and *all* his family, we
extend our deepest sympathy today.' There was an emphasis on
the *all* that left no doubt of its meaning.

'He's on our side,' Sandra thought. 'Someone is giving us
the benefit of the doubt.'

There was more sympathy from the people who gathered

in the church hall for the sandwiches and cakes. 'We're all praying for you,' one old lady said, causing Stuart to clear his throat and search for words. 'There, there,' she said, seeing he was overcome. 'It'll come right in the end.'

But could it come right, Sandra wondered, as she nodded and smiled at strangers. She was remembering some of the words that had swum out at her from the computer last night. Something about the Family Courts being at the heart of the adoption system, and their hearings being conducted behind closed doors. What had Sue Reid said in that article? 'This secrecy threatens the centuries-old tradition of Britain's legal system – the principle that people are innocent until proved guilty.' The old lady believed that right always triumphed in the end, but Sandra had her doubts.

CHAPTER 30

Celia

There was a faint breeze from the sea when she came out on to the balcony again, and she turned her face to it gratefully. The night sky was giving way to day, but it was doing it grudgingly. There was a silver line along the horizon where sea met sky, and in the distance the mountains were vague and ghostly. *Blue remembered hills.* She closed her eyes, hearing the words in her head once more.

The familiar mix of pleasure and guilt which had assailed her ever since Paul Fenton had arrived overcame her once more. What had she done! In spite of the warmth, she shivered at the thought. She tried to concentrate on the lights of a plane winging its way above the coast, destined for the airport. Soon the sky would be alive with such planes, one every few minutes. In seven hours' time, she and Gavin would be aloft, on their way back to London. Once she got home, she would work it all out; perhaps never see Paul Fenton again.

He had left last night. They had gone to the airport to wave him off, and he had kissed her cheek, and thanked her for 'two magical days'. Then he had shaken hands with Gavin and promised they would meet again soon.

'OK,' her son had said, as though meeting his mother's men was commonplace. What must he be thinking? Could he possibly know that, while he slept, she had been sharing another man's bed? She would die if he knew.

Yet the days with Fenton had indeed been magical, and the sex had been gentle and long-lasting, arousing in her feelings she had thought would never come again. But neither of them had said, 'I love you' – and what was sex without those words?

On his second day they had gone to the flea market in the

Cours Saleya. She had enjoyed telling him about something he had not known existed. 'Six days a week it's a flower market … you can smell the fragrance for miles. And then, on Mondays, the flowers vanish and it's a flea market. Millions of stalls, all different.' So they had wandered the Cours Saleya and then bought food and wine to carry to a nearby deserted chateau, where they could picnic. And in the evening, as the air cooled, Paul had taken Gavin paragliding.

She had demurred at first. Gavin's brow had grown thunderous, and a pet lip threatened. 'You're always the same, Mum. Everything that's good fun is dangerous, according to you.'

Paul had calmed her fears. 'He and I will go up together. The most he'll get is wet feet. Look, there are people doing it all along the coast. You just jog for a little, and then you're lifted up and away. He'll be strapped into the harness, with me right there behind him, hanging on to him for grim death. Sorry, wrong word. Grim life. Fifteen minutes later we'll be splashing back down, and you'll be glad you said yes.'

'I didn't say yes.'

'But you're going to.'

And of course she was. She hardly breathed for half an hour, and then her son was hugging her, his face triumphant. 'It was lush, mum. Paul will take you up too, if you want to go.'

She had declined the offer and tottered back up to the Promenade.

Now she closed her eyes and pictured the scene again. She had watched man and boy rising into the air, their bodies blended together, half of her thankful that someone was giving her son a good time, the other half regretful that the man in question was not his father. She and Paul had made love again that night; no need to ask this time, just eyes meeting in the restaurant, each knowing what the other was thinking.

But first they had sat on the terrace after Gavin had gone up, talking about travel and politics and work. He had asked about the progress of the campaign, and her meeting with Glenda's clients. And suddenly it was easy to launch into the stories of Kath, and the other women. 'She was just a kid, Paul. Thin as a rake, bitten nails. "Not much to tell," she said, when I asked her about her life. The social worker had promised her an "all-time mummy and daddy," but it didn't happen. She was pregnant as soon as she came out of care, and then they swooped.'

'On what grounds?' This time he looked more sympathetic.

'They said she had to go on a parenting course, only there wasn't a place for her. Apparently, that's quite common: they make a demand that they know can't be met. They said that, with her, the baby would be deprived, but I don't think it wouldn't have been. She's a wreck now, so it's too late. She'll go on fighting, but the likelihood is she'll get pregnant again to fill the gap, and that one will go, too.'

'You make it sound pretty Kafkaesque.'

'It is. And it's gets worse. The second woman was older, 48. She'd brought up four grandchildren because her daughter was a waste of space. Eventually she applied for guardianship. It was granted in the case of the three older children, but the youngest, an 18-month-old she had cared for from birth, has been put up for adoption.'

'Which is crazy.' He was frowning now. 'I mean, she's …'

'… competent to look after all four, or none? Exactly. They want the baby for adoption because the whole thing is becoming money-orientated. Trevor is trying to get reliable figures, and the paper means to go big on it.'

He had touched her hand, then, and changed the conversation to something light. And afterwards they had made love. Now she looked down on the Promenade, wondering how it had come to pass. She had thought never to make love with a man again. And then Paul had risen up from the Negresco banquette, and everything had changed.

She stood up suddenly, appalled at how even the memory of his love-making aroused her. He was a skilful lover, much practised. 'It doesn't mean anything,' she told herself, and then tried to work out whether or not she wanted it to.

In the end she gave up wondering, and went to start getting dressed.

She felt better once they were safely ensconced on the plane. She had been right to escape for a while: she had now got the whole Charley thing into perspective. It was his job to seize the initiative with news. If the *Record* hadn't printed it, neither would he have done. All the same, it would always come between them. Just for once, could he not have let it go? To honour a principle?

She turned her thoughts to the upcoming court case. If the Blenkirons won, then perhaps she could forgive Charley in time. If they lost – but that didn't bear contemplation. How must Sandra feel now, back at home, with a criminal prosecution hanging over them, and almost definitely prevented from seeing the children? 'I shouldn't have gone off and left them,' Celia thought, and was ashamed.

'It was good, Mum.' She turned to see Gavin regarding her. 'Especially Èze, and the paragliding.' He thought for a moment. 'He's all right, Paul. But thank you for taking me to Nice. It was dead good. I'm going to finish that book now because the film on here is crap.' Too late he realised she wouldn't appreciate the word he had used. She contented herself with raising her eyebrows, and he buried his embarrassment in *Empty Cradles*. Twenty minutes later he closed the book and turned towards her.

'I know it was a long time ago, but I still don't understand. People must have known, but no one stopped it.'

'It is hard to understand, darling. You have to remember that the people who did that – and even the people who took Sandra's children – think they're doing the right thing.'

'They just get it wrong?'

'Yes. The real problem is that no one looks into it properly ... makes sure they've got it right. Because people do have to have their children taken, sometimes.'

'If they do bad things to them? Like Baby P.?'

'Yes, like Baby P.'

'But they didn't take him away, and he needed it – so why have they taken Sandra's kids when they don't?'

'I wish I knew, darling. That's what we're trying to work out.'

'You mean Charley?'

'Yes, and Trevor and the others. We want to make sure that people always get it right. Anyway, try not to worry about it. But I'm glad you care that it's happening. Dad would be proud of you.' He didn't reply but she could see that he liked the idea.

She brought *The Globe* and the *Record* at Heathrow, to glance through on the shuttle. Jane O'Neil had a piece on the Blenkirons, although they were not identified by name. 'Couple who abducted children facing charges,' said the headline. It went on to paint a sympathetic portrait of Sandra and Stuart, and gave reasons why the writer hoped the court would show mercy. Celia folded the paper and put it in her bag.

She tried to map out the evening ahead of her: put washing in, check cupboards, get some bread ... but something was nagging at her. She took out the paper, and began to read the article again.

'Sandra Blenkiron had an emotionally starved childhood, living in foster homes and hostels, and never meeting her GI father.' Had Jane O'Neil caught up with Sandra, and pumped her for information? That couldn't have happened before they left for Nice, or Sandra would have told her. While she'd been away, then? Maybe, but surely Sandra would have checked with Gracie first? No use blaming Charley this time, because he hadn't known details of Sandra's childhood. Or had he? What exactly had she told him?

And then they were in a taxi and speeding home to an ecstatic welcome from a dog gone mad at the sight of them, and Sean grinning all over his face, and pointing at a huge bouquet on the hall table. So Paul had sent her flowers as a thank-you! She felt her cheeks flush, but kept her face impassive. If she gave Sean an inch, he'd have the whole story out of her.

'Lovely flowers,' he was saying meaningfully.

She plucked the card from its holder, but the name on it wasn't Paul's. The card said: *'Welcome home. Charley.'*

CHAPTER 31

Sandra

They were up and dressed by seven, which left them an hour before they must leave if they were to reach London by 11 a.m.

'We could get something to eat in London?' Sandra knew Stuart was trying to cheer her up, so she nodded with as much enthusiasm as she could muster. We're playing a game, she thought: each trying to cheer up the other. Once the suggestion of eating out would have been a treat. Nowadays she preferred to be at home, the door locked and her safe in her 'jamas and dressing-gown. In a funny way, life had ceased to happen. She still got out of bed, washed, dressed, cleaned up a bit, even shopped, but it was all just marking time. She had felt like that ever since the funeral. She couldn't explain it. It just was.

Today they were going to London for a final meeting with *The Globe*'s solicitor. She knew Stuart was hoping for progress, new evidence, something that would make everything come right. He had been quite chatty last night, and she had tried to respond, but it hadn't been easy. She had finished a book she had ordered from the internet. It lay on the arm of the sofa now: *A Mother's Nightmare* by Louise Mason. Its subtitle was 'My fight to get my children back'. The writer had fought and won but had not yet got all her children back. One of them had been apart from her for so long that it wouldn't be fair to uproot it. 'I'm trying to come to terms with the fact that the mother-child bond is not there as it should be with K, and I'm trying to do what's best for us all. The Social Services have said they think things may work out naturally when K is eleven – it seems a long time away to me ...' Is that how it would be with the baby? Even Bobby? He had asked for his foster mother when he felt stressed, even though she, his mother, had been there.

Sandra had recognised in Louise's book the feeling of coming up against an implacable organisation that would not let you win, no matter what you did. Like Kate Austin, the poor mother who had lost her child to her ex-husband, and might never see him again. She had read *A Promise to Keep my Angel* locked in the toilet in case Stuart saw, because he had gone on and on about her reading other women's stories, especially when they ended with her in tears. He spent hours on the internet, looking up cases that wound him up – but he claimed that was different.

He was obsessed with the internet, now, Googling every night in search of evidence and, particularly, for articles by the man who was now his hero, Christopher Booker. 'Listen to this, Sands: "It is not generally appreciated how adoption and fostering, organised by social workers, have become big business. Adoption payments and access to a wide range of benefits can provide carers with hundreds, even thousands of pounds a week." He had looked up and then back at the screen: '"Last week it emerged, from an official register, what the occupation is of a woman who adopted another woman's stolen children. She is a social worker."'

What if some social worker, somewhere, had taken a fancy to Ann Marie? Or Bobby? Terror gripped her. 'Come on, love. Time to get going.' His hair was still wet from the shower and plastered down in the way he liked it for formal occasions.

Sandra smiled at him, sliding the book behind her as she spoke. 'I just need to spend a penny, and I'm ready.'

In London, they parked in a side street, in the one miraculously vacant bay. 'See,' Stuart said, 'it's our lucky day.'

They had to wait a few minutes before Laurence Cohen was free. A secretary offered them coffee or tea, but they both declined. They were nervous enough, without trying to balance cups and saucers.

Ten minutes later they were installed in solicitor's office, and he was beaming at them from across his desk.

'We don't yet know what the charges against you for taking the children will be. By rights, I should advise you to plead guilty to the charges, as you manifestly did take the children. But by pleading not guilty we get a chance to ... if you like ... restage the original court hearing. Are you prepared for the fact that, if you do that, it might alienate the court, and make them act more severely?'

They both nodded, and he smiled his approval. 'Good. That means we can bring up matters that should have been dealt with in the Family Court, but were not. You did well to get the school's head teacher to give evidence for you. My clerk has talked with him, and that's all fixed. The even better news is that the doctor who will give evidence on your behalf is sure he can prove that the symptoms ... the metaphyseal fractures ... which Social Services put down to deliberate injuries, or to twisting, have natural causes. It's difficult for laymen to take in – I struggle myself. But the expert knows his stuff, and that's what matters.'

Stuart was leaning forward. 'Why didn't our last solicitor get this expert?'

'He probably didn't want to rock the boat. I imagine he gets all his work from the local council, and can't afford to fall out with them. And he probably thinks there's no smoke without fire.'

'We never hurt Darren!' Sandra's voice was anguished.

'I know that. But we have to convince the court. When a diagnosis is uncertain, as in this case, background evidence comes into its own. You put it to the court: is it likely that parents who were loving and attentive in every way would suddenly snap and break a baby's limb, or shake it long enough and forcefully enough to make its brain rattle in its head? Your previous solicitor failed to present evidence that you were loving, caring parents to your other children, and to the baby.

The hospital records show that your baby was well-nourished, and free from any external injury. Your older children were in perfect mental and physical condition. A proper defence would have asked whether it was likely that parents who cared for their children so well would suddenly vent their fury on a baby. I don't think the hospital comes out of this too well, either.'

'They believed we'd done it, right from the first moment. You could see it in their faces,' Sandra said.

'I've heard that before, and too often. Still, that was then, this is now. And we have the head teacher, and the nursery group leader. You say you approached your health visitor?'

'Yes,' Sandra said, intervening quickly in case Stuart vented his spleen on the subject. 'We always got on well with her, but she said her position didn't allow her to take sides.'

'We weren't asking her to take sides.' The words burst from Stuart. 'We only wanted her to tell the bloody truth.'

'I know,' Laurence Cohen said sympathetically. 'Well, she will have to live with her conscience. I want you to try to relax in the next few days, and not wind yourselves up. Your demeanour in court is important: you are innocent, and you need to look innocent. Anger in court, however understandable, suggests hot temper. There is quite a lot in the reports about your temper, Stuart. You don't need to tell me you were provoked, but I am afraid that is not an excuse. Eyes will be on you, looking for signs of aggression. You're not naturally an aggressive man, so don't give a false impression ... no matter what the provocation. You have a barrister who believes in you, and will fight all the way.

'Go away now, spend a little time sight-seeing, and then go home and relax. I'll see you in court.'

Stuart took Sandra's hand as they emerged into the sunlit street. 'What'd you think?'

'He sounds confident,' Sandra ventured.

'That worries me a bit. Is he too cocksure?'

'He knows what he's doing, Stu; Celia told you that. *The Globe* wouldn't have picked him if he hadn't been top of his trade.'

'I wonder what they're paying him? A king's ransom, probably. Thank God you wrote that letter to Celia.'

They turned in at the park they had visited before. 'There's a lot happened since we were here last time,' Sandra said.

'Yeah.' Stuart sounded a little guilty, and she knew that, like her, he was thinking of their crazy dash north, and that nightmare journey back. 'I shouldn't've done it, Sands.'

She squeezed his hand. 'We both did it. I could've stopped you. Anyway, it's water under the bridge. Remember what Mr Cohen said: we need to relax and unwind. I fancy an ice-cream. There's the kiosk. Your turn to pay.'

Just like last time, there were children playing in the park while mothers looked on. Almost all the benches were occupied, but once they had their ice-creams they found a seat next to an old man. He didn't look up as they sat down, intent, Sandra noticed, on watching squirrels in a nearby tree.

For a moment they concentrated on licking the cones fast enough to stop the ice-cream from dripping, but after a while Stuart said: 'We didn't do enough of this when we had the kids, Sands. When we get them back, let's make time just to enjoy having them.'

Beside them, the old man sighed, and rose to his feet. The next moment he had shuffled off, allowing them more ease, with the whole seat to themselves. Stuart took out the newspaper he had bought from home, and started to read the sport on the back page. But Sandra caught sight of the headline on the front page.

'*Judge furious as council splits up abused siblings.*' She waited till Stuart had finished with the sports section, and then she took the paper from him. 'What are you reading?' he asked as she devoured the print. She started to read aloud:

'"A High Court judge has hit out at the council responsible for the Baby P. scandal for preventing seven abused siblings from seeing each other after their parents were sent to prison. Mr Justice Holman said he felt a 'sense of the utmost despair' after it emerged that social workers at Haringey council organised a 'goodbye meeting' last year. In doing so they ignored a legal order made in 2012 to allow the brothers and sisters to stay in contact.' The judge added: 'It simply shouldn't have happened that way. It was a frankly catastrophic situation'."'

She read on. '"The eldest five were in foster homes and the youngest two are to be placed with an adoptive family. The judge had said the council's failings 'almost beggar belief', and accused it of a 'flagrant breach' of the order that ensured the five older children would remain in touch with their siblings, aged two and three. 'I can only say I part from this with a sense of the utmost despair. A terrible thing has happened'."'

'That's what the social workers could do with our kids, Stuart. They're a law unto themselves; they do it all the time. Not even a legal order stopped them.'

Their brief period of relaxation was over. They got to their feet, and started for the car. They were almost there when Stuart halted and turned to face her. 'Bugger this, Sands, we're coming at it from the wrong angle. We've got people on our side now, people with clout. And that Judge is speaking out. You have to believe right triumphs in the end. You'd go under if you didn't. I know I'm a bloody Jonah most of the time, but today I've got a feeling things are changing. Get in that car. I don't know where we're going, but we're going somewhere for a bloody good drink.'

CHAPTER 32

Celia

Gavin had obviously given Sean a blow-by-blow account of their time in Nice.

'So you had company?' Sean asked, as he lurked in the kitchen. He had come down on the usual pretence of running out of bread.

'You're so original,' Celia had commented; but sarcasm was wasted on Sean.

'That telly guy,' he continued. 'That must have been nice for you?'

'Do you want me to wrap the bread so you can take it upstairs?'

'No, ta. I might as well just eat it here. Save time.'

'Feel free. There's the butter and marmalade, but don't let eating get in the way of the third degree.'

'I won't,' he said amiably. 'Anyway, you've got a nasty mind. I'm only asking if you had a good time.'

'I did, thank you. The telly man, as you call him, went home before we did; and, no, he and I are not an item. I wish it could be more sensational for you, but that's all there is. Was. Two friends bumping into one another in a foreign city.'

As Celia spoke, she could feel the flush mounting her neck and cheeks. There had been no bumping into one another: Fenton's visit had been purposeful and, she now admitted to herself, significant. It was odd to sit at her own breakfast table, with the normality of her kitchen around her, and remember having sex with another man. A week ago, she would have thought such a thing inconceivable. Except that there had been times in the days leading up to that flight north ... she felt the blush rising in her cheeks again, and got to her feet.

'I can't sit here gossiping. I've got to get back to work.'

'Don't let me stop you. I mean, if I don't get the facts, I have to use my imagination ...'

'And we all know how lurid that can be. Don't judge everyone by your own standards. And remind me to buy you a loaf each day: it'll save wear and tear on the stair carpet.'

'You should be writing for the *Now* show. They're always looking for gags! Anyway, I've got to go, too. I'll pop down tonight, just in case you need a shoulder.' The tea towel she flung just missed his head, and he was humming as he went on his way.

She had offered Gavin the chance to accompany her, but he had preferred to stay with the dog. So she journeyed to *The Globe* alone, and made her way to Anxious Alley, where Gracie was waiting, coffee at the ready.

Celia gave her a brief account of their time in Nice, trying to make Fenton's presence there seem like a casual event; but Gracie didn't seem inclined to pursue the matter. That was unusual enough to cause Celia to ponder, but so much mail had accumulated that she had to put conjecture aside and get down to work. They went on sorting the piles of letters and emails, and choosing the seven that would go in the next column, for what seemed like hours; sometimes uttering little gasps of astonishment, more often saying 'Not again!' in world-weary tones.

They were almost ready to stop and go in search of lunch when Trevor appeared. 'Good break?'

Celia told him that Nice had lived up to expectations, and then raised her eyebrows at the piece of paper he was holding. 'Need any help?'

Trevor pursed his lips. 'Well, more of an opinion, really. You saw Monday's piece – well, you probably didn't. We ran a list of the children let down by Social Services ... Victoria Climbié, Rikki Neave, Baby P., Heidi Kosega, you know the score. Why, we asked, were the social workers so good at missing real cruelty, and so bad at spotting loving parents who simply needed support? The online response was mainly on our side, but this arrived this morning. It's an email from a male reader whose wife is a social worker, and he's not a happy bunny.'

Celia took the letter from him.

'Sir,' it began. 'My wife gave up a well-paid job to pursue a career in social work, as she naively thought she could make a difference! Your campaign is nothing short of an assault on social workers, it would be laughable if it wasn't so serious! Are these the words of a person who is completely devoid of any semblance of what it takes to be a competent social worker, sometimes 14hr days to the detriment of her own family.' Celia looked up from the letter. 'He's certainly forthright.'

'Read on,' Trevor said. 'It gets hotter.'

Celia obeyed. 'Why does it take isolated cases as Baby P. to bring out uneducated morons who have no idea what a fantastic job social services carry out in the UK. Apart from your experience of being journalists what qualifies you to voice your uninformed views on such a dedicated and qualified group of professionals. We should be ashamed to even suggest that these dedicated people should be highlighted for anything but good things, but I suppose this is a great democracy and any idiot without anything to back it up can spout off.'

'He doesn't mince his words,' Celia said. 'Will you answer him?'

'Not sure. The letter's polite, but it's also abusive in places. I understand his wanting to defend his wife, but what he's really saying is that no social worker is less than perfect because his wife is perfect. I don't think we can let him get away with that.'

Celia nodded understanding as he continued: 'So I'm thinking of running his letter along with our reply. What do you think?'

'I like that. I can see where he's coming from: he's bridling just as we do when the press is criticised. But loyalty has made him blinkered.'

Celia could see Gracie nodding in agreement as she too read the letter.

Trevor was holding out another bunch of emails. 'These are all from social workers.' He picked out the first one. *'I agree with you when you say Family Courts rubber-stamp social workers' reports.'* He looked at a second. *'I was a foster carer, but felt I had to resign rather than be part of the appalling practice of taking babies away from their mothers soon after birth.'* A third said: *'I am a qualified social worker, and I can assure you that when the social worker wants a child removed, the court always does it. My manager always gets her own way, and some of her decisions are frankly disgusting.'*

His face displayed satisfaction. 'We've got a stack more of these. So I think we'll do a sidebar showing just how many "morons" there are in his wife's profession.'

But when Trevor went off, keen to begin his next assignment, something was niggling away at the back of Celia's mind. Something that didn't fit. Something to do with Sandra.

They popped out to the nearby Pret a Manger, and had coffee and sandwiches. 'Your break has done you good,' Gracie said, eyeing her. 'You look relaxed. It was what you needed.'

'Yes, it was rather nice. And Gavin loved it.'

'How does he get on with Fenton?' There was an unusual caution in Gracie's voice, but her bland expression said it would be useless to question her.

'Very well. Considering that Paul's never had children, he's good with them.'

'Well,' Gracie said with a sigh, 'that's nice, then.'

When they got back to Anxious Alley, Celia cleared space on her desk. 'Have we got our reports on the Blenkirons' dash north? And I'd like the *Record*'s too, if you can find them.'

Ten minutes later the cuttings were on the computer screen in front of her and she began to read.

Eventually she picked up the phone and dialled Sandra's number. 'Hi, how are you both? Good. Look, you haven't talked to any other journalists, have you? Apart from Trevor? No, I thought not. No, it's nothing to worry about. Oh, that's excellent. I told you Laurence Cohen was good at his job. See you soon. Take care. 'Bye.'

Gracie was regarding her with open curiosity.

Celia said: 'I can't work out how it came out as it did, Gracie. No one in here would talk, so how did the *Record* get hold of the story in the first place? It could have wrecked everything, if the police had got to the Blenkirons before I did. And there were things in the O'Neil piece that only I knew. Well, I'd told Charley some of them, but he wouldn't talk to Jane O'Neil. Would he?'

Gracie looked scornful. 'Spill to our bitter rival? You've got to be joking. And you should have seen him when he heard that the *Record* had the story – he was gutted!'

She went back to her desk, and Celia continued to study the cutting. Jane O'Neil had mentioned Sandra's GI father – but no one had known about him, not even Charley. Had Sandra lied to her; had she, in fact, talked with the *Record*? She gazed at the screen, unseeing. There was only one person whom she had told about the GI father. Only one.

She reached for the phone, and dialled Fenton's number. It was ringing out when she hesitated – on second thoughts, this was better done face to face. Twenty minutes later she was standing on his doorstep.

He smiled when he opened the door and saw her standing there. 'Celia! I was thinking about you.'

'Cut the crap, Paul, and answer a question. Did you tell Jane O'Neil the things I told you about the Blenkirons?'

'So that's what this unexpected visit is about. For a moment I thought you couldn't live without me!'

'Straight answer, Paul. Yes or no?'

He was silent for a moment and half-turned as though to end the conversation. Then he spoke. 'Grow up Celia. This is the media – it leaks like a sieve. Everyone knew about the

Blenkirons running off with the children.'

'Not everyone knew about St John's church or Sandra's GI father, Paul. I was the only one who knew that, and you were the only person I told. Jane O'Neil's by-line is dated the day after I spilled things to you. And again, in Nice, when I'd told you even more.'

'Jane is an old mate of mine. I might have said … anyway, what does it matter? It won't affect anything. You did a wonderful job. The children are back. It will be sorted …'

He was still talking as Celia turned on her heel.

When she got back to Anxious Alley, she sat down at her desk, shuffling papers in an effort to find something, anything, to distract her. Had he really kissed her goodnight and then got out his phone to ring Jane O'Neil? Had he even left her bed for a cosy chat with his ex? Was he still shagging Jane O'Neil? Or was it just that he couldn't resist appearing to know it all, to be the imparter of real gen? '*Guess what, Jane. The mother was a GI's bastard – and that's a real scoop I'm giving you.*'

When she looked up, she saw Gracie was regarding her sympathetically. 'I wondered how long it would take you to work it out.'

So Gracie knew, and if she knew, who else? Did the whole workforce know what a fool she'd been?

She'd worry about that tomorrow. For now, all she could think of was how she was going to find words to apologise to Charley.

CHAPTER 33

Sandra

It was their first day in court, and suddenly the possibility of imprisonment seemed very real. 'Celia will be here,' Sandra said. 'I know she'll get here.'

They were sitting together in a small room, its window high up in the wall – 'In case we make a break for it,' Stuart said bitterly, when they first saw it. They had reported to the police an hour before, as instructed, had gone through a security check, and been told to wait. Laurence Cohen had appeared, then, along with his clerk and another man who looked like a teacher but turned out to be the medical expert who would give evidence on their behalf.

'Pleased to meet you,' Sandra had said, and tugged at Stuart's sleeve.

'Yes,' he'd said. 'Thank you.' His voice was flat and devoid of hope. The uplift in spirits he had felt in London had lasted for days, but it was over now

'I'm going to do my best for you.' The expert was smiling at Stuart, but his words were addressed to Sandra.

'I know,' she said. 'Thank you.' Her voice, too, sounded flat and somehow false. How could that be, when you only wanted to tell the truth?

He was leaving now, and Cohen was shepherding him towards a door. Was her coat and dress what you wore for court? Sandra had looked at him, fearing to see disapproval in his eyes. Tidy and respectable, he had advised; so had she got it right? She had wanted confirmation, but he had simply smiled at her. And then the formal surrender of bail had been gone through, and now they were alone.

She looked at Stuart. 'Celia's been good to us, hasn't she?'

Last night she had switched on the television in the hope of lightening his mood, but the programme had been Davina McCall re-uniting mothers with the babies they had had to give up years before. She would have switched channels but Stuart had stopped her. 'Watch it, Sands. Maybe we'll be on here in 50 years' time, seeing our children ... the children we had pinched from us for no good reason. They're all sitting blubbing at the screen now and saying, "Eee, isn't it touching?" but they don't give a bugger for lost families in the here and now.'

Before they had slept in the early hours, she had quoted all the examples Celia had given her of parents who had fought and won – but it was useless. Every time she had woken in the night he was awake, too, sometimes sitting on the side of the bed, once just staring out of the window. And when at last he did sleep, it was obvious he was having troubled dreams.

She was still deep in thought when a man appeared in the doorway. It was the barrister they had been told about, and Cohen was behind him. 'All ready?' he asked when they had been introduced. He was smiling reassuringly, and she tried to respond, but her face felt stiff. 'I'm afraid,' she thought. 'Stuart's right. We haven't got a prayer.'

A moment later both men were gone, and she sat silently trying not to give way to terror.

Suddenly a woman in a black gown was in the doorway, calling out their names. Time to go. They followed her down a long corridor, and up two flights of stairs. A heavy door in front of them opened, as if by magic, and the court lay before them.

They were ushered to two seats. Stuart looked at her, and she knew what he was thinking ... that they should be standing in the dock, gripping the rail in front of them, burly policemen behind them, or at least nearby, in case they ran amok. Members of the public were filing in, looking curiously around them. Who were they? Mere sightseers, or people who were somehow concerned in the case?

The two police officers who had interviewed and then

arrested them after they had brought the children back were sitting on the right. And there was a row of people she recognised as coming from the Social Services department. Not the people like Mrs Harker, who had particularly harassed them, though. Presumably they would be giving evidence, and were hidden away somewhere until they were called.

Suddenly Laurence Cohen was with them again, whispering information, telling them who was who. The bench over there contained the press – only two of them, a man and a young girl. And then they were joined by another man, older and rather bad-tempered-looking. What would he write about them?

Everyone in the court seemed to be fiddling with mobile phones. 'Switching them off,' Mr Cohen whispered. 'Cardinal sin to interrupt proceedings, if your phone rings.'

Sandra looked at her watch: 10.32. The judge was late. And then Laurence Cohen was squeezing her arm and slipping away, and a man in a black gown was calling out: 'Silence in court. All rise.'

The judge was coming in.

'Let him have a kind face,' Sandra prayed. But the face beneath the wig was neither kind nor unkind. It had no expression at all.

'This Crown Court now stands open.' It was the man in the black gown again.

Then two men in uniform were there, urging them towards the dock.

'Sandra Elizabeth Blenkiron, you are charged ...' She saw Stuart's knuckles tense, and wanted to reach out to him, but that was probably forbidden. She sat still as the charges against them were read out.

And then the prosecutor began to outline the case against them. He spoke briefly of the need to remove the children to a place of safety, of the order that had made the children the property of the local authority. And then, his voice sombre, he spoke of the wickedness of their removal from the place of safety.

Sandra tried to penetrate the official language, but what was being said bore no relation to what had really happened. She had held her baby close, and followed her husband, that baby's father, out of the door. That was all. She hadn't harmed them or stolen them, because they belonged to her. What was being said sounded like a Hollywood film about kidnappers taking children for ransom. She wanted to cry out in protest but, even if she had had the courage, her mouth was too dry for any sound to come.

She turned slightly to look at the rows of spectators, and suddenly she saw Celia. A friendly face; eyes saying, 'Hang in there.' She tried to smile her thanks, and turned back to face the judge.

She had felt optimistic the night before, but as the local authority's case unrolled she felt her spirits plummet. They were outlining her shortcomings in detail, saying Ann Marie had had rotten teeth, even though the dentist had advised leaving them in place till her second teeth came through. The judge's face was still impassive. 'I wouldn't give them back if I heard all that,' Sandra thought.

She looked at Stuart. There was almost a slight smile on his lips, a bitter acknowledgement that he had been right to fear the worst.

Suddenly she realised that the judge was looking at her, right at her. Should she meet his eye? That might look brazen. But if she dropped her eyes, that would look as though she couldn't face him. What were you supposed to do when faced by a judge? In desperation she looked away, only to see that the eyes of the jury were fixed on her, too. There was no escape.

She tried to examine the jury without appearing to be doing so. Most of them were women: was that good or bad? Would women believe that it would have been impossible for her to harm her child? Or would they be even more critical than men, feeling she had somehow behaved in a way that disgraced all women?

Lunch-time came, and they sat in the small room, trying to wash down dry sandwiches with stewed tea. Laurence Cohen came in, and seemed remarkably hopeful. 'The prosecution are having their say,' he said. 'Wait until it's our turn. I know this is gruelling, but it gives you a chance to put your case to an impartial forum, which you would never get in a Family Court. It may not feel like it … and I'm not recommending making off with kids as a wise course … but at least it's giving you a platform.'

As soon as he was gone, Sandra looked at Stuart. He was smiling, but it was a grim smile. He hadn't believed a word of it.

The afternoon followed the same pattern as the morning. Witness followed witness: Mrs Harker, and then her boss, Mrs Stonebridge, with another long recital of their shortcomings. Sandra's lack of a family background; her emotional deprivation while growing up; Stuart's short temper: all were couched in sympathetic terms, but deadly just the same. 'I tried to establish a rapport with them,' Mrs Stonebridge said, looking saintly, 'but there was no co-operation.'

At least their barrister managed to fluster her, asking, in an apparently kindly way, questions that were really rapier thrusts. A tiny flicker of hope arose in Sandra's heart, but it was quickly extinguished when the medical expert took the stand. The prosecutor asked him to give details of X-rays taken when Darren had been admitted to hospital.

'The X-rays showed metaphyseal fractures at the head of the right femur. Metaphyseal fracture is a fracture observed almost exclusively in young children, children under the age of two. It is considered pathognomonic for non-accidental injury, occurring in around 50 per cent of cases.'

The prosecutor was almost purring with pleasure. 'I hate you,' Sandra thought, and then dropped her head in case her face mirrored her feelings. The prosecutor was asking how such fractures might be caused. If he said she had hit her baby, she would shout out, 'Lies! Lies!'

She saw that Stuart was staring at her lap, where her hands were clawed like talons. 'Calm down,' his eyes said, and she tried to relax and listen to what the man was saying.

'Shaking is the force most probably applied, for example holding the child around the trunk while shaking, with the limbs moving back and forth due to the ferocity of the shaking. That's when the micro-fractures occur in immature bone. The infant lacks the capacity to protect its limbs during the onslaught.'

Onslaught? The man was still speaking, but all Sandra could think of was that word 'onslaught'. Who would carry out an onslaught on a baby? She looked at the jury, but their eyes were on the witness, their faces sombre. 'They believe him,' Sandra thought, and felt her shoulders slump.

But their barrister was on his feet now, hitching up his gown and fiddling with papers on the desk in front of him.

'Surely there are strong clinical grounds for doubting that these alleged metaphyseal fractures are characteristic of abuse, in this case? The case notes show that there were no relevant clinical signs of injury. Are you asking us to believe that a small baby, who has allegedly been the victim of an onslaught' – he was pausing to allow his repudiation of that word to sink in, and inside Sandra a tiny flicker of hope stirred again – 'that this baby, savagely shaken, should none the less have appeared well, with no physical signs of injury, such as bruises, or soft-tissue injury such as a sub-dural haematoma? That absence is also recorded in the case notes: "*Baby appears contented and well nourished.*"

'I put it to you: is it likely that parents, otherwise respectable and with two other children who are manifestly thriving, parents who, furthermore, have no history of mental illness or psychopathology, should suddenly seize their small baby and subject it to ... I use your word ... an onslaught?'

The expert was mumbling something about the X-ray evidence being irrefutable, but the certainty had gone out of his voice. Even when the prosecutor pressed him to reaffirm his findings, he sounded less certain. Glancing sideways, Sandra saw that Stuart's chin was no longer sunk on his chest.

Witnesses came and went after that, but it was the prosecutor who made the running. He wants to win, Sandra thought. He has to make us lose in order to justify his fee. Her mind wandered off into all the accounts she'd read of barristers paid millions of pounds in divorce cases; breaking up marriages for a living. That was marginally less awful than breaking up families, which was what this one was bent on doing.

Their barrister intervened occasionally, but he didn't seem particularly effective now. 'Maybe we've got the wrong man,' she thought. He had really only seemed to exert himself with the medical expert. We need him to fight for us, she thought – but why should he, really? When the case ended, he would go home to a wife and children, in all probability. They would go home to an empty house.

Or perhaps they wouldn't go home at all: Stuart would be led one way, she another. Doors would clang shut. Why hadn't they pleaded guilty, and got some leniency for that? It was what all the people who had intruded into their lives had suggested: *'Just admit it ... or tell us it was Stuart. That way you'll be co-operating.'* Weasel words, that's what Celia had called them.

And then suddenly they were all on their feet, the judge was sweeping out, and it was over for the day.

'Let's get out of here,' Stuart said. 'I've had about as much as I can stomach.'

Officials were ushering them through doorways, and down steps, issuing instructions about surrendering to bail and other things that she couldn't comprehend. Their words came out like bullets. They're in a hurry to get rid of us, Sandra thought, as though we were dirt. In fairness, though, the officials couldn't afford to get involved, couldn't try to work out who deserved to be in the dock and who didn't. It would drive them crazy if they allowed themselves to care.

'How did it go? I thought it went well. What do you think?' At the sight of them, Celia had risen from the stone wall on which she was sitting.

'It didn't,' Stuart said. 'Go, I mean. We never had a prayer. There was a moment ... but it was just a flash in the pan.' There was a grim satisfaction in his voice at having his worst fears confirmed.

'It's good of you to have come.' There was a wobble in Sandra's voice, and Celia smiled and reached out to squeeze her hand.

'I wouldn't have missed it. I hope to see you get justice. Laurence Cohen seems quite hopeful, Charles Lewin tells me.' And then Mr Cohen himself was there, taking in the mood.

'It's not even half-time yet,' he said. 'Wait till our side gets the ball.'

He spoke briefly with Celia, and then she was shepherding them towards a pub. 'You need a drink,' she said. 'And what did you have at lunch-time? Try to eat something. I know you probably don't feel like it, but it's important.'

They refused anything to eat, but accepted a drink. 'I'll get them,' Stuart said, but Celia was already at the bar. Once she was back and they were settled, Sandra felt herself begin to relax. But with relaxation, feeling returned. 'I'm going to cry,' she thought, and steeled herself not to let tears flow.

Stuart had been tracing a pattern on the table top with a beermat. Now he looked up. 'At least Mr Cohen doesn't cosy up to the social workers like the last one did.'

Celia nodded. 'I know what you mean. Did you pick your previous solicitor from the local authority list?'

'Yes.' Sandra was nodding. 'They said they were all good

solicitors. We just took the one at the top. It was a bit of a waste of time.'

'It was more than a waste.' Suddenly Stuart had come out of his gloom. 'He was working for them, not us. He wanted it over and done with, nice and neat. "Prepare for the worst," he said, that last time. He could hardly keep the grin off his face.'

'He wasn't that bad, Stuart.'

'He was, Sands. Face it. You're pissing me off by not facing it. He set us up to fail, and we have.'

'Not yet,' Celia said firmly. 'Your barrister is not in anyone's pocket, and he hasn't had a chance yet. You've got the head teacher, too. And the woman from the toddler group. It's not over, not by a long chalk.'

Celia walked to the car with them. 'I'll be here tomorrow. It'll be different, you'll see.' But as they drove back towards home they didn't speak to one another. There was nothing to say.

It was the same when they got home. Stuart didn't even switch on the television, usually his first move when they entered the house. They were sitting in silence when the phone rang. Stuart didn't move to answer it, and Sandra also listened to it ringing without moving. No one who mattered would be ringing; it would be one of those stupid messages – '*This is an important announcement*' – that turned out not to be important at all.

But it was not some anonymous voice on the answerphone. It was Celia.

'Trevor has just rung me. There's been a breakthrough. Your health visitor, the one who said she couldn't testify, has rung the newsroom and said she was prevented from speaking up for you. Threatened with the sack, in fact. But she can't live with herself. She says you were marvellous parents, and she's willing to say that in court.'

CHAPTER 34

Celia

Celia was up before dawn, tense at the thought of what the day might bring. For two days they had listened to evidence for the prosecution, and now it was going to be the defence's turn.

On the kitchen bench, Paul Fenton's flowers were propped in a bucket. They had been there when Celia got back from court, Sean hovering over them with eyes like saucers. 'Proper posh. This lot didn't come from a garage. He must have a bob or two.'

'So you know who they're from?'

He was unabashed. 'I just happened to notice the message as I took them in.'

She looked up from studying the card. 'And now you want to know what "*Forgive my big mouth. Don't let it spoil things*" means? Well, want will have to be your master. And don't come down for any bread later on, because the answer will be the same.'

Something in her voice must have alerted Sean to the fact that this was serious, because, to his credit, he didn't push it.

Left to herself, Celia would have binned the flowers, but that would give Sean more reason to probe. When Sean scented a mystery, he was remorseless. Above all, she didn't want Gavin to know anything about the whole miserable affair. She carried her coffee through to the computer, and brought up her emails. The last one in the in the box was from Gracie.

She opened it. There was only one line: '*Thought you might like to see these.*'

There followed a series of quotes from judges in the Family Courts. Lord Justice Thorpe had said: 'There is nothing more serious than a removal hearing, because the parents are so prejudiced in proceedings thereafter.' Lord Justice Wall had criticised as 'quite shocking' the determination of some social workers to place children in an 'unsatisfactory care system', away from their families. Lord Justice Aikens had described the actions of social workers in Devon as 'more like Stalin's Russia or Mao's China than the West'.

Baroness Hale had seen it in a wider context: 'Taking a child away from her family is a momentous step, not only for her, but for her whole family ... Families in all their subversive variety are the breeding ground of diversity and individuality of the state'. Mrs Justice Pauffley had been 'profoundly alarmed' at the discovery that Family Courts were effectively working with Social Services through 'clandestine arrangements' that undermined the independence of the justice system. 'It is patently wrong, must stop at once, and never happen again.'

Gracie had meant the list to cheer Celia up, but it had the reverse effect. If all those eminent men and women were saying that bad things happened, and that no one put a stop to them, what chance did anyone – even a national newspaper – have? She sat gazing at the screen for a while, but her thoughts kept turning to Paul Fenton yesterday. Now she could see that he had been weak rather than wicked. He needed to be in with everyone, even discarded girlfriends. She had been one more on the list, nothing more. He hadn't meant to harm the Blenkirons – he just hadn't been particularly bothered about their plight. And it seemed that the general public agreed with him: if they didn't, they would surely be lobbying their MPs, or taking to the streets? But Fenton's actions could have ruined any chance the Blenkirons had of regaining their children, and Celia couldn't forgive him for that.

Abruptly she stood up, and went back to the kitchen. If she did something practical, like preparing breakfast, it might improve her mood. Frasier padded in behind her, sat down, and looked at her expectantly. 'You're not supposed to be here,' she said sternly. The answer was an uplifted paw. Sean had taught him well. 'You're a scrounger, like your Boss,' she said. But she opened a tin of chopped pork and gave him a sizeable slice.

'It'll be all right, you'll see,' Sean said, when he came down and saw her gloomy face.

Gavin was equally optimistic. 'When that health visitor woman tells how the authorities shut her up, everyone'll see who the baddies are.'

Celia smiled at that. It wasn't a case of goodies and baddies – that would be simple. But the Blenkirons were locked in combat with people who believed they were doing the right thing – and who often were. That's what made the whole thing so impossible to unravel.

Gracie was waiting for her in Anxious Alley, and from the look on her face she wasn't the bearer of good news. 'There's a message for you from Glenda Forbes. It's about someone you met the other day – one of the mothers. Kathy.'

'I remember her. She's just a kid.'

'She *was* just a kid.'

Celia's heart sank. 'What's happened?'

'She topped herself. Overdose. Decided she'd never get her kid back, and topped herself. Glenda sounded in bits. She wished you luck for today, though.'

At her desk, Celia sat remembering their meeting. 'This is Kathy,' Glenda had said and the girl's voice had shaken as she said, 'I don't know where to begin.' And now it was ended. 'I'm still fighting,' she had declared. 'Glenda says there's a chance … but that's all'. There had been despair in her voice, and Celia had thought: 'She knows she's had it.' What was the last thing she had said? 'Once they've got you it's useless. They play this game, come here, go there, do this, do that – but it's all a farce. They've got your bairn, they've decided where it's going, and that's not home with you.' Now she had ended her life, alone in a bed-sit, probably with her baby's photograph in her hand.

She was still going over it, finding no sense in it, when a figure loomed up beside her. It was Charley. 'I just wanted to say "good luck". I hope it goes well. Give my best to the Blenkirons. Trevor is psyched up to do the piece on them, as soon as they're free to speak.'

Celia nodded. Neither of them dared to voice what Trevor might write if the Blenkirons went down. And she also felt embarrassed – she wanted to apologise for doubting him, but an apology would have to reveal that she had thought him guilty of disregarding the Blenkirons' welfare just to further his journalistic ambitions.

'Let me know how it goes, and ... well ... take care of yourself.' Charley sounded unusually uncertain.

'That's an odd thing to say. I'm not in any danger.'

'I know. I just – well, put it down to editorial anxiety.' And with that he was gone.

Gracie materialised from nowhere. 'He fancies you.'

'Eavesdropping again, as well as crazed!'

'I can't help it if my hearing's sharp. And the crazy one round here is the one who can't see what's under her nose.'

Celia tried not to think about anything on her way to the court. She felt empty. She also felt scared: what would she say to the Blenkirons if it went against them? Laurence Cohen had been honest the last time she spoke with him: 'It will have to be a guilty verdict, because they did break the law by taking the children. But pleading not guilty has opened up the whole thing. It all depends on the judge, now.'

She was still thinking about his words, and the apparent inability of judges to effect change, when someone came up to her. It was the social worker who had been thoughtful on the day that Sandra and Stuart had surrendered the children to her and her colleague.

'I saw they were down for today. I hope it goes well for

them.'

Celia couldn't conceal her surprise. 'So you think the Blenkirons are innocent?'

The woman raised her palms in incomprehension. 'I don't know. But they struck me as two decent people lost in a nightmare. So I wish them well.'

'That's good of you, very fair. Sometimes, to an outsider like me, it can seem that social workers make snap judgements, and then won't go back on them.'

She was nodding. 'I think that does happen. But that is partly society's fault. Can't you see the headlines? *"Social workers get it wrong again?"* So, yes, there can be a tendency to prove ourselves right at all costs. To escape the flak. If the media would allow us to say that we made the right decision at first, but now that we've investigated further we find no cause for alarm, so we're changing it, then a lot of misery would be prevented.'

'Would you be prepared to say that in print? I think it would be enormously helpful if you would.'

'I'd have to ask my manager, but, yes, given the nod, I'd be prepared to say that. We need to get people on-side. Do you know how many vacancies there are for social workers? Local authorities can't hold on to front-line staff: new graduates are dropping out after six months. They can't face the aggro. There are over 4,000 social-work jobs being advertised at the moment, and no one to fill them, so we're stretched too thin.'

Celia sympathised, and promised to keep in touch, and as the social worker moved on, pondered what she had said. Larger workloads and fewer people to shoulder the burden would be making a bad situation worse. But she couldn't worry about that now. It was time to take her seat.

The court began by hearing more evidence from the defence's medical expert. 'It's difficult to compare the skeletal surveys of injured children with a random group of healthy controls, because of exposing them to the potential hazards of unnecessary radiation, which wouldn't be ethical. But a study performed on 78 children who had died of Sudden Infant Death Syndrome revealed suspicious appearances that were not the result of abuse, in over 50 per cent.'

That sounded interesting. Celia tried to concentrate, but he was talking about the angles at which X-rays were taken ... something about axial planes and orthogonal views, and that was all definitely beyond her. And then he was talking about birth trauma, and the dangers of making a diagnosis on a single X-ray, which was something she could grasp. 'Injuries, including subdural haemorrhages, were present in ten per cent of 111 infants who had an MRI scan within 48 hours of delivery,' he was saying. 'There is no difficulty in recognising how readily a fracture sustained at birth, but not identified on a skeletal survey till two or three weeks later, could then be wrongly attributed to child abuse.'

Soon after that, the Blenkirons' health visitor was in the witness box, looking uneasy, but determined to speak.

'I was asked at a Care ... a Social Services ... meeting whether or not the Blenkirons' older children should be placed on the "at risk" register, and I said no. I said I'd been with the parents through both births, and didn't believe that either would deliberately harm any of their children. I was quite firm about it, because it was the truth; but I could see the others around the table didn't like it.

'Later, when the suggestion of going for care proceedings in respect of all three children was put forward, I disagreed with it. I said it was wrong – but my superior overruled me. Which I didn't think was right, because she had never met the family, and I had. She told me the medical evidence was overwhelming, and that there was expert opinion around the table, so I should agree with it. I suppose I got scared – I mean, they were the experts. So I just caved in. But it's been on my conscience ever since.'

The court was quiet now, and Sandra was looking towards Celia. She looked tense, but when their eyes met, she responded with a half-smile

The nursery leader was in the box, now, not as confident as the other two, but saying that Bobby was a well-loved child who had given them no trouble. She tilted her chin at the end, and said, almost defiantly, 'I think it was a happy family.'

Celia looked at Stuart as the woman left the witness box. Was that the end of it? But he was staring ahead, lips tight, big hands knotted together on the front of the dock.

Defence counsel was speaking again. 'The social worker, Mrs Harker, made much of the father's irritability. This would seem to be contradicted by the testimony of the several people concerned with the children, so you need to consider whether or not his irritability was due to the intervention of social workers into his life. Mrs Harker, throughout her evidence, seemed to give the impression of being partial, and punitive to the parents. Time and again, as she gave evidence, she seemed unable to answer yes or no, so busy was she in making a case for a placement order. I put it to you that she had formed a view against these parents even before the parenting assessment was started. A "permanent alternative family" for the children was her goal.

'Now I turn to the Guardian, and the paucity of visits made to the parents, even for the purposes of preparing a report. She seems to have relied upon the word of others. Without that contact, how could she bring her independent judgement to bear? I ask you to consider whether or not these parents have been treated with the efficiency and consideration they had a right to expect.'

'It's going well,' Celia said, when she met up with the Blenkirons. They looked tired, but they nodded agreement.

'At least they are hearing our side of things.' Stuart was attempting a smile as he spoke, and Celia put out a hand to pat his arm.

She had waved them off, and was turning to go when a car

drew up alongside her. 'Get in,' Charley said, pushing open the passenger door. 'And don't ask me what I'm doing here. That attack dog you keep left me no option.' And then, in case he had sounded ungracious: 'I would have come anyway, but you know what Gracie's like.'

They drove back into London, and settled in a bistro in Soho. She had phoned home on the way, and promised not to be late. Now she sat back and tried to relax.

'Want to talk about it?' Charley asked, when they had ordered.

'In a moment. I'm getting my breath back. It was OK, though. Now that it's our side, the whole thing seems less frightening.'

She had thought she wasn't hungry, but the risotto was good and the wine perfect. Charley had ordered without fuss, and she felt herself relaxing. Dining with Paul Fenton had been an experience. This was just ... she sought for the right word ... nice.

'What's amusing you?'

'I was thinking about the word "nice". My English teacher said it was a nothing word, never to be used. In fact, most of the time it says it all.'

They talked of humdrum things: Gavin's school, the dog, Charley's passion for the west of Scotland. 'There's still space there, Celia; room to think. God knows I wish I could get up there more often. Moidart in the spring! Heaven! You should see it.' As he spoke, he took off his glasses and rubbed his eyes.

'You're tired,' Celia said, concerned.

'I'm always tired – and do you wonder, herding that rabble, and trying to produce a decent paper. As for the agony aunt ...'

'Pish and tush,' she said. 'Can I have some more wine, please?'

CHAPTER 35

Celia

According to Laurence Cohen, it would all be over today. She ought to feel relief, even jubilation, because yesterday the culmination of the defence had been good. But the words of Maddie Simpson, the social worker she had talked to weeks before, reverberated in her brain: '*I came into this job to do good, to make things better. Now, when I mention what I do, people treat me as though I were Cruella Deville.*'

She had discussed it with Trevor, afterwards. 'Maddie was very fair. She made me realise that a lot of good people are working to help children. It's easy to be moved by the desperate letters I get, and think that all social workers are, as she says, Cruella Deville. Some of them can't stick it – like that earlier one who wrote to me, ages ago. She said she'd given up working in child protection, "because the mothers were on a hiding to nothing".'

Trevor had pulled a face. 'So she left, rather than make a stand? Not very brave.'

'She's trying. She advises people; acts as a McKenzie friend sometimes. And Maddie said something else that made me think – that nothing, nothing in her training, had prepared her for the lies her clients told her. She made me see that it's not clear-cut. The parents are innocent? Guilty? How do you make sure?'

Trevor had been less sympathetic. 'Removing children without just cause is a form of child abuse, Celia. This campaign has woken me up. We can't let it go on. Social workers have to be better at owning up when they make mistakes.'

'Suppose they did admit they were wrong – the media would pillory them.'

'True ... and we journalists could improve there. But trying to prove that black is white, because you daren't say you got it wrong in the first place, is unforgivable behaviour.'

Celia liked Trevor when he had his crusader cap on. She'd seen it first when Blair and Bush had invaded Iraq; and, for him, this was just as big a fight.

She was still mulling it over in her mind when court proceedings began again. Soon both sides would give their final statements; the judge would then sum up, and the jury would retire. Laurence Cohen was expecting a quick verdict. 'No option,' he had said, before they came in. 'The Blenkirons are guilty as charged. But we've got the whole thing into the open, now. I'm hopeful.'

There seemed to be a lull in the proceedings; and then the prosecution barrister was standing up, hitching up his gown, and starting to outline all the reasons why Stuart and Sandra should be taken out and shot.

Celia looked at the two in the dock. Stuart was sitting erect, head held high. But it was Sandra who looked somehow different. 'Almost serene,' Celia thought. Perhaps her GP had given her something? Whatever it was, something had changed.

'I ought to feel afraid for them,' Celia thought, but somehow she was past fear. What would be, would be. The prosecution barrister spoke for what felt like hours, but, when she looked at her watch, it had actually been 25 minutes. Then it was the turn of the defence barrister. He was persuasive, and he had obviously done his homework. But the judge's face remained expressionless.

Defence counsel was speaking again. 'How can it be proper procedure,' he was asking, 'that a psychologist was asked for, and was prepared to provide, during the course a *single* working day, on the basis of papers supplemented by a telephone conversation with a local-authority professional who had never met the mother, a report that could play a material part in deciding the fate of a family?'

Celia looked at the jury. His words seemed to be having an effect there, but still the judge's face remained impassive. And ultimately, he was the one who would decide the real outcome: not the punishment for the flight north, but whether or not the Blenkirons would remain a family.

When the barrister sat down, the court rose, and Sandra and Stuart were shepherded away. Laurence Cohen came up to Celia. 'I hope we get a verdict today, but it may go into tomorrow.' When he had gone, Celia thought: if the verdict comes today, the Blenkirons could be behind bars tonight. Should she hope the verdict was not reached, so they could have one more night of freedom? But even before she could decide, they were all being hustled back into court, and the summing-up had begun.

The judge began by referring to each witness, and pointing up, for the jury, the parts of their evidence that he thought significant. Then his tone grew heavier.

'The defence has tried to prove that the children should not have been taken from the parents, and that therefore the parents were entitled to remove them from their legal guardians. That the children should not have been removed from the parents may well be true, in the light of what we have heard. But that is not a matter for you today. The fact of the case is that, on that day, the children were the subject of a court order. If you find that the parents did indeed remove them from the custody of those empowered to enforce that order, then you have no option but to bring in a guilty verdict.'

He paused for a moment before he spoke again. 'You may, however, leave their punishment to the discretion of the court.'

A moment later the man in the black gown was calling 'All rise', and the court was emptying. Laurence Cohen was again waiting for Celia when she emerged from the court.

'He's already pronounced them guilty,' she said.

Cohen smiled. 'He had no option but to do that. However, he's sent the jury a coded message that he's going to let them off lightly. She clocked it, the old bird in the glasses who's the foreman. She actually nodded. It'll be a suspended sentence, or I'm a monkey's uncle. And, if we're lucky, a strong recommendation that the Family Court look again at the case.'

Celia went into the pub to lunch, but she couldn't eat. Somewhere Sandra and Stuart would be sitting, waiting to know their fate. She downed two gin and tonics, and walked out into the open air.

The court reconvened at 2.15. The jury were filing back. Surely they couldn't have made up their minds already? Celia felt protest rise in her throat – but then the foreman, the spinster lady who had nodded at the judge's hint of leniency, was on her feet. She gave the verdicts in a firm voice. To the question of Stuart's behaviour, she pronounced him guilty. Then it was Sandra's turn, and the verdict was the same. The jury foreman sat down again, and Sandra's head dropped to her chest. Stuart stared straight ahead, as though unmoved.

For a moment there was complete silence, and then the judge was speaking, addressing the two of them in the dock.

'You have rightly been found guilty of removing your children from the care of the local authority, which was legally their guardian. There can be no excuse for wilfully disobeying the law. Nevertheless, I recognise the sense of injustice under which you were labouring. We have heard medical experts disagree as to whether or not you harmed your child. Where there is such disagreement, we need to look carefully at the background to the case. Much has been made, Mrs Blenkiron, of your own upbringing, but it would seem to me that you have overcome any lack of nurture in your childhood and made, as we have been told by witnesses, a stable and happy home for your children. I think that if a health visitor, someone who has been in the house and viewed the family closely, says: "I cannot believe they would hurt their children," that seems to be evidence I would want to weigh, and take into consideration.

'I remind myself that, in child-protection cases, the burden is on the local authority to prove each element of their case, and the overall threshold condition.' He paused then, and gazed down at the area where representatives of Social Services were sitting. 'We start with section 31 of the Children Act 1989. The court can only consider making a public-law order at the welfare stage if the threshold is met. I am not satisfied that in this case it was met, and I will be calling for the relevant documents from the Family Court to be re-examined. I will take a keen interest in this myself.

'Nevertheless, a crime was committed, and a jury has found both defendants guilty. Stuart Blenkiron, I sentence you to one year's imprisonment, suspended for 12 months. Sandra Blenkiron, I sentence you to six months' imprisonment, suspended for 12 months.'

Celia had been holding her breath. Now she let it out in a slow gasp. Sandra was turning her head, searching for a friendly face. 'It's over,' Celia mouthed, and saw Sandra struggle to smile.

She waited for what seemed like hours before they emerged from the court. Stuart was jubilant, but Sandra was more composed.

'It's all right now, Sandra, it's over. It'll take time, maybe more trips to the Family Court. But things have now changed. I know it's hard to believe, but I think the judge meant what he said about taking another look at the evidence – and they won't dare ignore a judge. Once that's done, I'm confident you'll be a family again, and can put all this behind you.'

But Sandra was looking at her calmly, and when she spoke her voice was even. 'It's OK, Celia, I've got it sorted.' She saw Celia's puzzlement, and continued. 'Stuart got the Webster case up on the internet last night, and I read all about it. They lost their children, but they haven't lost hope. She says she's waiting for the knock on the door when the children come to find her.

I hope you're right, and it'll get sorted, but if it doesn't, we'll still be parents. They can't take that away from us. We'll go on like the Websters, hoping that one day we'll see our kids again.'

Celia hugged her, and held on long enough to stem her own tears. This was no time for crying. When she released her, Sandra spoke again, and this time her tone was sombre. 'Even if we get them back, I will never feel safe again.'

Long after she had seen them into the car and watched it thread its way on to the main road, Celia stood, reflecting. Life went on remorselessly, even while people's lives were being torn apart. Would the Blenkirons ever recover from the events of the past months? How long before the children knew they were in a place they could really call home? And if one or other of the children found they couldn't adjust, whose fault would it be?

At last she turned and made for the pub on the corner. She ordered a whisky mac, and drank the strong, pungent liquid in two gulps. 'Another,' she said, 'please.' She felt empty – and she felt ashamed. She had betrayed Michael with a worthless man, and in doing so she had jeopardised the safety of a family.

Afterwards she went out into the street. For some reason she didn't want to go home yet. Instead she walked until she came to a park. It wasn't much of a one – a bowling green, some swings – but at last she came upon a little enclosure. 'Scented Garden', the sign said. She sat there for a long time, as the sun sank lower in the sky and birds flew homewards. Where did London birds spend the night? There were too many of them to roost in trees. Where did they lay their eggs, if they had no nests? Surely not on stone ledges? Birds needed safe nests to rear their fledglings, just as people needed safe nests to nurture their children. If once that nest was violated, could they ever feel secure in it again?

At last she took out her phone and called her home number.

'They won, darling. Well, not on paper, but it's going to be all right. They'll get their children back, although it may take a little time.' She could hear the excitement as he relayed the news to Sean, whose whoop of joy set Frasier barking.

'I'll be home later,' she said. 'But it's quite a long drive. Go to bed. I love you.'

It was growing dusk. She ought to get on her way to London. Charley had told her to order a car. 'I'd come myself,' he had said, 'but there's a COBRA meeting about terrorism, so I need to stay by the till.'

She was walking aimlessly forward when her phone rang. It was Gracie, who said excitedly, 'It's over, I hear. Trevor told me. So get yourself back to London. A car is on the way to collect you. Keep your phone on, and they'll ring when they get there.'

Celia moved on. In a few hours she would be back in a London preparing for nightfall. In tower blocks, in stately homes, in little eyries high above offices and shops, in rows of terraced houses, lights would spring up. Behind those lighted windows would be people struggling, celebrating, striving to do their best, and occasionally failing. Sometimes being blamed for crimes they had never committed, sometimes knowing loss they did not deserve. Like her, like all those mothers in contact centres, they would put a brave face on things, because you couldn't cry aloud.

Her phone was still in her hand, and suddenly she knew what she had to do. She dialled the number of the one person whose voice she wanted to hear, and, when she heard it, she spoke.

'Charley, I think they're coming home.'

DENISE ROBERTSON BOOK CLUB

If you've enjoyed this book and would like to find out
more about Denise and her novels, why not join the
Denise Robertson Book Club. Members will receive
special offers, early notification of new titles, information
on author events and lots more.

Membership is free and there is no obligation to buy.

To join simply send your name and address to
info@deniserobertson books.co.uk
or post your details to:
The Denise Robertson Book Club
PO Box 58514
Barns,
London
SW13 3AE.